CH

VILLAIN

VILLAIN

MICHAEL GRANT

KATHERINE TEGEN BOOKS
An Imprint of HarperCollins Publishers

Katherine Tegen Books is an imprint of HarperCollins Publishers.

Library of Congress Control Number: 2018933266
ISBN 978-0-06-246787-4

Typography by Joel Tippie
18   19   20   21   22   PC/LSCH   10   9   8   7   6   5   4   3   2   1

First Edition

To my daughter, Clara

And I stood upon the sand of the sea, and saw a beast rise up out of the sea, having seven heads and ten horns, and upon his horns ten crowns, and upon his heads the name of blasphemy.

And the beast which I saw was like unto a leopard, and his feet were as the feet of a bear, and his mouth as the mouth of a lion: and the dragon gave him his power, and his seat, and great authority.

—Revelation 13:1–2

California's governor and legislature are rushing to replace the iconic Golden Gate Bridge, which was destroyed in a battle between police and a superpowered mutant calling himself Knightmare....
—The New York Times

The Port of Los Angeles is still conducting damage assessments following the battle involving several mutant creatures, but early estimates run to the billions of dollars....
—Press Office, Port of Los Angeles

The president has issued a tweet criticizing late-night comedy shows for portraying him as paralyzed in the face of this novel threat....
—Associated Press

Ministry of State Security (MSS)
People's Republic of China
Electronic Communications Intercept (ECI) #42-8909
The following conversation took place between Deputy Undersecretary of US Homeland Security Peter Stroudwell (PS) and Angela Britten (AB), a senior advisor to the Homeland Security General Counsel, at a restaurant in Washington, D.C.

PS: The president has suggested asking the population to take direct action. His words. Direct action.
AB: What action? Does he want the whole country hiding

in shelters indefinitely?

PS: Not that kind of action. He's calling for a Second Amendment solution.

AB: You're kidding. He's suggesting every gun nut in the country go on a mutant-killing spree? Come on, Peter, you must know—

PS: Of course I know! Jesus, Angela, why do you think I'm talking to you? You're in the counsel's office, you're a lawyer, you need to do something to head this off.

AB: Right, because I can somehow stop POTUS. I need a drink.

END OF ECI

Madam Chairman, to be honest, we haven't got the first goddamned clue how to stop these monsters.

—Secret testimony of FBI director

CHAPTER 1
It Rhymes with Villain

"HEY, FREAK? WHAT are you looking at?"

The drunk tank, the catch-all common room used as a first stop for drunks and druggies, was a large space lined with a wall-mounted steel bench. The floor was bare cement, sloped down to a drain in the center of the room. There was a single window with both bars and thick wire over filthy glass, allowing neither sunlight nor cheer, but a grim, gray reminder that there was an outside world.

The walls of the drunk tank were painted a sickly yellow, the color of baby puke, which went perfectly with the reek of vomit.

There were maybe fifteen adult men in the room, and the barely eighteen-year-old Dillon Poe, and Dillon felt very, very bad. Bad to a degree he had never felt before.

Is this what a hangover is? Oh, my God!

Dillon being Dillon, part of his mind was already looking for the potential humor in the situation. And it wasn't hard to

find. He'd gotten very drunk the night before, after walking
into a bar and asking for whiskey like some cowboy in an old
movie. Having no choice or will of his own at that moment,
the bartender had poured, and Dillon had gagged down the
first fiery shot, then another, and . . . and the next thing he
knew was right now, waking up with throbbing eyes and ach-
ing head and a mouth that tasted like he'd spent the night
eating roadkill.

No, not roadkill, that was generic. It was funnier to be specific. Like a dead beaver? Like a dead opossum? Rats were
overdone. Like a dead raccoon?

Yeah, dead raccoon. His mouth tasted like he'd spent the
night chewing on dead raccoon.

It was an absurd situation: an eighteen-year-old walks into
a bar. Like the start of a joke where a priest, a rabbi, and an
imam walk into a bar. . . . And, yeah, he admitted wearily, his
brain was not quite up for writing jokes.

"I'm nah lookin' chew," Dillon managed to say to the belligerent man, a sandpaper tongue thick in a cotton mouth.
Dillon sat up, rubbed sleep from his eyes, and instantly vomited on the concrete.

"Hey, asshole!" This from the same man who'd challenged
him. He was a big, very hairy white man, though it was hard
to comment on his complexion given that he was almost
entirely covered in tattoos. Including the tattooed tear at the
corner of one eye that testified to a murder committed. Chest
hair that included some gray sprigs spouted from a lurid chest
tattoo of an American flag where the stars had been replaced

by swastikas. "What's the matter with you, boy?"

Dillon stood up, wobbly, weak, and deeply unhappy.

"Nasty little punk, stinking up the place!" Tattoo said.

This, Dillon thought, was really not fair: the place already reeked of puke and piss and worse. There was a man passed out facedown on the bench, a brown stain in his trousers.

Tattoo swaggered over, grabbed Dillon's T-shirt, and kicked him in the knee. Dillon dropped to the floor, landing painfully on the concrete. "Clean that up, boy!"

What? *What?* How had this happened? How was he here, on his knees? Part of him counseled quiet submission: the man was bigger and had friends. But part of him, despite the alcohol-fueled misery in his brain, simply could not shut up.

"Can I use that mop on your head?"

First rule of stand-up comedy: never let a heckler get the upper hand.

Tattoo, whose limp salt-and-pepper hair did, arguably, resemble a mop, gaped in astonishment. Then he grinned, showing a row of overly bright, cheap false teeth. "Well, I guess I get to hand out my first ass-kicking of the day!"

Dillon closed his eyes and focused and almost immediately the brutal hangover faded, and subtle but utterly impossible changes began to transform Dillon's body and face. He said, "Ass-kicking, or ass-kissing?"

This earned him a hard kick meant for his stomach, but which deflected off his arm, knocking his hand into his own puddle of puke. Bad. But on the other hand, his hangover pain was fast receding.

A relief, but not the point, really. The point was that Dillon Poe was changing. Physically. The change was subtle at first and mostly visible in his eyes, which had shifted from brown to a sort of tarnished gold color. His pupils narrowed and formed vertical, thin, elongated diamond-shaped slits. His hair seemed to suck into his head, which now bulged at the back and tapered to a version of his own face rendered in the green of a new spring leaf.

Dillon knew about the physical change, or at least thought he did. He'd caught a terrifying glimpse of himself in a barroom mirror, seeing a reptilian version of his face visible past the bottles of booze.

But he had also begun to guess that there was something about this snakelike version of himself that caused more fascination than revulsion. If anything, the few people whose reactions he'd been able to gauge seemed to find him attractive, even mesmerizing. They stared, but not in horror. Even his fellow denizens of the drunk tank did not recoil in fear or disgust, but turned fascinated, enthralled faces to him.

Dillon was not in a happy or generous frame of mind. He had clearly screwed up the night before, outing himself as a mutant. And now he was in a cage with men, every single one of whom looked meaner and bigger and tougher than he—well, aside from the weeping tourist in the chinos and canary-yellow polo shirt. But it didn't matter, because Dillon Poe—this hypnotic, serpentine version of Dillon Poe—was more than capable of dealing with Tattoo.

Dillon looked up from the floor at the man and said, "You

clean it up, tough guy. In fact, *lick* it up. Start with my hand."

Without hesitation Tattoo stuck out his tongue and began licking Dillon's scaly green hand, as avidly as a dog welcoming his master. It was fascinating watching Tattoo's rheumy eyes, the expression of brute incomprehension, the alarm, the anger, the . . . impotence. The panic he was helpless to express.

"Now lick up that mess on the floor," Dillon said. Instantly Tattoo dropped to his hands and knees. He said, "I don't want to do this!" but without hesitation lowered his head, his long, grizzled hair trailing in the mess, and began lapping it up like a dog going after a dropped table scrap.

The entire room stood or sat frozen in stark disbelief. It was like they were an oil painting, all open mouths and wide eyes and expressions of disbelief. One man moaned, "Is this a hallucination? Is this real? Am I really seeing this?"

Dillon stood—his morph came with a lithely muscular body several inches taller than his own, an athlete's body—facing Tattoo's two buddies, who advanced, belligerent but nervous.

One said, "Hey, Spence, come on, man, stop that! Get up off your knees! Get away from that thing!" He tugged at his partner's shirt, but Tattoo—aka Spence, apparently—would not stop licking the puke. In fact, *could* not stop. He tried to speak but only incomprehensible grunts emerged—it's hard to talk with a mouth full of another person's vomit.

The other thug snarled at Dillon. "What did you do to him, freak?"

"I am really not in the mood to be picked on," Dillon said.

His voice, too, was subtly different now. His normal voice was a bit too high-pitched to ever be authoritative, and he had a slight lisp on "s" sounds. But this voice? This voice was like a musical instrument in the hands of a master. This voice persuaded, cajoled, and seduced.

The man frowned and stopped, then shook his head in confusion before finding his anger again. "I don't give a damn what you're up for, freak!"

Dillon turned to this fellow, younger than Spence, with a tweaker's emaciated body and rotting teeth. He would have tolerated any number of insults, but that particular one, "freak," was something he'd heard too many times in his young life, both at school and at home.

Freak for having no friends.

Freak for his physical awkwardness.

Freak for the way he looked at girls who would have nothing to do with him.

Freak for being the only one of five siblings who rejected walks and hikes and camping and biking and all the other physically tiring wastes of time his family loved.

Freak for sitting in his room for days on end watching stand-up comics like Louis, Maron, Frankie Boyle, Seinfeld, Chris Rock, Jeselnik, Jimmy Carr, and the few surviving videos of the godfather of stand-up, Richard Pryor.

And of course, *freak* for being a survivor of what people called the Perdido Beach Anomaly, but which Dillon, like all the survivors, called the FAYZ.

"Dude," Dillon said, "don't ever call me a freak again."

"Okay," the tweaker said.

"Say that you promise?"

The tweaker frowned and grimaced, but said, "I promise."

And Dillon almost stopped there. Almost. But Dillon's life was filled with times when he almost did the sensible thing or the smart thing or the right thing. A whole lot of almosts, and an equal number of "what the hells." Of the two, "what the hell" was always funnier.

The truth was he was rather enjoying the fear in the eyes all around him. Fear and confusion and mystification, expressed in frowns and mutterings and the sorts of threats not meant to be heard by the person being threatened—coward's threats.

Yeah, Dillon thought, *you losers should fear me. Every breath you take is because I allow it.* A nasty smirk formed on his lips.

"I'm not sure I trust you," Dillon said. "Let's make sure, huh? Let's make sure you never call me or anyone else names again. Bite your tongue in half."

A spasm went through the room. They leaned forward, disbelieving but enthralled. After all, a tough guy was licking the floor, like a dog determined to get every last chunk of Iams.

"You can't make me . . . uchhh ggghrr can't ma . . . ," the tweaker said.

"Sorry, having a hard time understanding you," Dillon said savagely.

The tweaker concentrated hard; you could see it on his

face. He was trying to fight, but putting far more energy into obeying. His jaw muscles clenched until the veins in his neck stood out. Blood dribbled from his mouth.

"Jesus Christ!" someone yelled. Then, "Guards! Guards!"

"Grind your teeth back and forth and bite down hard," Dillon said. The sound of dull teeth grinding on gristle was sickening, and Dillon might have relented had he not caught sight of the swastika tattoo on the tweaker's arm.

No pity for Nazi tweakers.

"Hey, can you say *sieg heil*?" Dillon asked.

Blood now gushed from the man's mouth. Tears streamed from his eyes and mucus from his nose. His eyes were trapped, desperate, terrified.

"Come on, mister tough guy, gimme a *sieg heil*."

"Ssnk thth stnch ccchuch . . ."

More prisoners were shouting, agitated, some wide-eyed and fascinated, others appalled, even sickened. And Dillon was sickened in a way that had nothing to do with his hangover. There was something electric about the feeling, but in both senses of the word. The power was shocking, and it shocked him in return. It seemed impossible, just absolutely, batshit impossible, and yet he could hear teeth on gristle. . . . *Life shouldn't be like that,* he told himself. *That could not be it. Could it?*

"Guards! Guards!" The cries went up with mounting hysteria, and men banged on the bars, all of which was fine with Dillon. He wanted guards to come, because he was more than ready to leave.

A portly guard came sauntering along, her face a mask of weary indifference. Then she took a look through the barred door and immediately keyed her radio. "Backup to the tank! Hats and bats! We have a situation!"

"Open the gate, guard," Dillon said in his calm, mellifluous voice.

The guard fumbled for keys, found the right one, and turned the lock just as two other guards came rushing down the corridor, helmets on heads, truncheons and Tasers in hand.

"Open all the gates, all the doors. Do it now," Dillon said, and heard the clanks and the buzzes, all the noises of unlocking doors. He stood in the open doorway and glanced at the denizens of the tank, shrinking back from him.

It was a strange moment, and Dillon recognized that it was the end of one life and the start of another. It was as if some giant, animated meat cleaver—shades of Terry Gilliam—had come down out of the sky and announced with an authoritative *thunk!* that life was now divided into "before the drunk tank" and "after the drunk tank."

The only way now was forward.

That could be a tagline. I could build a bit around that.

He had only realized he had this power two days ago. He'd tried it out—gently—on one of his brothers. Then on his father, a bit less gently, but all the while in ways that revealed nothing and raised no suspicions. He had intended to approach the matter after thinking it through, deciding on just how to use the power, if at all. His first thought had been to use it to get stage time at the LA Comedy Club, which despite the name was here in Vegas, and not just on an open-mike night. But that seemed a bit small for such a huge power.

There was not much point in having power if you didn't use it, and no point in using it if it didn't give you an edge. Right? That was the point of life, after all, wasn't it? To do the best you could for yourself, and perhaps for those loyal to you? And to deal with doubters and haters and enemies?

But then he'd been dumped by his girlfriend, Kalisha, which was not a heartbreak—he could barely tolerate her; the girl's sense of humor went no further than slapstick—but it was a humiliation. They'd only been going out for two weeks, and she was his first girlfriend. In the context of the senior class at Palo Verde High School, he would be reduced once again to the status of total loser. The unloved *freak*.

Dillon didn't do well with humiliation; he found it intolerable, in fact, as he had found it intolerable in the FAYZ. There, he had been just another thirteen-year-old kid without powers. He'd been forced to work in the fields, braving the carnivorous worms they called zekes, picking cabbages for hours in the broiling sun, at least if he wanted to eat. The kids with powers—Sam Temple and his group, Caine Soren and his—had never treated Dillon as anything more than a nuisance, another mouth to be fed, another random, powerless nobody to be ordered around by Albert and Edilio and Dekka, the big shots. Another nobody who might be crippled or killed if he happened to get between Sam and Caine in the ongoing factional war.

And then, after the end of the FAYZ, his parents had moved to Las Vegas. He had coincidentally enjoyed a big improvement in his internet speed, and he had learned of the dark web: the sites that sold illegal drugs and guns and even arranged meetings with hit men. And there he had come across someone supposedly selling pieces of the "Perdido Beach Magic Stone." That's what the ad had said. A hundred dollars an ounce, to be paid in Bitcoin. He had assumed it was fake, but he gave it a try anyway, and sure enough, a chip of rock had arrived in the mail. He had slept with it under his pillow for a full month before concluding that it wasn't working, and he'd been on the verge of throwing it out when something told him to try one last thing.

He had practically destroyed the blender. And he'd had to finish the job with a mortar and pestle that left the rock tasting like the basil that had been the previous thing crushed in the mortar. He had gagged it down.

And the next day he had made his brother do things, and his sister go change sweaters three times, and he had made his father go online and order a new and expensive VR headset.

But later that same day he'd gotten into a loud argument with his mother, and he had stormed out of the house and ordered a passing motorist to drive him to the TGI Fridays, where, using his new serpent's voice, he told the bartender to pour. That was a mistake, clearly, because passed out he had no power at all, obviously, and the result was this drunk tank and this very public revelation of his power. There would be video from the cell, video revealing him as a mutant, one of the so-called "Rockborn," he was certain, which meant police and who-knew-what government agencies would have his name, address, picture—both of his faces—fingerprints, credit report, and, worst of all, his most recent psych evaluation, which had labeled him a borderline personality—psych-speak for *freak*. The FBI would be interviewing his "known associates" before the day was out, and they would, to a boy or girl, roll their eyes and retell all the old stories of Dillon the loser, Dillon the freak, Dillon the virgin.

Terrible timing, terrible planning. He had not previously used the power for a violent end, and now that he had, he could expect to be treated no more kindly than the creature who had torn up the Golden Gate Bridge, or the monsters who had blown up the Port of Los Angeles.

The tweaker's rotting teeth finally came together, and he spit a hunk of bloody pulp from his mouth onto the floor, where it looked like a piece of calf's liver. Tattoo, still on hands and knees, looked quizzically at Dillon as if to ask whether he should lap the meat up as well.

Yes, life going forward would not be the life he'd led to this point.

Oh, well.

"I'm out of here, ladies and gentlemen," he said. "You've been a great audience, but . . ." He grinned as the old Marx Brothers ditty came back to him, and he sang, *"Hello, I must be going. I cannot stay, I came to say I must be going . . ."*

There was no applause. He could have made them laugh and applaud, but no, some things were sacred, and he would earn his laughs the hard way, the right way. All the people he admired had been freaks in high school, and they had all become admired and beloved and rich.

Louis C.K.: $25 million net worth

David Letterman: $400 million

Jerry Seinfeld: $800 million

"Ta-ta!" he said with a jaunty wave. Then an afterthought: "Oh, you can stop licking the floor now."

And with that, Dillon Poe—six foot two inches tall and decidedly green Dillon Poe—walked out through the cell gate, down the hall to the open security door, past guards he silenced with a word, past the jail's grim waiting room, out into the lobby of the county building, and out into brilliant Las Vegas sunlight.

A pretty young woman passing by gave him a definite once-over that was certainly not the way she should have looked at a green, scaly creature with yellow eyes, and he smiled at her in gracious acknowledgment.

Could I work the whole snake thing into my act?

It was mid-morning in Las Vegas. The air was only hot, not blistering, but the sun was blinding, a sharp contrast with what Dillon felt inside. Because in his head he was having visions again, like he had last time he had changed . . . well, maybe not visions, more like voices. Only the voices never spoke.

No, not quite visions or voices, he realized, more like the neck-tingling sense of being *watched*. It was more than just the faint apprehension you might get when you thought

someone on the street was eyeballing you; this was both more
real and insistent, and yet impossible to make sense of. It was
as if somewhere inside his head was an audience, sitting in
complete darkness and absolute silence, watching him act on
his own personal stage.

Dillon was an empirical guy, not someone given to mys-
ticism or even religion. He tested things. He sought truth,
because all the best comics traded in truth. His suspicion was
that the dark and silent audience had something to do with
the changes—the morphing, as he had heard it called. So now
he tested the hypothesis by de-morphing: by resuming his
unimpressive human physique. And sure enough, the invisible audience disappeared.

"Huh," Dillon said, which a passing homeless person took
as an invitation and held out a dirty styrofoam cup.

"Sorry, I don't have any money," the now-normal-looking
Dillon said.

No money, just power. But Dillon was cynical enough to
understand that in much the way that matter and energy are
really the same thing, so are money and power. He could
make anyone do anything. *Anything.* Which meant he could
have anything he wanted.

He, Dillon Poe, ignored FAYZ survivor, was quite possibly
the most powerful person in the world. In light of that, he
asked himself: *Now what?*

And the answer was: *Whatever you want, Dillon; whatever
you want.* The only way now was forward.

CHAPTER 2
Friends Don't Let Friends Scream Alone

"AAAAAHHHH! KILL ME! Kill me, oh, God, please kill me!"

Once upon a time, Malik Tenerife had argued convincingly that the idea of hell, of a place of eternal torment, was nonsense, an impossibility. Sooner or later even being boiled in a lake of fire would get dull and repetitive. After a year? Ten years? A million years?

He knew now the flaw in his argument: it only worked if you experienced *time*.

Malik did not experience time. Everything was now. Now! NOW! Right *now* he felt as if he'd been skinned alive and left raw. Right *now* he felt as if wild beasts had gnawed on him. Right *now* his brain could barely form a thought before a crashing wave of agony would wipe it away, leaving nothing but screams.

He'd heard some of what the nurses had had to say since Shade and Cruz had rushed him to the hospital. He was vaguely, distantly aware that the shape-shifting chameleon Cruz, assuming several disguises, had been with him throughout. He knew that she had filled the one request he had managed to form and articulate in a single scrawled word on a pad of paper. The word: "Rock." But to say that Malik *knew* or *thought* was a gross exaggeration—Malik's memory, his thoughts, his essence as a human being were a bunch of scraps swirling in a tornado. He could glimpse but not hold a thought.

Cruz had indeed been with Malik throughout. She had the power to appear as any person she could visualize, and had passed as a doctor, a nurse, an orderly. She had stayed by his side as much as possible because, even though she knew it was nothing compared to Malik's agony, she had her own problems. When in morph, the Dark Watchers were always with her, always insinuating themselves in her mind. Sometimes she just locked herself in the bathroom, returned to her normal, true form, and cried.

She had given Malik the rock, ground up in a cup of water, and he'd managed to drink it through a straw. And then she had waited.

At first the third member of their little group, Shade Darby, could come and go, using her super-speed to be effectively invisible, nothing but a blur and a gust of wind. But now Malik's room was heavily guarded. There were Los Angeles police just outside his door, two SWAT members, all kitted out in black jumpsuits and machine pistols, at each end of the hallway. They knew Malik was with Shade and Cruz.

They were looking for Shade and Cruz, unaware that Cruz had been there the whole time.

Cruz had picked up some useful if depressing facts. She'd become a well-informed amateur on the subject of burns.

Pop quiz: Do you want second-degree burns or third-degree?

Tricky answer: It depends which bothers you more, permanent disfigurement or pain. The second-degree burn hurts like hell but will heal. The third-degree burn destroys nerves and may actually deaden sensation, but you'll be wearing your very own Halloween mask.

"Pleeeeeaaase! Kill me!"

Cruz had also learned that there is a such a thing as a fourth-degree burn. That's when a burn goes all the way through the skin and eats into muscle, fat, tendon, and even bone.

After giving Malik the rock, Cruz had reopened the morphine line, allowing the soothing drug to flow into Malik's veins. But she knew now that it was like sprinkling water on a forest fire. There was no drug capable of killing this pain. The doctors were getting ready to put him in a medically induced coma, basically turning off all his brain functions so that, pain-free and unaware, he could glide to his death.

"Oh, God, make it stop!"

Cruz rose from the hard, narrow chair and gave the hanging bag a squeeze, pushing morphine more quickly into the catheter in the back of his hand.

Malik had second-degree burns. And third. And he had

fourth degree, and there the scalding pain of second-degree burns became the marrow-deep, consciousness-twisting pain of muscles eaten into like he'd been attacked and half consumed by a tiger. The superheated steam and napalm from the great fire beast—sometimes known in the media as Napalm or Dragon, and also known as Tom Peaks—had burned through clothing and skin, had snapped and curled the tendons of Malik's ankles, had melted the muscles of Malik's calves; it had splashed up and burned away parts of his thighs and buttocks. His lower back was second-degree burns; third-degree burns spread up his back.

The fire had exposed the tendons of his wrist. Most of his face was untouched, but a burn spread from his neck up the left side of his head, so that his ear had melted and now lay flat, a sort of bas-relief of itself. His face, as well as most of his chest and private bits, was intact aside from spot burns. The unburned bits were like islands floating in a magma sea.

One thing was clear: no one—not a single nurse, doctor, or specialist—had any doubt that Malik would die, probably within hours.

So Cruz had made the solution of water and pulverized meteor fragments that carried an engineered alien virus with the power to disassemble and reassemble DNA like a kid playing with Legos. The rock, as it was called, had created the Perdido Beach Anomaly, the place survivors of that impossible dome called the FAYZ.

The rock had turned Tom Peaks, ruthless government bureaucrat, into a massive, liquid fire–spewing beast; the rock had turned an obnoxious-if-talented young artist named Justin DeVeere into the armored, sword-armed monster called Knightmare; the rock had turned a disturbed young man named Vincent Vu into the vile creature that called itself Abaddon.

This was also, of course, the rock that had given Shade her power, and Cruz hers. No one could predict what the rock would do to Malik. No one could be certain it would do anything at all. But the alternative was to simply wait for him to die, either screaming in agony or in a coma from which he would never wake. So Cruz had run down to the hospital cafeteria to get a straw so he could drink, and held it to his trembling lips.

Malik had swallowed all he could. And then he had fallen and fallen and fallen into hell, because taking the rock had meant turning off the morphine drip so that he could swallow without choking, and within seconds, as he felt the gritty water slide down his throat, the pain rose beneath him like a tidal wave, like some terrifying volcanic eruption, an irresistible force.

The rock changed those who consumed it, but how would it manifest in Malik? The alien virus was clever, subtle, and opportunistic. It had used the DNA of Dekka Talent's own cat to shape Dekka's morphed self. It had used starfish DNA to grow Vincent Vu into a monster. But the rock had other tricks as well—it had turned Tom Peaks into a fearsome creature that was surely not the product of any earthly DNA, but rather a creature of half-remembered movies whose images lay buried in Peaks's memory. And an unfortunate child in Islay, Scotland, had been transformed into a creature from a children's board book, a creature that had had to be annihilated by shells from a Royal Navy destroyer.

Cruz herself, formerly known as Hugo Rojas before she'd come to accept the fact that "Hugo" was simply never going to be authentic as a male, had acquired a power that had no analogy in nature: she could appear as anyone. Anyone she had seen, or even seen video of. She had only to form a picture in her mind, and as if she was some sort of overhead projector, she could reflect and embody that image. Nature was brilliant at disguise and could make an insect look like a leaf, but nothing in nature matched what Cruz could do.

Had the rock virus used her own gender transition as a text in creating the morphed Cruz? It would almost imply that the virus had a sense of humor.

Cruz had stayed in morph for hour after hour while Malik was in the hospital, playing various roles, shifting her appearance with increasing ease and speed. And for all of those hours she had endured the vile, insinuating attentions of the Dark Watchers, those voiceless, faceless, formless observers who emerged any time a morphing happened. At times it was like being whispered to by a pervert—not words, just slithering, leering tones. At times she felt she could almost glimpse them. Like when you suddenly turn your head and have the feeling that you just missed seeing something out of the corner of your eye.

Shade Darby had come and gone several times. She would stand by Malik's bed, talk in quiet tones to Cruz, wince at

Malik's pain, and brush tears away with quick, impatient gestures, as though her tears were an irritation. Eventually Shade managed to convince an exhausted, emotionally wrecked Cruz to come with her to their latest stolen vehicle in the hospital parking lot and eat something, and hopefully sleep. She settled Cruz into the passenger seat of the Mercedes and tucked a woolen throw around her, like she was putting a child to bed. Shade turned on the engine and the seat warmers, and despite being sure she could not sleep, Cruz did just that. After several hours Cruz woke from a troubled sleep and found Shade sitting in the driver's seat, opening a Subway bag.

"I have an Italian cold cut and a ham and cheese. Also chips."

Cruz said nothing, but pushed open the door, leaned out, and vomited onto the concrete.

Without a word, Shade handed her a bottle of water. Cruz swirled and spit, then drank the entire bottle and dropped the empty. Then she took the Italian cold-cut sub, wolfed down half of it, swallowed, and mumbled, "Thanks."

Shade nodded and looked away.

This was a new Shade Darby. Cruz had always seen her strange, brilliant, ruthlessly determined friend as two people in one body: there was the pretty, vaguely punk-looking girl with the interesting scar up one side of her neck. That Shade Darby was amused, kind, a bit distant but supportive. Then there was what Cruz thought of as the shark, the cold, calculating young woman with the brilliant mind.

This was a different girl, neither easygoing Shade nor the

shark. This was a wounded Shade, an uncertain Shade. A girl who had made decisions that destroyed her relationship with her only surviving parent, dragged Cruz into a life of felonies piled upon felonies, and, finally, left Malik screaming in unbearable agony, a charcoal and melted-flesh version of the boy Shade had once loved and been loved by.

"How are you?" Shade asked, practically cringing, as if she expected Cruz to berate her.

But as Shade had come to recognize the damage she had done, Cruz had come to accept her own complicity. No one had put a gun to her head to force her to follow Shade. Cruz had been the new kid in school, a mid-semester transfer after being kicked out of a Catholic school for wearing dresses. Evanston, Illinois, was still a bastion of relative tolerance, but the nastiness that had come to be a part of American life, even at the highest levels, had threatened her. Until Shade. Shade's friendship had spread an umbrella of safety over Cruz at school, and Cruz had leaped at the chance to have a friend. She had quickly seen that Shade was obsessed with the death of her mother on the day of the Perdido Beach Anomaly four years earlier, when the FAYZ dome had fallen. And Cruz knew that Shade's head was filled with fantasies of revenge against the monstrous being called Gaia who had used her powers for slaughter. But Cruz knew as well that Shade's revenge fantasies were just that, fantasies. No one can get revenge on a dead thing, and Gaia, that evil child, had died, destroyed in the end by the courage and sense of justice of an autistic child called Little Pete, and the charming sociopath Caine.

And yet, step by step, Cruz had gone along with Shade. She had chosen to take the rock herself, to become Rockborn. She had then acquired and learned to use a superhuman power. And she had raised nothing but the most token objections as Shade used her super-speed to steal money and cars and phones to keep them going.

Mea culpa. Mea maxima culpa, Cruz thought, an echo of her upbringing in the church. My fault. My most grievous fault.

Hero, villain, and monster, that was the three-part taxonomy of superhumans, according to Malik. Shade was meant to be a hero, intended to be a hero, wanted to be a hero, and Cruz, to the extent she'd really thought about it, imagined herself as a sort of Robin to Shade's Batman, a sidekick.

I'm not even starring in my own life.

But at the moment, the hollow-eyed, quiet, sad girl beside Cruz did not inspire notions of heroism. She looked like Cruz imagined soldiers must look after far too long in battle.

"What do we do?" Cruz asked, hating herself for the question, hating the weakness that made her turn to Shade for the answers even now, even with Malik a few hundred yards away with tubes in his throat and veins, with tubes collecting his bloodred urine, with acres of gauze and gallons of salves hiding the horror show his body had become.

Shade lowered her head to look through the windshield and up at the hospital. "I guess they'll do skin grafts and—"

"No," Cruz said. She shook her head. "They're not thinking of fixing him, they're waiting for him to die."

A spasm twisted Shade's face, squeezing her eyes shut,

making a grimace of her mouth. Tears rolled down her cheeks, and these she did not brush away.

Cruz said, "His only hope is the rock. Too much deep-tissue damage. His legs . . . I was there when they changed the dressings. His legs are just bones with chunks of burned meat attached, like, like those turkey legs they sell at fairs. It was awful. Terrible. There's no coming back from that, Shade. Malik is dead unless the rock . . ."

Shade cried silently for a while, her forehead on the steering wheel, hands limp in her lap.

"I don't know what to do," Shade said finally. "I don't—"

But Cruz did not hear the end of the sentence because at that moment a wave of unspeakable pain assaulted her with a suddenness and violence that wrung whinnying, panicked screams from her mouth.

Shade, too, shrieked in agony, her face distorted like a figure from some medieval painting of hell's torments.

And it wasn't stopping; it wasn't lessening; the two girls writhed and shook and bellowed in pain as if they were burning alive inside the car. Shade screamed and slapped at her body as if she was on fire. Cruz pushed open the door of the car, panicked, believing the car had caught fire.

It was the worst thing either had ever felt, and it would not stop. And through a mist of tears and with senses twisted by mind-shattering agony, Cruz realized that they were not alone: people were streaming from the hospital, crying, screaming, rolling on the ground, tearing the hair from their heads.

"Morph!" Shade yelled. "Now!"

Cruz understood, though holding on to even a snippet of thought was almost impossible. Agony lent wings to the transformation as Cruz, the six-foot-tall trans girl, became to all appearances a large young black woman with dreadlocks. Cruz had gone to the first image that popped in her mind, their fellow Rockborn mutant, the FAYZ survivor Dekka Talent.

Shade at the same time had changed even more drastically. Her face narrowed and seemed to sweep back, like a person in a wind tunnel. Her russet hair became a solid punk-rock-looking wedge. Her body seemed to be covered in something like plastic, like she was a less slick version of a Power Ranger. Her knees reversed direction, making a noise like wet stones tumbling, becoming insectoid, inhuman.

In seconds Shade was the vibrating speed demon she could become at will. And Cruz was Dekka. The pain was subdued, lessened, manageable, but it was still right there, like a physical force, like standing beside a rampaging river and feeling its power even if all that hit you were drops of spray. They were no longer in that river but felt its devastating power and knew that one slip . . .

"Malik," Shade said, slowing her speech to normal time so that Cruz could understand. It was like dragging a finger on a vinyl record to slow it down, words slurring but understandable.

Shade blew away, raced through the emergency room, a hellish scene of patients and their doctors and nurses all writhing in torment, crying, roaring, letting go of every bodily fluid. She went on, down corridors where patients dragged themselves out of sickbeds in a desperate need to do something, anything, to escape. She saw a nurse just about to jab herself with a syringe and took a millisecond's detour to snatch the syringe away.

Finally, Shade arrived at Malik's room.

And there he was: Malik.

Of all the things Shade expected, this was none of them, because Malik stood. *Stood.* He had pulled the tubes from his throat and was unwinding gauze and peeling off compresses, revealing his own healthy black flesh, undamaged, unscarred.

Impossible!

From every direction the terrible screams lessened, giving way to moans and cries of shock.

Shade could do nothing but stare as the full horror of what she was seeing came home to her. The rock transformed those who took it. The power the rock granted came with the necessity of a physical transformation—a morph.

This Malik, the one with flesh and muscles, was not Malik, it was a *morph* of Malik, like some desperately unfunny joke. He had become not himself but a version of himself, a living memory of himself.

"It's gone," Malik cried. "The pain's gone! I'm better, Shade! I'm fixed!"

CHAPTER 3
Veterans of Past and Future Wars

"YOU WERE CLEVER to come in through the back window," Astrid Ellison said to her guests. "We've been under surveillance for the last four years, but it was pretty sketchy. You'd see a cop every now and then, or maybe an FBI car. But the last weeks it's been more intense."

"Any chance the place is bugged?" Dekka Talent asked, accepting a cup of tea.

Astrid made a humorless laugh. "Of course it's bugged, but we found the bug with some help from a guy Albert sent us. He tied the bug into a YouTube channel, and if anyone's watching or listening they're probably getting awfully tired of listening to autoplays of Tim and Eric."

"Albert, huh?" Dekka said with a glance at Armo.

Armo, short for Aristotle Adamo, was very large, very strong, and not terribly bright despite his given name. He was a pathologically oppositional white high school boy who had ended up being thrown together with Dekka. And oddly enough, the partnership between the tough, serious, unshakable African American lesbian and the impulsive, reckless, impossible-to-control straight white guy seemed to work. Neither could have explained why. So long as Dekka was careful to avoid sounding as if she was giving orders and always gave Armo the option of disagreeing, he would mostly end up doing what she needed done.

And there was value in a crazy person who could become a sort of weird, not-quite-polar bear. His power was little compared to Dekka's, but in a fight it never hurt to have some batshit berserker on your side. And no one was more berserk than Armo once the fighting started.

"Who's Albert?" Armo asked.

Sam Temple sat opposite them in an IKEA Poäng chair, brown leather and blond wood. "Depends who you ask. Most people in the FAYZ despised him. But they ate because Albert figured out how to feed them." He shrugged. "The FAYZ revealed unsuspected depths in some. Albert's what, like, seventeen, eighteen years old now? He's at very least a millionaire, and if he's not a billionaire by the time he's thirty, I'll be shocked. His company—FAYZco—owns four McDonald's franchises down in Orange County and one in Oakland. And his second book is number one. Still."

"*Business Secrets of the FAYZ*," Astrid said with a curled lip.

It would be wrong, Dekka reflected, to suppose that time had matured Astrid—Astrid had always been an adult. Dekka pictured Astrid at three years old already delivering lectures and secretly imagining herself to be the smartest person in the room. Then again, Dekka admitted, Astrid generally *was* the smartest person in the room. Once upon a time she'd been known as Astrid the Genius. Of course, Astrid the Ice Queen, Astrid the Bitch, and even less polite sobriquets had also been used at times. And had also been at least partly true.

Dekka had never much liked Astrid, but Astrid had changed over time, both in the FAYZ and after. On a superficial level she'd grown from quite pretty to stunning. The weight of pain and fear, and a small dose of humility, had added depth to her judgmental blue eyes. And a diet of something other than rat and cabbage had given her a complexion too perfect to be natural, though Dekka detected no makeup. Astrid was manipulative, controlling, and superior, but also in the end an oddly perfect match for Sam Temple. Dekka was glad Sam had her watching his back—Astrid could be fierce.

The strength of the bond between them even impressed itself on Armo, who quite enjoyed looking at Astrid. Armo had read a book once—just one—and it had been about the Vikings, who he considered "his people," his heritage. Give Astrid Ellison a sword and a chain-mail coat, and she would be exactly what Armo imagined a Viking shield maiden would look like. But Armo kept his admiration discreet. Dekka had told Armo about Sam, and while Sam could no longer simply raise his hands and burn a hole through you, there was a gravity to him. Armo might be (by his own cheerful admission) all kinds of difficult and headstrong, and he would never pretend to be the smartest person in any room, but he honored warriors, and, if Dekka was to be believed, Sam Temple was the living, breathing incarnation of a warrior king, some combination of Cnut the Great, Cyclops from the X-Men, and George Washington.

Dekka saw that Sam had put on weight. Not fat, but thickness in his shoulders and arms. Sam Temple at age fourteen had had terrifying power and staggering responsibility dropped on him. He had made mistakes, he had failed at times, but he had become a great leader, an inspiration. Dekka had become his strong right arm, his soldier, his advisor. Dekka and Sam were connected in ways that only two combat soldiers who've shared a foxhole can be.

For no particular reason, Sam reached across the coffee table and took Dekka's hand. She squeezed back and held it for a long minute as memories flowed invisibly between them.

"Sammy," Dekka said, shaking her head.

"Dekka," he said.

"Bad shit happening, Sam."

He nodded. "Yeah. It's the same thing, isn't it? The FAYZ, I mean."

Dekka nodded. "The same asteroid or whatever it was, the rock, more of it has come, and more may be coming. I don't know. I don't know if anyone knows—maybe Shade Darby. But the powers . . . that's all changed. I don't know if that's because of the dome, or because Little Pete held the gaiaphage back, but whatever, this stuff is out of control now. The main difference is that you need to physically morph."

"Like Orc?" Astrid asked.

"Maybe. But turned up to eleven. And we can turn it on or off. I can become this . . . this thing. This *creature*. By choice. When I am the creature, when I am in morph—which is what we're calling it for some reason—I can make things come apart. Shred things. People, too, if I'm not careful. Armo came by a different path, but he's one, too, now, a COR, a Child of the Rock. Rockborn or Rockborn 2.0, some people say." Dekka's lip curled. She had never been a big fan of social media, and after years of being referred to as "the black lesbian" and much worse, and now frequently identified as "Lesbokitty," her opinion had not improved. "You and Astrid are being labeled as O-COR—Original Children of the Rock. The Rockborn 2.0 include people like Shade Darby and her friend Cruz. And as you've seen on TV, a bunch of, um, unpleasant people."

"We saw the video of the Golden Gate and the Port of LA," Astrid said.

"And there's this . . . *thing*," Dekka said in a low tone. She tapped the side of her head. "When we change, when we morph, we . . . I was going to say 'hear' but we don't, we just feel or sense or are aware of these . . . well, we've been calling them Dark Watchers. I think it's them. I think it's the same creatures who fired the damned asteroid toward us."

"Dark Watchers?" Astrid said, narrowing her eyes. "Interesting. Probably just a coincidence."

Her husband looked at her expectantly.

"It's an old California legend," Astrid said. "The Dark

Watchers. I think it started with the Chumash Indians and was picked up by the Spanish, who called them *Los Vigilantes Oscuros*. Supposedly they are nonhuman creatures who only appear at twilight in the area around Monterey down to, well, down to Perdido Beach. Steinbeck actually referenced them. . . . Anyway," she concluded, sensing that her lecture was getting a bit lecture-y, "probably coincidence."

A long, tense silence fell, broken finally by Armo, who said, "I'm sorry, but do you have anything to eat?"

Astrid patted Sam on the shoulder and said, "Why don't you make some sandwiches?"

Something passed between Sam and Astrid, something tinged with frustration and regret. Sam nodded finally, like a condemned man accepting a judge's just sentence. He left and Armo went with him, leaving Dekka and Astrid alone.

Astrid wasted no time. "You are not dragging Sam into this, Dekka."

Dekka felt a surge of irritation—a very familiar feeling when she dealt with Astrid.

"He doesn't have the power anymore. He's just a guy, a regular human being." Astrid stopped herself, seeing Dekka's raised eyebrow. "Okay, he's still *Sam*. But he has no powers. He'll go with you if you ask him, you know he will. And he'll die." Her voice cracked on that last word. "He had his war, Dekka."

Dekka heard the echo of her own voice saying just about those same words to Tom Peaks, the man who had run the monstrous HSTF-66 facility called the Ranch before being fired and choosing the path of the rock to become the monster Dragon.

"I don't want him to come," Dekka said. "Not really. I mean, look, does part of me sort of automatically reach for him when the trouble starts? Yeah, Astrid. If I live to be a hundred, whenever the shit hits the fan I'll still probably be thinking, 'Get Sam.' But you're right. And I know it."

Astrid sighed. "So does he. He knows. He's barely voting age and he feels he's washed up. He doesn't know what to do. We have money from the book and the movie, so we're not struggling, but Sam needs to find a place for himself in the world, and it can't be with you, Dekka."

Irritation drained away. Dekka hung her head and said, "You know, I don't like you, Astrid, I never have. But you stand by Sam. You love him, and I honor the hell out of that. If I ever meet someone who loves me half as much as you do him, well, that would be pretty great. I will never do anything to hurt Sam."

Strange, Dekka thought, two young women who could not be more different, talking about Sam Temple as if he was a fragile child they had to protect. Sam and Armo came back in, laughing at some shared joke, and set sandwiches down. Armo had one halfway down his throat already. Both young men caught the mood, and Sam shot a look at his wife and then at Dekka.

"Ah. So the decision's been made," he said with a mixture of rueful acceptance and frustration. He shrugged. Then he held up the hands that had once had the power to blast a beam of light capable of cutting through steel. Nothing happened. "Honestly, I wouldn't be of much use."

Dekka said, "Right, you're all done for, useless and pathetic." She shook her head. "Don't make me slap the crap out of you, Sam. I am not going to feel sorry for you, and if you feel sorry for yourself, I swear to God I will kick it right out of you."

To Dekka's delight and Astrid's relief, Sam burst out laughing. "I have missed you, Dekka. You, Edilio, Lana . . . Breeze."

Dekka felt the familiar catch in her throat on hearing that last name. Brianna, the Breeze, Dekka's one-way, unreciprocated, hopeless, doomed, magnificent love. "We kicked more than our share of ass," Dekka said.

Sam looked intently at his friend. "You've got something else to tell us, Dekka."

"He hasn't gotten any dumber," Dekka said to Astrid, trying for a light tone.

"Well, he couldn't, really," Astrid said, playing along. It was an old joke between Astrid the Genius and Sam the surfer dude.

"Spill it," Sam said, undeterred.

Dekka folded her hands, twining the fingers. "I don't think it showed up on the public footage, at least not the stuff I've seen."

Sam waited, and Astrid, as if sensing the need, stood up.

"Drake," Dekka said. "Whip Hand is back."

ASO-6

ANOMALOUS SPACE OBJECT Six was not a large chunk; in fact, by the time fiery reentry had burned off a bit, it would weigh just forty pounds on impact. The impact had been carefully calculated to be in the Atlantic Ocean, four hundred nautical miles west-northwest of São Miguel Island in the Azores.

But the loose grip of astronaut Heidemarie Stefanyshyn-Piper changed that. During a 2008 space walk, astronaut Stefanyshyn-Piper had accidentally let go of a briefcase-sized tool kit.

Because ASO-6 was smallish, it picked up a bit of a wobble when it smacked into that orbiting space garbage, and went off in a different direction than its original trajectory. It hit water thirty miles off the coast of the Kings Bay submarine base in Georgia, just north of the Florida line.

The water wasn't deep by Atlantic Ocean standards. The rock would likely be recoverable. But the vessels intended to carry out the recovery were all about two thousand miles from the location, a trip that would take them days to complete.

In the meantime the Coast Guard cutter *Abbie Burgess* was dispatched to monitor the scene.

Fourteen hours later, with the undersea research flotilla steaming toward them, the *Abbie Burgess* sank, with the loss of twenty-one lives.

The only radio message to be heard from the *Abbie Burgess* was, "Oh, God! Oh, G—"

A Coast Guard helicopter sent to the scene found only a few bits of floating wreckage. And no bodies.

CHAPTER 4
And Coming In at Number One . . .

BRIGADIER GENERAL GWENDOLYN DiMarco did not like the office Tom Peaks had vacated at the Ranch, the secret research and development facility in the hills east of Monterey, California. It was too bland, too office-like, too normal.

Normal. Not a word to be applied to Tom Peaks himself, who had salved his hurt feelings at being demoted by taking a large dose of the rock and turning into a massive, fire-breathing, magma-vomiting, reptilian creature who'd burned down much of the Port of Los Angeles before being dragged into the channel by an even more bizarre and dangerous creature created out of starfish DNA.

Peaks had concealed the crazy within, and perhaps, DiMarco thought, his dull, cubicle-like office was part of the disguise. She had chosen a space closer to the action, and the action at the Ranch was all underground. Anyway, she'd never been much of a sun worshipper.

Her office now was a singular structure occupying one

end of the great cavern, the combination cave and excavation that hid all their work from electronic eyes on satellites and drones. On Google satellite maps, the Ranch looked like what it had once been: an older, repurposed army facility.

Should call it the Iceberg, not the Ranch, DiMarco thought, nodding with grim pleasure at what she took to be a rather clever joke. Because more of it was underwater than above. Although not water, but land, earth. Dirt. Or at least a giant hole in the dirt. So, an iceberg if you meant that . . .

Well, DiMarco knew she was not a natural wit.

Her office was a long rectangle originally built as a construction office for the contractors who had excavated and built the massive underground facility. The location had the great advantage of being up high on a granite outcropping that formed a shelf a hundred feet above the cavern floor, just twenty feet below the jagged stone roof. She'd had it totally remodeled, of course, so the old corrugated-tin cladding had been replaced by reinforced concrete eight inches thick. The small, dirty windows that had been enough for the construction supervisor had been replaced with a single long window, twenty-four feet from end to end and six feet tall. Level 8 bulletproof glass, of course, just a hair over six centimeters thick, and capable of shrugging off five rounds from a high-powered sniper rifle.

Within the Bunker—as DiMarco's office had been instantly nicknamed—were just two interior walls. One, on the left end, closed off DiMarco's adjutant, secretary, and security detail. On the right end DiMarco had her private bathroom.

But occupying fully two-thirds of the square footage was her own office, dominated by a massive steel desk partly made of armor recovered from a Russian tank that had come to misfortune in Ukraine. The desk was painted olive drab, a very military contrast to the rest of the office, which had expensive Persian carpets and rich mahogany bookshelves stuffed with everything ever written about the Perdido Beach Anomaly and the emerging field of exobiology, and a great many books on arcane aspects of genetics and the hacking of same.

Major Mike Atwell, DiMarco's adjutant, walked in, five long strides from his own office, stepped off with careful precision to bring him just before her desk, where he executed a pivot that faintly snapped his heels together, and lay the morning briefing book on her desk.

The paper copy was a formality, of course; DiMarco already had the digital version open on her computer.

"Have a seat, Mike," DiMarco said.

Atwell, a thirty-one-year-old West Pointer with not one but two PhDs—genetics and military history with a focus on China—was a man who would never manage to look as good as he should in his impeccably tailored uniforms. He was getting full at the waist, had shoulders that were more vertical than horizontal, and had been cursed with a face that screamed "nerd."

"Let's run down the top-ten list," DiMarco said.

Atwell nodded and began from memory. He might not have shoulders, but he had prodigious recall.

"We are well beyond ten at this point," Atwell said, earning a sharp look from DiMarco, who hated being told what she already knew. "Vincent Vu, who calls himself Abaddon the Destroyer, has been spotted subsequent to the Port of LA battle, as himself, as a kid, at a 7-Eleven in Long Beach and a Target store in Glendale, as well as appearing as Abaddon and, for reasons that remain obscure, destroying half a mile of used car lots. Three dead."

DiMarco nodded. "I'm not sure Vu is target number one, but go on."

"In second place, your predecessor, Tom Peaks. He's being called Dragon in the press. Sometimes Burning Man or Hot Lizard in social media."

"*He's* number one," DiMarco said. "You can't just assess according to damage done, you have to consider the mental capabilities as well. Vu is genuinely mentally ill, and a teenager to boot, who knows nothing and certainly has no larger plans. But Peaks?"

"Yes, ma'am," Atwell said, though he was far from convinced that ill was any better than evil. "In third place we have Shade Darby, with her super-speed. Very powerful and very smart, a bad combination. We've analyzed the videos, and the best guess is that she can hit speeds in excess of seven hundred miles an hour, which, depending on atmospheric conditions, can mean Mach 1, the speed of . . ." He let that trail off, seeing the warning look from DiMarco, the look that said, *I know what Mach 1 means.*

"Next up, Dekka Talent. She's very powerful, reasonably bright, and more experienced at actual physical combat than any of the others, and probably more than any soldier currently serving in uniform, frankly. In the media they're calling her everything from Catstein to Catzilla to Lesbokitty."

DiMarco nodded, and her upper lip disappeared behind her lower lip, a clenched-jaw expression that often preceded an angry eruption.

No eruption this time. Not yet.

"Fifth place is Aristotle Adamo, aka Armo."

"I *made* that boy!" DiMarco snapped. "I gave him power beyond anything he could imagine, and offered him . . ." She waved a hand to encompass the world of pleasure she'd tried to use to control the uncontrollable brat. This one DiMarco took personally. Dekka had been Peaks's special project, Armo had been hers, and it was not a happy reality that the two had apparently teamed up.

"Six is Hugo Rojas, aka Cruz. She's a trans female or gender-fluid male—we aren't sure yet—a follower, not a leader. She seems to have the power to alter her appearance at will. She can appear as any person, old, young, big, small, any race, any gender."

"Huh." DiMarco grunted and turned on a sour smile. "I'm sure he, she, or *it* enjoys that."

Atwell quashed his instinctive disgust at her sneering bigotry. "Seven is Francis Specter. She's just fourteen, mother and father both members of a meth-dealing biker gang known to have been one of the gangs drawn to the Perdido Beach cave. No idea whether she consumed some rock or was down there in the hole long enough to be affected less directly."

"What do we have on her powers?"

Atwell blew out a sigh. "Damned little, I'm afraid. She seems to be able to pass through solid objects, or allow solid objects to pass through her. We just located a seven-second snippet off a traffic camera in Glenrio, New Mexico. May I?" He indicated the remote control on DiMarco's desk. He clicked the button to open a sliding panel that revealed a large TV monitor. A few more clicks, and they had choppy, grainy black-and-white video of a girl with jet-black hair crossing a busy highway. A car came into view, swerved madly to avoid her, and was followed by a Costco tractor trailer that slammed into her at sixty-four miles an hour.

And passed right through her: the entire length of the tractor trailer. Francis Specter had walked on out of camera range as if nothing had happened.

DiMarco had him replay it twice. "Fascinating. My first thought was that she alters her density, or the density of solid objects, but we'd see an increase in apparent size then. The lab's current working theory is that she moves into an unseen dimension and essentially moves *around* the object through a fifth dimension of space-time."

"The truck driver says all he saw was like a blurred rainbow."

"A what?"

"He says that in the split second he saw her, she looked like a walking, blurry rainbow."

"Why don't we see it on the video?"

Atwell said, "Well, one, the driver could be hallucinating,

or two, she's got her back to the camera and the effect is only on her skin."

DiMarco drummed her fingers and looked at the freeze-frame blur. "Criminal parents. If she's bending space, it will be impossible to lock up or restrain her in any way. Pity. She's a KOS."

KOS. Kill on sight.

"Glenrio is hard on the New Mexico–Texas border," Atwell said. "New Mexico authorities will not cooperate, but the gang frequently crosses into Texas, and we have people in the Texas Rangers who can . . . can do what needs to be done."

Atwell, as a student of military history, understood that he was being given an illegal order, an order that violated the law and the Constitution. And his oath as an officer. It made him queasy. Just not queasy enough to refuse.

"KOS! And I'm not concerned with blowback. We have assets of our own, we don't need to lean on the police," DiMarco said. "Eighth place?"

"The Perdido Beach survivor Drake Merwin, aka Whip Hand, known to millions from the Ellison book and the movie. He's teamed up with Peaks, which is bad enough, but worse, ordinary people think he's Alex Pettyfer, the actor who played him in the movie. In reality he is worse than could be shown in a PG-13 movie, much worse—a psychopath and a sadist. A murderer, rapist, torturer, an all-around nasty piece of work."

"KOS?" DiMarco frowned. "No, I think not—we want him. I assume you've read-in on him? The whip arm thing is not the power that interests me; he is apparently indestructible. You could run him through a blender and pour the bloody goo in the ocean, and a few days or weeks later he would be back. No, no KOS on Drake Whip Hand—he may yet be useful."

Atwell made a note, concealing his disapproval. Atwell understood the need for drastic measures, but working with vicious animals like Drake Merwin was not why he had enlisted.

"Number nine is Malik Tenerife. A college freshman at Northwestern, high IQ, devoted, we think, to Shade Darby. We have only very preliminary information about him. He was badly burned by Peaks in the battle at the port. Doctors gave him a zero chance of surviving, but somehow he walked out of the hospital, seemingly healthy. He had an unusual effect. I just this minute got some video . . ."

DiMarco rapped her knuckles on her desk, an impatient signal to get on with it.

This time the video was from a professional news camera, showing a middle-aged nurse with a tear-streaked face.

"*It was horrible, horrible, I felt as if I was on fire. The pain . . . I could look down and see that I wasn't hurt, but the pain, the agony . . . It was unbearable. I honestly thought that if it didn't stop very soon, I would kill myself.*"

"Huh," DiMarco said thoughtfully. "We want Mr. Tenerife if we can get him. Let's see just how devoted he is to the girl who dragged him into all this."

"Finally, number ten is still Justin DeVeere, aka Knightmare."

DiMarco gave him a hard look. "Young Justin is in custody and working for us now." She stabbed a finger in the direction of the cavern outside her window. "He's caged and tagged, and enlisted as a private in the US Army. And not even that sword of his can cut through a foot of reinforced concrete and six inches of electrified Vanadium steel."

Atwell licked his lips nervously. "Ma'am, I think we should remember that both Dekka and Armo were formerly held here, and both escaped."

"They escaped Tom Peaks, not me!" she said, adding grit to the last two words. "Anyway, if we're going to start counting our own kept monsters, hell, we've got worse than Knightmare locked up down here."

Yes, Atwell thought grimly, *and may God forgive us all.* The Ranch had been doing crash research in numerous avenues: they had tried to weaponize and control the rock by feeding it various strands of animal DNA. Sometimes—Armo—it had worked. Other times it was as if the rock was mocking them, using entirely different DNA—a passing mosquito, say—to create unsustainable monstrosities. One had morphed into a human-mite hybrid, a brainless slug unable to move its bulk on eight tiny, distorted human legs.

The Ranch had also pioneered cyborgs—human-machine blends: robots with human brains, weapons systems with a human head attached, or sometimes just a brain.

Silence descended as DiMarco templed her fingers and rested her chin on her fingertips, a sign she was thinking. For a solid five minutes Atwell sat looking into space, trying to convince himself this was all right, trying to believe that years from now he would still be able to look his daughters in the eye and justify what he was doing. General DiMarco made that harder with what she said next.

"We are being handcuffed by rules and regulations that are totally inappropriate for this moment in history. We need to be able to shoot first and ask questions later. These are not street criminals, these are superpowered terrorists, mostly very young because God knows only a teenager is dumb enough to deliberately swallow a mutagenic alien virus. But young or old, they've already done billions of dollars in damage, not to mention cost hundreds of lives. KOS. Kill on sight! That should be the default, and we only exempt those we can use. Work for me, or take a bullet."

"Yes, ma'am," Atwell said, flashing mentally on the Wannsee Conference, the notorious meeting that had led to the Holocaust. There had been gutless apparatchiks there, too, nodding and saying, "Yes, sir."

Then came the bad news he had to deliver. He'd been hoping for a good moment, but DiMarco was not in a good mood. "There's another matter, General. The Mother Rock. We've got it secured here, as you know, but we've only just recovered data from the *Okeanos Explorer*, and there is a discrepancy."

Her eyes practically burned a hole through his forehead. "Discrepancy?"

"They weighed the rock on board. We've now weighed it. And there is a discrepancy of nineteen pounds, four ounces."

"Almost twenty pounds has gone missing?" Silence again, broken by a slammed hand on the desk that made Atwell jump. "Godammit! That's 320 one-ounce doses! That does it. I'm tired of playing by the rules. Prepare a request for a national mobilization of the National Guard and a State of Emergency. We need to be kicking in doors! And let's start with everyone who was aboard *Okeanos*. I want them questioned, and I don't give a rat's ass about how that questioning is carried out."

Atwell sat forward, alarmed out of his calm composure. "But ma'am, the White House would have to approve that!"

DiMarco's sneer was like a dictionary illustration of the word "cynical." "Do you really think they won't? This White House? We'll have the approval in six hours, twelve tops. And I'm not waiting."

Atwell smoothed the concern out of his expression and nodded.

DiMarco drummed her fingers on the desk. "The bigger problem," she said, "is not the monsters we know, but those that are to come."

Atwell frowned. "General?"

"Do you really think this crop of Rockborn is the end of it? We know that several pounds at least of the the original Perdido Beach rock are in private hands—biker gangs, treasure hunters, thrill seekers. We know Shade Darby has some or all of ASO-3. And we know something has happened to twenty pounds of the Mother Rock. And that's not even getting into foreign threats! My God, Atwell, do you not realize what this is?"

"I think I—"

DiMarco's hand slapped the desktop again, hard enough to make her souvenir mug jump. "This is an alien invasion,

Atwell. It's come in the form of a mutagenic rock, not little green men, but it is still an invasion. The only way we survive is total, complete annihilation of anyone who uses the rock without working for me!"

She swiveled her chair away, turning her back to Atwell, and gazed at the wall-sized map of the world. "If we are strong and ruthless, we can stop each of the ones we have, one by one. But somewhere out there may be a mutant too powerful for us. That is what worries me, Atwell: the unknown villain."

CHAPTER 5
Crackers with a Lunatic

TOM PEAKS, FORMER head of Homeland Security Task Force 66, had emerged from the water at the Port of Los Angeles exhausted and defeated. For all Dragon's power, he had been defeated in the end by some kid like a giant starfish. It had been humiliating, and unfortunately Tom Peaks's companion was not one to be gentle.

"You got your ass kicked," Drake had said.

"We need a place to hole up," Peaks said.

Drake laughed contemptuously. "The big man who thought he'd make me his sidekick. Your face is known, Peaks. Everyone in the world is gunning for you. I have a place, I have a place where I can hole up, but what hole do you have?"

Peaks stared blearily at Drake. The sadistic psychopath was as angularly handsome as ever, untouched by the passage of time or by the terrible injuries he had sustained. He was cruel and vicious, and Peaks didn't need Drake's ten-foot-long python arm to convince him. Nor did you need to have seen coroners' photos of his victims over the last four years, as Peaks had. You could see it in Drake's eyes.

Peaks thought, *I'm the Dragon, but he's the monster.*

But Peaks knew he needed time to recover. His mind was barely functioning, like a remote control with a nearly dead battery—sometimes the buttons worked, sometimes they didn't. If he were a normal human being, he'd have self-diagnosed as suffering from depression. So he let Drake take the lead. They stole a car and drove into the desert, back to Joshua Tree National Park, to the emptiness of the Quail Mountain area, where Drake led them up and up, deeper and deeper into dust-dry hills, into wild piles of boulders, through tangled thorn and Velcro-leaved succulents, to a crack that looked too small for a man to push through. But it proved doable, just barely.

It was a cave. Peaks felt the relatively cool air and the scent of musk and mildew and carrion, rotting meat. It was dark as night, and for a moment Peaks wondered whether Drake had led him here as a trick. But the truth was, if Drake had wanted to kill Peaks, he probably could have done so at any time.

Then Drake struck a lighter and held it to a candle. Then a second and a third. The revealed interior was nothing, a thousandth the size of the great cavern at the Ranch. It was a space more vertical than horizontal, narrow at the opening and at the far end, shaped like an envelope that bulges in the middle. The roof of the cave was invisible, a darkness that called to mind tall Gothic cathedrals. The floor was perhaps twenty feet at its widest, four times that deep, with tumbled rocks leading to solid stone at the end. In daytime a faint light might filter in, but it was night when they arrived, and the only source of illumination was the candles.

Peaks wished there were fewer candles, for what they illuminated was a nightmare. Drake had used railroad spikes to crucify three people. Three bodies hung from the stone walls, the fat rusted steel spikes driven through their wrists. They'd had no support for their feet, so they would have hung with all their weight from the bones of their wrists. One was a male in a state of advanced decomposition, stripped naked, flesh little more than beef jerky, face like a drum skin stretched over a scream.

The other two were women, one almost as decomposed as the male. The other was . . . fresher, for lack of a better word. Despite being in a cave in the middle of nowhere, the flies had found her, and maggots grew fat and white in her eye sockets.

"Jesus Christ," Peaks whispered.

Drake nodded. "Yeah, the Romans had some skills at making death take a long, long time."

"You murdered them!"

Drake laughed. "Nah, I just nailed them up there. Had a little fun with them, sure, but it's hunger that killed them. You want to give them water from time to time, otherwise it's too quick. Thirst will kill you in anywhere from three days to a week. But hunger? Hell, that can take up to four or five weeks. Longer if you give them the occasional bat or coyote turd to eat."

His cruel lips smiled. "That bitch there, the redhead? She

took thirty-four days. Screaming, begging, crying. Like my own personal sound system."

Peaks felt sick. He had known what Drake was. He had seen pictures of people, mostly women, flayed by the Whip Hand. He'd heard or read all the stories from the FAYZ survivors. He'd even seen the movie based on Ellison's book. But pictures and stories and movies still did not prepare him for the reality. For one thing, only reality smelled.

What have I gotten myself into?

In his arrogance, Peaks had always imagined using Drake as a convenient tool, as if the sick bastard was a screwdriver he could just pull out as needed. He'd also thought he could use and control Dekka Talent.

Note to self, he thought wryly, *don't assume that young equals weak or compliant.*

Still, he reassured himself, Dragon was within him, and if Drake tried anything . . . and yet, for all that, Peaks was scared all the way down to his liver.

"Speaking of starving to death, do you have any food?" Peaks asked, trying to sound unimpressed.

Drake nodded. "A little. I don't need to eat, but I sometimes like the taste. And Brittany Pig likes to chew on a cracker sometimes. Can't swallow, of course." He whipped off his T-shirt, revealing a tight, lean body with six-pack abs and the bulge of a girl's face rising like a hideous wart on his upper chest.

Long ago Drake had become fused to Brittany. Brittany had once, many years earlier, been one of Sam and Edilio's "soldiers," a moral, religious, decent girl who been driven hopelessly mad. The metal wires of her broken braces still protruded from the mouth that liked to chew and then spit out the occasional cracker or cookie.

It was testimony to the horror of the cave, candlelight flickering off bleached bone and tattered skin, that Peaks barely bothered to notice Drake's . . . companion.

Drake whipped his python arm through the air and snatched a box of Ritz crackers and tossed it to Peaks. "You can have these, but feed one to Brittany Pig."

And Tom Peaks—once one of the most secretly powerful people in the country—realized he lacked the strength of will to refuse. Gingerly he fed a Ritz to the wire-jutting mouth and watched with morbid fascination as she chewed and let the results dribble down Drake's belly.

"So now what, mastermind?" Drake asked. "You promised me Astrid. I've got room for her on my wall."

"There's security on Ellison and Temple, and it'll be doubled or tripled now," Peaks said through his cracker crumbs. "But a month from now?" He shrugged. "It's all coming apart now, Drake. Civilization is cracking and crumbling. Law and order won't be sustainable."

Drake tilted his head, genuinely interested. Crumbling civilization sounded like just the thing for him.

"We thought we could contain this, but we can't," Peaks said.

Drake's whip snapped again, and from the darkness emerged a warm can of beer, which Peaks drank gratefully.

"Tell me," Drake said. "Give me your play-by-play."

Peaks considered. "Well, look at it this way. The Perdido Beach Anomaly, the FAYZ, was a massive blow to everything humans thought they knew. And the more we learned, the worse it got. What happened inside that dome was impossible under the laws of physics. Which means the laws of physics are either bullshit, or they are like computer code and can be hacked, or"—he shrugged—"or everything is an illusion."

Drake nodded. "We're their TV."

"The Dark Watchers?"

"Whatever," Drake said. "Brittany Pig says they're gods, right, Piggie?"

The mouth on his chest gnashed and a whispery voice, speaking in gasps, said, "Gods of hell, not heaven."

"See? She's fun to talk to."

I'm going mad, Peaks thought. *I'm going absolutely insane. I'm in a cave decorated with crucifixion victims, chatting with a serial killer who feeds crackers to the girl who lives on his chest.*

"So," Drake pushed, "what happens if civilization crashes and burns?"

Peaks shrugged. "Then we're back to evolution, survival of the best adapted, the most fit. People who adapt survive; those who don't, don't."

Drake had lit a collection of twigs and now had a small fire going. Peaks watched the smoke rise. There was another opening to the cave, that was clear, something that acted as a chimney.

"What is it you want, Drake?" Peaks asked.

"Me? Just my usual fun."

"That?" Peaks nodded toward the hanging bodies.

"And more. See, thing is, Tom, I can't be killed. Everyone's tried. But somehow I just keep coming back. It's kinda weird until you get used to it. Like when Brianna chopped me up and scattered pieces everywhere. I reassembled. Then Sammy boy burned me to ashes. But there was a chunk of me left from Brianna's work, and that's all it took." He shook his head as if remembering better times. "I didn't have, you know, thoughts or anything. But when that last piece of me started to grow, well, pretty soon, bam, I was back to being me. Me and Brittany Pig. So, see, I'm not worried about adapting or evolving or even surviving."

"So, you won't be going to college," Peaks said, deadpan.

Drake showed wolfish teeth. "I'm a simple boy with simple needs."

"Torture. Rape. Murder."

"Don't knock it if you haven't tried it. You know that guy, that rich tech guy who disappeared a couple years ago? That's him." He nodded at the crucified man. "Day one he offered me a million dollars. The next day he offered to give me a *billion* dollars." Drake smiled, enjoying memories. "What are you after, Peaks?"

Tom Peaks thought it over. He'd been a respected and powerful man. He'd had a family, a career, things he liked and cared about and enjoyed. But that was all gone now.

"Survival," Peaks said. *My God,* he thought, *is that really it? Is that what it's come down to? From running HSTF-66 to praying for mere survival at any cost . . . in just a week?*

Drake laughed. "You aren't me, Peaks. I can't be killed, but you can be. Sooner or later they'll get you."

Peaks wanted to argue, but something inside him was crumbling like a stale cookie. He felt sick, sick down to his soul. He had lost his family . . . his career . . . his meaning in life. He had shocking power as Dragon, but he knew what assets the government had, and he knew Drake was right. They would find him and they would kill him.

"You don't even know how to process this, do you?" Drake mocked. On his chest, Brittany formed a leering, metallic grin. "You'd have lasted about six weeks in the FAYZ. Caine Soren would have had you licking his shoes for a hunk of boiled rat. You think you're all bad-ass with your Godzilla thing, but you barely survived Dekka and Shade Darby. Be glad ol' Sammy doesn't still have his powers. Wimp."

That insult caused a flare-up of pride, and Peaks almost said something. Almost. The truth was, he was scared. Scared of the future, scared of what he'd done. Scared to death of Drake. He now truly understood Dekka's extreme reaction when he'd first told her Drake was alive.

But along with the sneers, he sensed that Drake was looking for leadership. Drake had no plan, never would have any plan, beyond his next murder.

"We need the same thing they need if they are to survive. We need chaos. Without chaos, the government will eventually prevail. This has to become a fight of all against the government."

Drake raised an eyebrow. Brittany slavered.

"Without a complete breakdown of civilization," Peaks said, "we will all be hunted down, one by one."

"Uh-huh," Drake agreed. "I'll bet you could use a drink with a bit more kick." He whipped his tentacle out and came back with half a bottle of vodka. "Here you go. Liquid courage."

Peaks twisted off the cap and took a long drink. Then he said, "I need to know everything you know about the Dark Watchers. What do they want? And more importantly, will they help?"

"They don't help. They just watch. Sometimes they get impatient; sometimes they laugh. Sometimes you can kind of tell they don't want you to do something. But they don't interfere. See . . ." He leaned forward, casting house-of-horror shadows on his face. "This whole thing, the rock, the FAYZ, all this? It's a TV series, Tom. They're just waiting to see how it all comes out."

CHAPTER 6
Do You Feel My Pain? How About *Now?*

"MALIK, HOW . . . ARE you okay?" Shade asked.

It had not been hard to get Malik away from the hospital. Everyone in or near the hospital, from the parking lot attendant to the armed guards oustide Malik's room to the chief of medicine had been literally knocked to the ground by a blast of crippling agony.

Shade drove. Cruz sat in the back behind Malik, who rode shotgun. The wave of projected pain had ceased, and Malik was Malik again.

Mostly.

In sidelong glances, Shade saw the subtle differences. Malik was not quite Malik, he was a version of Malik, a reconstruction of Malik from his own memory, a Malik morph. A scar was gone from his lip. His shoulders were wider. His face was sleeker. He was a very realistic avatar of Malik.

Shade knew Cruz's view was even more disturbing. Seated behind Malik, she saw the back of his head and neck, areas Malik had not seen every day of his life and therefore did not picture, so that back there his hair was less detailed, like a blurry photograph or cheap animation.

Shade understood: When Cruz was in morph she could pass as anyone whose picture she had seen, or who she had met in real life. But the front, the part cameras saw, was invariably more detailed than the back. Sometimes, if she had only a front picture, the back was so vague as to be empty space, so that she could easily appear to be a flawless Morgan Freeman, but with nothing from the ears back.

It was Malik's clothing that was the least convincing part. It looked too clean and too crisp. Like paper rather than fabric. And his loopy, curly, poodle hair, one of many things Shade had loved about him, now had the too-sharp look of black ribbon.

"I'm . . . different," Malik said. "I'm . . . I don't feel the pain, but I know it's there. It's like it's on the other side of frosted glass. I . . ." He seemed to drift away for a moment. Too long a moment.

Shade sought Cruz's eyes in the rearview mirror. They were heading northeast, away from the Pacific, away from Los Angeles, with no destination in mind but *not here*.

Malik spoke again, and his voice was smaller somehow, as if it came from a distance. "This is a morph, isn't it?" He tapped his arm and rubbed the skin.

Shade felt her insides turn to lead. She wanted to weep. Wanted to end her life, to escape the weight of guilt that crushed her, that she knew would go on crushing her, that would never leave her alone.

"Yes, Bunny," Shade said. Long ago that had been her

affectionate name for him, back when they had been close.

Malik nodded. "I'm afraid I'm a bit confused."

Shade nodded, but could not speak. She brushed as unobtrusively as she could at tears.

Cruz saw this and spoke up. "Malik, you were burned. Badly. Very badly, my friend." Then she added a word weighted with sadness. "Fatally."

"But . . . ," Malik said. Then he was silent again, working it through, seeing the terrible truth of it. "If I de-morph, I'll die. I'll die in terrible pain, won't I? Shade?" Panic put a sharp edge on his words.

Shade gripped the steering wheel so hard her fingers were white. "Yes, Malik," Shade whispered.

The silence stretched again, each silence more damning than the one before, each one like a razor's cut on Shade's heart, on her belief in herself. She wanted to say that she was sorry, so terribly sorry, but those words would mean nothing to him, or to her.

"I never saw myself the way I am now, did I?" Malik asked. "Burned, I mean."

"You were bandaged up," Cruz said.

"I feel them," Malik said.

Both girls knew what he meant, but Shade asked anyway, because not to would have made her seem indifferent.

"Them?"

Shade was not indifferent, she was destroyed inside. But she had to drive the car. And she had to figure out what to do next. So she had to understand Malik, which meant understanding what she had led him to, which meant coming face-to-face with the human cost of her own stupid, stupid, reckless decisions. And that way lay only more guilt, more self-loathing. The cold, dead-eyed shark that Cruz always said was the other half of Shade struggled to rise within her, but the weight of self-loathing was too much. Shade felt herself on the edge of a precipice, teetering beside an endless black hole.

"The Dark Watchers," Malik said. "I won't ever be able to get away from them, will I?"

"I don't know," Shade said.

"What did I do back there? People were screaming. I think I did that, didn't I? Did I hurt those people?"

Shade again sought Cruz's eyes in the mirror, pleading.

Cruz said, "You have a power, Malik. I think, maybe, you can . . ." Shade heard her hesitation. She knew, and Cruz knew, that she was pronouncing a type of death sentence. "It seems like you can project pain. Shade and I felt it. It was . . . unbearable. Like being on fire. Your pain, I think. Somehow you can inflict it on people. In morph we were mostly immune, like you were talking about with frosted glass, like we knew it was there, but it didn't quite get to us."

Malik's voice was childlike in its hurt and disbelief. "You mean I hurt people?"

"Not hurt, not injure," Shade said quickly. "It's just pain."

"Just pain? *Just pain?*" Malik said, and suddenly began to cry.

Shade had never seen Malik cry. It seemed at once impossible and not at all impossible. Malik was strong, but he was a decent human being all the way down to the bone, one of life's good guys. And now he was a good person who could cause terrible pain to others.

"Is it still happening?" Malik asked, his voice a child's sob.

"No, it stopped," Cruz assured him. "It was a few seconds, maybe a minute. It may be something you can control. Something you can, you know . . . *use.*"

Everything about this conversation was wrong, like walking through a psychic minefield.

"*Use?*" Malik said. "Like torture? That's my power? That's my escape from death? I can bring people pain?" The childish tone was falling away, replaced by growing outrage. "I'm going to live the rest of my life with the Dark Watchers in my head? And the only thing I can do now is hurt people? That's my life? That's what I *am* now?"

The words were on the tip of Shade's tongue, but she would not say *I'm sorry*. To say it implied she thought the words meant something. As though some stupid words would lessen the enormity of what had happened.

What had happened because of *her*. An apology would be a request for forgiveness, and she neither wanted nor deserved forgiveness.

"I want to see," Malik said. "I want to see what I really am. My real body, not this . . ." He flicked a finger against his biceps as if expecting to discover that he was insubstantial.

"Malik, you can't de-morph," Cruz warned. "The pain would—"

"*Aaaaahhhhhh!*" Malik cried, and to the horror of both

Shade and Cruz, he was de-morphing, too-sleek flesh seeming to swirl and re-form.

"Stop it!" Shade cried, and yanked the car onto the shoulder of the road. "Stop, stop, stop! Don't do it!"

But Malik's clothing had turned to smoke, and the illusion of healthy flesh had given way to a creature of charcoal and angry red meat and bleached bone, and Malik screamed and screamed as Shade shouted, "Stop it, stop it, stop it!"

"Look at me!" Malik screamed, staring at the hideous stumps of his legs. "Look at me!"

Cruz said, "Change back, Malik! Right now!"

"Look at me!"

For just a second, the harder Shade emerged long enough to snap, "Goddammit, Malik, morph! *Now!*"

Her voice cut through the blinding, deafening, brain-shattering agony, and Malik began to change. Cruz watched in fascinated horror as flesh crept over his bones, eerily reversing the damage that superheated steam and liquid fire had done.

"I'm sorry, I'm sorry, I'm sorry." The futile words came at last because the only alternative was silence. And they evaporated, irrelevant, insufficient. Pointless. Shade gripped the wheel like she was trying to break it in half, unable to look at him. Then she turned and with one hand gripped Malik's reconstituted shoulder. "Do it to me. Make me feel it! Make me feel it! Hurt me! Just *me!*"

Malik was shaking his head no, no, but Cruz said, "Do it, Malik. See if you can focus it."

"I don't want to hurt Shade!"

"She needs to feel it," Cruz said, shaking her head in wonder at the madness of it all, the madness and the gutting feeling that everything, everywhere was spiraling down and down and down, that the whole world was staggering to a finish line that would bring nothing but destruction.

"I'll try," Malik said.

Shade steeled herself.

One . . . two . . . three . . . Cruz counted off seconds, expecting to be hit with the brutal agony she'd experienced earlier. But nothing. *Four . . . five . . . six . . .*

"*Shhhh shhhh ah ah ahahahah aaaarrrrrgghh!*" Shade screamed suddenly. "*No, no, nonononono! No! No! No!*" Her screams bounced around inside the car, deafening. She scrabbled madly at the door with hands she could not control, nothing but escape on a mind reduced instantaneously to an animal state.

Then Shade sagged and fell silent but for gasping breaths.

For a long while no one had anything to say. Sweat poured down Shade's face, joining bitter tears. Finally Shade pulled back out into traffic.

"Where are we going?" Cruz asked.

Shade jerked her chin forward. "That way."

They drove toward the mountains, toward the great dry mountains, toward the desert, away from people, away from the Port of Los Angeles, away, away, but never away from the one person Shade most wanted to leave: herself.

And yet, buried as she was under a mountain of guilt,

shattered as she was by the pain Malik had again revealed to her, nevertheless, deep down in the lowest depths of her mind, the shark began to move, somehow liberated by the pain, as if it was penance. There was no other way forward. Malik was not in a state of mind to make decisions. And Cruz? Well, Shade thought, Cruz had been amazing, but only in a support role. Cruz was not willing to take responsibility. She was not willing to lead. Only the shark could lead them now.

Because I've done such a great job so far.

They were three fugitives on the run from the entire US government, and possibly one or more mutant monsters. None could go home. None had a family anymore; they were beyond all of that. They were no longer daughters and son, they were no longer children at all, no longer anything they had meant to become. Monsters, the three of them. Monsters who had meant to be heroes.

"Cruz," Shade said. "I'm taking this turnoff to Desert Hot Springs. Google houses for sale. Find us one that's been empty for a while, at least two weeks."

Desert Hot Springs, like every Mojave Desert town, was flat and sparse. Few if any buildings extended above a single story. Houses were all ranch-style; businesses were marked with indifferent, sun-bleached signs. They drove past developments of gated trailer parks, gas stations, modest family restaurants, always heading toward dry mountain ridges that never seemed to get any closer.

Cruz found a house listed for sale, and they drove there. It was not in a gated development but stood somewhat forlorn, well off the main road, a single shaggy palm tree standing guard over a yard otherwise devoid of vegetation.

Shade pulled past and parked a quarter mile away. "Excuse me," she said, morphed, and ran. Thirty seconds later she was back. "Totally empty. I got in through a back window. We can hide the car in the garage."

Inside, the house was clean and completely empty, and smelled of carpet cleaner and fresh paint. But the water was still on. The water heater was not, but there was no such thing as really cold water in this part of the world. Cruz practically ran for the shower and stood for half an hour beneath a lukewarm stream, wishing the water could flow through her mind, cleaning away memory and self-doubt, anger and fear, leaving her as clean inside as out. When she was done she dressed in her old clothes, there being no towels.

Shade glanced up as Cruz reappeared. "I need a store. A big one. There's a Target, but it's a bit far, so I'll drive there rather than run. Back in an hour."

Malik and Cruz sat on freshly vacuumed beige carpet and leaned their backs against beige walls. The electricity was still working, and Cruz turned on the air-conditioning. She found an old red plastic Solo cup in the back of a cupboard, rinsed it out, and brought a glass of water to Malik, who gratefully gulped it all down.

"Shade will figure something out," Cruz said, wincing as she realized how weak that sounded.

"Yes," Malik said. But he wasn't listening. Not to Cruz, anyway.

"Watchers?" she asked.

Malik nodded slowly, eyes fixed on nothing. "It's like . . . like . . . like being touched. Molested. Inside your head. I feel them in there. They're pushing into places . . . memories . . ." He shook his head. "I guess you already know all that. When I resist them, they laugh at me." He tapped the side of his head. "In here. It's like I have other people inside my brain, Cruz, like . . ." Tears came again, bitter, helpless. Defeated.

The agony of his burned body, or the agony of a mind invaded. Those were Malik's choices now. He could see it all clearly: pain or madness. Because in the end, Malik knew, the Dark Watchers would defeat him. They were tireless and relentless, dark tendrils reaching inside him, through him, treating him like some sort of video library where they could just punch up his memories and watch them play out like his short life was a biopic.

"Malik," Cruz said softly. "Maybe this is stupid . . ."

No answer.

"Maybe it's nuts, but . . . but if they can watch you, maybe it goes both ways. You know? Maybe you can learn about them."

She was rewarded by a narrowing of Malik's eyes, the first familiar thing he'd done since the hospital.

"Maybe," he said, but shaking his head no.

And a minute later, "Maybe." And this time he did not shake his head.

Shade reappeared, heralded by the sound of the car pulling into the garage. She had sleeping bags and prescription painkillers, whose sudden absence from the shelves following what felt like a burst of wind would baffle the pharmacist. And she had food, orange juice, and a bottle of vodka.

They ate and drank, and Malik popped a handful of pain pills, just in case he de-morphed in his sleep. Oxycontin wouldn't do anything more than dull the sharpest edges, but it was all they had.

Malik fell asleep first.

Shade and Cruz watched him, then their eyes met.

"I know what you're feeling," Cruz said.

Slowly Shade shook her head.

"Well, I can guess," Cruz said impatiently. "But Shade, you cannot let this destroy you."

A quirk appeared at the corner of Shade's mouth but collapsed into a downturn. "But it already has, Cruz," she said. "It already has."

CHAPTER 7
There's More than One Kind of Predator

"WANT A HIT, kid?"

Francis Specter, fourteen, had earbuds in, and Lars Frederiksen was singing about growing up "on the farms" and being raised by bikers.

Francis had not spent time "on the farms," a euphemism for juvenile prison, but she was definitely being raised by bikers. Bikers like "Mangohead" Briscola, her mother's current "old man," who had earned his nickname by wrapping his bike around a streetlight pole and cracking his head open. The surgical repair job had left him with a segment of skull that was raised a quarter inch above the rest of his scalp, and from that six-inch slab, his normally dark hair grew a sickly orange, hence, "Mangohead."

Mangohead Briscola was forty-five years old, which was fairly well-aged in biker gang culture, and had a full, greasy beard dotted with Cheeto dust, a pitted, unhealthy face, and rotting teeth. Many meth-heads had rotting teeth, one of several reasons Francis Specter could think of to say . . .

"No."

"Awww, come on, young-and-tender, get some of this up your nose"—he held out a vial filled with white powder—"and we can have us a party."

"I'm fourteen years old, you creep."

Mangohead grinned. "Old enough to bleed . . ."

Francis walked away on stiff legs, followed by his raucous catcalls. "Sooner or later we're gonna party, you 'n' me!"

Francis had nowhere particular to go; there weren't exactly a million choices. The gang—the Mojave Huns—had what they liked to call a compound, which was three trailers; two tin shacks; a rust-weeping Winnebago up on cinder blocks; a reeking, vile outhouse; and a rusting LPG tank badly painted with the gang's logo, which was a stylized depiction of a very blond and very white Hun swinging a battle-ax.

Francis had read about the original Huns online. They had come from Asia and were definitely not white folks, but she had never been reckless enough to point that out to Mangohead, or to her mother, and certainly not to the pack's leader, who flew a Pepe flag over his trailer. Nor were the original Huns drug dealers.

The compound was only a few hundred feet off the 392, which fed into Interstate 40, and Francis could, if she chose, walk a mile along the two-lane road through red-sand nothingness to Russell's Truck and Travel Center, a truck-stop restaurant, convenience store, and gas station. Beyond that it would be a very, very long walk—seventy-five miles—to Amarillo, Texas. That was it aside from little no-account "towns" that were nothing more than fast-food restaurants or gas stations.

Her only escape, her only window on the world, was through her phone and a desperately slow internet connection that took a full minute to load a single Wikipedia page.

It had been sheer boredom that had led Francis to take some of what the gang called the Jesus Rock, a few chips of stone from some place called Perdido Beach. The rock glowed faintly green in the dark, and the gang had decided it was their inspiration, a sort of lucky totem. The gang held nothing sacred but loyalty to the gang, silence to the police, and a sort of negligent, unfocused, half-mocking worship of the rock, whose true power they knew nothing about. Only Francis was clever enough to connect the gang's "sacred" stone with the monster who had annihilated the Golden Gate Bridge.

She had taken one of the rock flakes out into the desert one night and spread a blanket, lain on her back smoking a joint and looking up at the one true wonder to be enjoyed in the New Mexico emptiness: a magnificent sky filled with a million more stars than any city dweller ever saw. There, mildly high and mellow, for reasons she would never be able to explain except that "I was bored," she'd ground the rock flake to powder using the hilt of her knife. And then she had snorted it.

Two days later, Francis had gone with her mother to the Lowe's market in Tucumcari. They'd taken the ancient baby-puke-yellow Chevy pickup truck, detailed to shop for groceries for the nineteen people in the compound. Francis's assignment had been to shoplift steaks—they had money for some things, but definitely not steaks.

Francis had been caught with two packs of ribeye steaks in her backpack and had run from the store clerk and the fat security man. Her mother, who was supposed to provide a distraction should such an unfortunate event occur, had passed out, and was sitting splay-legged amid crushed boxes of Cheerios and Wheat Chex.

Francis had raced for the front of the store and been cut off, turned and headed for the back of the store, intending to run through the storage area and escape out through the loading dock. But a large man had loomed up out of nowhere, and she'd had nowhere to go.

So she had . . . well, she had no words to explain what had happened next. She remembered a feeling of panic, knowing that if she was busted, the gang had no means of (and very little interest in) bailing her out. In her fear she saw things differently. Weirdly. The exterior wall of the grocery store, lined with cartons of bleach and six-packs of paper towels, had seemed to *twist*. It was impossible to describe, she had no words for it. But it felt as if she had somehow slid up and over and around the wall and was suddenly in the parking area at the back of the store.

Since then she'd told no one. But when she could, when she was sure no one was watching, she had experimented. It was odd, because the world was absolutely as solid as it ever had been . . . unless she first got herself in what she thought of as *the right frame of mind*. When she did that, she saw the world differently. And to her shock she saw herself differently, too. Her skin seemed to shimmer, like sunlight on a greasy puddle. Like a rainbow.

She had passed her rainbow hand effortlessly "through" trailer walls; she had walked through—although it felt like sliding "around"—the LPG tank; she had lain on her flea-ridden cot in the shed and had dropped through it without effort.

Then, she had nerved herself up to the ultimate screw-you: she had passed through the gang leader's own trailer. Not through like she was *inside* the trailer, but sort of . . . *through and around,* like the trailer was a flat box within which she could see the Big Man eating a burrito like he was on TV and she was a 3-D person floating above it. But even that wasn't quite it, because she had not just seen him eating a burrito, she had seen the burrito going down his throat to settle in his belly. She had seen his heart and his lungs and both the inside and outside of him simultaneously.

She had even tested her nerve, as well as her power, by walking across a busy highway and letting a Costco tractor trailer blow through/around her.

Francis Specter had acquired a *power.* She was Rockborn 2.0.

She spent a long time online, her inquiries leading to pages full of talk about extra dimensions and even a holographic universe.

And then she had chanced upon a snippet of video show-ing someone identified as Dekka Talent, looking like an angry black feline walking erect, with dreads that ended in snakes' heads, but sitting on a very nice motorcycle. On a motorcycle while black, which the Mojave Huns considered a sort of race crime, as if bikes were only for white people.

Francis had long considered running away. No day passed without Mangohead or one of the others hitting on her; no day passed without being offered meth, mescaline, Oxy, occasionally cocaine. At fourteen she knew she should be in school, but her last day of school had been three years ago, back when her mother was a respectable school librarian, not a brown-toothed, haggard, hollow-eyed junkie.

But each time she'd dreamed of escape, the question was always the same: Where? She was a million miles from any-where. If she tried hitchhiking, the odds were she'd either end up busted or picked up by some leering trucker or discovered by some member of the gang. The gang would call it treach-ery, and she would take a beating, which, based on previous beatings, would leave her stiff and sore at best, bleeding and incapacitated at worst. A previous "traitor" was buried in the desert a few miles away from where she stood.

But the "dangerous" black cat-girl on the bike? Well, in Francis's imagination it was as if Dekka Talent was secretly waving her over. Dekka had become a destination.

Francis had started to plan. First things first: money.

On the next supply run to Tucumcari, Francis had wan-dered away to the Wells Fargo bank, where she effortlessly slid around the wall and into the bank. It had been a Sun-day, so the bank was closed and empty. She'd looked around inside for a while, opening drawers and finding nothing, before finally confronting the heavy steel vault door.

It did not matter how thick the door was; Francis saw it as a series of geometric lines that made her vaguely nauseous to see since they made no sense at all. But she slid around the door and into the vault. There she reached effortlessly into safe-deposit boxes. She walked—slid—away with $3,200 in cash, plus a stash of fake green cards, a very nice necklace that might be real gold, and a little pouch full of what Francis hoped were rare coins.

She noted with pleasure that while she was Rainbow—her self-mocking term for her extra-dimensional self—she could carry things with her—her clothing, for a start, which was extremely useful. But also, obviously, her loot from the bank.

She'd hidden her cache out in the desert under a flat rock. The spare key to Mangohead's chopper—a six-bend ape-hanger hog—was now in her jeans.

And she was waiting for night to fall.

"Night," as in people sleeping, seldom came before three in the morning, but finally the howling drunks and the jittery tweakers settled down, passed out, leaving no one alert but the gang's dog, a much-abused pit bull Francis had cultivated with occasional bits of "people food."

Once she was sure it was as quiet as it was going to get, Francis retrieved her cache of money and her other bit of contraband, a five-gallon water can. She then went from bike to bike, trembling with fear, pouring a few cups of water in each gas tank. People thought sugar in a tank would kill an engine, but that, Francis had learned, was an urban legend—sugar does not dissolve in gas. But water sinks below gasoline, gets into the fuel line and . . .

The motorcycles might start, but they weren't going to get far.

Then she stuffed the "sacred rock" into the deep pocket of her jacket, threw a leg over the saddle of Mangohead's bike, inserted the key, and with a deep, steadying breath, fired up the engine.

The dog barked. A voice somewhere in the night said, "Who the f . . . ," before fading out.

Francis accelerated away slowly, down the 392, savoring the vibration of the powerful engine, tortured by her own small but growing sense of hope. In the distance ahead was the sickly fluorescent glow of Russell's truck stop. But something was overhead, something unusual. She slowed and looked up in time to see a ghostly, pale gray shape zoom almost silently overhead, maybe two hundred yards up, maybe more. It looked like an airplane, but was too quiet.

She shrugged it off and rode on for mere seconds before she saw a blinding flash of light behind her, followed not quite immediately by a concussion that made the road surface jump.

In her rearview mirror, the compound of the Mojave Huns exploded in a ball of orange flame. It was not an unexpected end for the gang—cooking meth required knowledge and discipline if you were to avoid blowing things up. But at this hour? Who would have left a fire burning in the "lab" at this hour?

She pulled off onto the shoulder. Less than a mile, a one-minute drive, separated her from the flaming annihilation of the gang . . . and of her own mother. Francis squeezed her eyes shut, not wanting to see mental pictures of her mother blown apart, and at the same time desperately fending off a powerful but shameful emotion that swelled within her.

Relief.

She should cry, she thought. But tears did not come, nor did they seem likely to. She had long since given up on fantasies of rescuing her mother. Her mother had ceased to be a mother in any real sense. Francis had been on her own emotionally for years already.

"Bye, Mom," she whispered. And after some hesitation, added, "Love you."

I should cry. I should need to cry.

Heart in her throat, shaking with fear and the knowledge that she herself should have died, Francis motored on, passing Russell's and merging onto the freeway. There was very little traffic and, acutely aware that she had no license, she kept to the speed limit.

But a feeling of being watched nagged at her, and when she looked up, she saw the ghostly gray plane gliding overhead, outlined against the stars. It banked away, and Francis thought she was done with it. But then, in the sky, a flare of flame.

In the time of a single heartbeat, it all came together in Francis's mind. It was not meth cooking that had blown up the compound, it was the gray ghost in the sky, the gray ghost she'd seen on any number of news broadcasts: a Predator drone.

And it had just fired a second missile.

Francis punched the accelerator, and the bike leaped from sixty miles an hour to a hundred and ten in two blinks of an eye as the highway just a hundred yards back exploded. The blast wave nearly knocked her over, the bike fishtailing madly as she was pelted with gravel and felt the wave of hot air.

She roared on through the night, fear welling inside her alongside hope. The compound had gone up in smoke and flame. Her mother was probably dead, and maybe the day would come when she would mourn that properly, but right now it just meant that in all likelihood no one would be following her.

Except of course for whoever had just used a Predator drone to launch missiles, one of which had, incredibly, just blown a big hole in the westbound I-40. Her first thought after her mind returned to something like normal function was that the DEA, the Drug Enforcement Agency, was getting awfully damn serious about cracking down on drug gangs.

But her second, more dangerous thought was that the Wells Fargo bank's interior security cameras might still have been working on a Sunday. In which case . . .

It was after me!

She had some cash, a half tank of gas, an open road, and no goal but to somehow join up with that black girl on the Kawasaki.

That, plus a power whose uses she had barely begun to understand.

CHAPTER 8
The Symbiosis of Good and Evil

"ACCORDING TO GOOGLE Maps, it's 10.3 miles from here to the county line. Round trip just over 20.5 miles."

"And?" Cruz asked, indifferent.

They were in the backyard of their illegally occupied home, Cruz sitting on concrete steps, Shade pacing back and forth on what might have been a lawn once upon a time but was now a patch of dirt scarcely punctuated by the occasional weed.

"I want you to time me. I want to see how fast I am. And I want to see whether this works." She held up a tangle of black nylon straps and a tiny black camera.

Cruz shook her head slowly—not negation, disbelief. "That's what you think is most important? Really? We're squatting in someone's empty home, Malik is losing his mind, and—"

Shade gritted her teeth in frustration. "Listen to me, Cruz. Any time you want to take over and figure out our next plan, go for it. All right?" She slapped her chest angrily. "I don't want the job, okay? I'm in way, way over my head, do you get that, Cruz? Way the hell over my head! I'm doing what I can, trying to at least find out what powers I have."

Cruz let the anger burn out. "What's the camera about?"

"I have an idea, probably a stupid one," Shade said, calming herself. "Look, I think the more secrets the government can keep, the more trouble we're in. People think Rockborn are the big threat, and the government is the solution. We need them to decide the opposite, at least some of them. We need at least some people out there who don't think we're some new kind of cockroach that needs to be stamped out."

Cruz nodded, her expression cautious.

"I'm going to morph. I'll strap the camera on as tight as I can, and I'll take off as fast as I can. As soon as you see me disappear, push the stopwatch on your phone. As soon as I reappear, push it again."

It was not, in fact, Cruz's phone; it was a phone belonging to someone named Janice Harms. They had a routine for this kind of thing now, regular patterns of theft. Shade could snatch a dozen phones with a quick run through a mall or a Walmart, and inevitably one would have an easy password. Then they would quickly turn off the find-a-phone feature and use the phone for no more than twenty-four hours before replacing it. A lot of phones were stolen on any given day in the United States; not even HSTF-66 could track them all, let alone send investigators.

Shade turned her mind to the now-easy task of transforming. *Strange,* she thought, *how easy it has become. I radically change my body like some kind of instant puberty, but it has become almost second nature to me. I might even stay in morph, were it not for . . .* But that was a bad line of thinking because it led directly to the fact that Malik could *not* escape the Dark Watchers.

Shade closed her eyes for a moment, centering herself, trying to shut out everything else: Malik, Cruz, her father, all the people whose lives she had ruined. The instant she was morphed, the Dark Watchers were on her, like whispering ghosts.

She kicked off with a powerful thrust and ran, arms pumping, legs a blur, energy from who knew where. She ran down the highway, easily passing cars and trucks doing seventy, passing them so fast they seemed to be crawling.

Faster and faster until those speeding cars were mere blurs, until the desert landscape was nothing but a tan smear, until the jeans and T-shirt she wore over her angular, insectoid morph shredded, with a piece of it actually burning from the air friction.

The experience of moving at top speed was not like what she'd seen in movies. The passing world could be a blur, but because her perceptions were also accelerated, she could shift focus and see the passing world clearly as a series of still shots, like isolating one frame of a movie.

Sound was distorted, though, and there was no help for that. Her speed was nothing compared to the speed of light, but it was close to and occasionally exceeded the speed of sound. Sounds that were coming toward her from in front, from the direction of travel, arrived at a much higher pitch than normal. Sounds coming from behind were either low and draggy if she was below Mach 1, or fell away completely above that point.

She passed Mach 1, confirmed by the rumble that vibrated through her body, followed by a deepened silence, but as a regular thing breaking the sound barrier was a bad idea—it advertised her presence with a loud crack.

There were things to be learned about this power and how to exploit it. For example, she understood now that she could be effectively invisible, somewhat like an airplane propeller: an observer would feel the wind, hear the sound, and see something, but that something would be at most a blur. And the human brain had certain weaknesses that could be exploited, like persistence of vision, the human tendency to go on seeing what they've already seen; and confirmation bias, the human tendency to see only what they expected to see. People could be amazingly blind to what was right in front of their faces.

Ten miles. It passed in forty-five seconds. She decelerated for the last half mile, tapped the county line sign, turned around, and raced back.

"One hundred and seven seconds," Cruz said, holding up the phone as proof.

Shade said something in her hyper-speed buzz, then demorphed and repeated it. "About eight hundred miles an hour. Give or take. Faster in a straight line where I don't have to turn around."

"I suppose you've noticed you're about half naked," Cruz said.

"Yeah." Shade tugged at her jeans. The waist was broken at the back seam, the knees were gone, the cuffs were shredded. About all that was left intact of her T-shirt was the banded neck. "I need to find something stretchable enough to handle the morph but strong enough and tight-fitting enough to do distances at speed. Plus, I had to run part of the way with my hand on my head to hold on to the camera, so I need better straps. And probably boots, not sneakers." Her sneakers were in tatters as well.

"Look on Amazon under 'superhero clothing,'" Cruz said, the closest she'd come to a joke in days.

"I broke the sound barrier," Shade said. "It was weird. I found out something about the body, though: the morph, it adjusts automatically. I could feel that I was losing contact with the ground, and then the shape of my body changed. Like a spoiler on a race car. The faster I went, the more down-pressure."

"Swell," Cruz said. "So?"

Shade flopped down beside Cruz on the steps. "So, I don't know. I guess I thought it might clear my head." She sighed. "The thing is, Cruz, we have no way to win. No matter how clever we are, sooner or later the government will get us. They can make lots of mistakes and still be the government. One mistake and we're done."

"Is that really our number-one enemy now, the government?"

"The others like us, the mutants, the Rockborn, they aren't after us, not unless they work for the government. That starfish kid has no idea where we are and no interest in us."

"So, what, we're going to overthrow the government?" Cruz asked archly, obviously assuming it was snark. When Shade did not immediately shoot it down, Cruz's expression darkened.

"You've got to be kidding me."

"The world is changing, Cruz. Has changed. Too much of the rock is out there, not just here, but around the world. The creeps in Washington will decide the only safe thing to do is kill us all."

"Shade, we have laws, you know. The Constitution? All that stuff?"

"Do we?" Shade wondered aloud. She shook her head. "If you go about two hundred miles north from here you get to Manzanar, which is where the government locked up American citizens who happened to be of Japanese ancestry during World War II. The Constitution got over that, but lately it's been pretty tattered and beat up. No, the government will start killing us off unless we join them. They have to."

Cruz shifted uncomfortably, as the concrete had numbed her behind. Then she stood up, feeling the need to move. "So maybe we join up?"

"Do you really think the government won't start using the Rockborn against regular people? You would make an amazing spy, for example. I could blow through someone's house and pick up evidence—or plant phony evidence. Or kill someone, for that matter. The possibilities are endless. And they'd only accept us if they could control us, make slaves of us."

"Okay, so we run off to some tropical island where no one has ever heard of the Rockborn."

"Cruz, there is no place on earth where people haven't heard of us. Certainly no place the CIA or whoever can't follow us."

Cruz walked away for a few steps, turned, and came back. "So? So we just hide until they catch us and kill us?"

"No. We need the public. *People.* We need the people to back us; that will make it harder for the government to just murder us."

"And?"

Shade shrugged. "We need to do something big, something that will show that we can't be screwed with, and it has to be something good and righteous that will make people . . ." She petered out.

"Love us?" Cruz said wryly. "Love a white girl who can go eight hundred miles an hour, a trans Latina who can turn invisible or appear as anyone, and a black boy who can send out blasts of unbearable pain? We're not exactly the Avengers, here, Shade. So, unless you're planning on curing cancer in your spare time, I'm not seeing this."

But Shade wasn't listening; she was thinking out loud. "If we could take down and deliver Tom Peaks, or better yet, that starfish kid. Or if we could pull off some huge rescue, which, yeah, isn't so easy unless there just happens to be some big fire, earthquake, whatever, conveniently happening right where we are. Or . . ."

One of the depressing lessons they had learned was that life was not like comic books, where it seemed there was always some emergency requiring a superhero. When some extreme emergency occurred it was never near enough for them to do anything about it. Spider-Man could web-sling around Manhattan and always happen across some sort of crime being committed, but Malik—being Malik—had run the numbers, and it seemed statistically that Shade could race around any given city for a week and not happen to arrive just as a crime was about to start.

Malik's conclusion had been grim. "The fact is that superheroes are only really useful if there are supervillains. The whole super thing is a net loss for the human race. Basically Magneto had it right—humans will always hate and fear mutants with powers, and for good reason."

Shade had left that "or" dangling. Cruz almost didn't want to ask, but with a sigh said, "Or?"

"Or," Shade said, her lip curling, "we hit them so hard they're scared to come after us. And we expose them." She tapped the camera in her hand.

Cruz met Shade's angry, intense stare. "We're back to Malik's system: hero, villain, monster. Let's face it, we're all monsters—mutants, Rockborn, CORs, whatever name we come up with—we're monsters playing hero or playing villain." Then, as if worried that Shade might be taking the villain option seriously, Cruz added, "By the way, I vote for hero."

Shade nodded slowly. "The thing is, Malik's right; it's a symbiosis. If you asked regular people if they want super-powered creatures running around, they'd say no, kill them all, exterminate them. The only way they come to love us is if we're the only ones standing between them and something worse."

Then Cruz, words coming reluctantly, said, "I think . . . I think maybe you're right. Maybe all the comic books have it wrong with all that secret identity stuff. I mean, if you're just some freak in a mask, people don't see you as a human being, and why would any *normal* support a masked, unknown freak with superpowers?"

"We need an enemy, and what we have is HSTF-66, the government. And we need to give people a reason to support us, not them."

"So . . . ?"

"So, the Ranch," Shade said at last. "The place Dekka told us about, up north. We could break in, record everything, and upload it."

Cruz shook her head. "Why would that work?"

"Because what they're doing there is illegal and unconstitutional and *wrong*." Shade stood up, and her sidelong glance at Cruz was through shark's eyes. "Better yet, it's creepy and disturbing, and no one likes creepy."

And because we would create chaos, and in times of chaos, people look for heroes, Shade thought.

Cruz said nothing, just exhaled a long, slow breath. "It's all bad, isn't it? It's all bad choices. I just want to . . ." She made a frustrated gesture with her hands, like someone wrestling a glitchy Rubik's Cube. "I just want to roll time back."

"Back to before you met me." It wasn't a question, and Cruz didn't answer it.

Shade nodded, accepting Cruz's anger and frustration. "I'm going to find us something fast to drive," Shade said. "I don't want to run all that way, and anyway, I need you both with me. We'll leave in an hour. Tell Malik."

Shade walked away, shifting as she moved, then blurred and disappeared.

Cruz had her orders. And for the first time they had been just that: *orders.* Orders Shade had given; orders she knew Cruz would obey because she had no idea what else to do.

Nothing for her to do but help me dig the hole deeper still.

And be buried in it with me.

CHAPTER 9
Take Over the What?

"WELL, WELL, THIS is my lucky day!"

Dillon Poe came from a wealthy family. They had a five-bedroom, five-bath, swimming-pool, hot-tub, four-car-garage house in the Las Vegas gated community called the Promontory. Dillon had never been denied anything (legal) by his parents, and he'd certainly never worried about money.

Still, he had never before had a million dollars, and it was an interesting experience. The million was in stacks of chips formed into unstable towers between himself and the roulette board with its numbers from 0 and 00 to 36.

The croupier waved his hand over the rows of numbers and said, "No more bets."

Dillon had ten thousand dollars on number 32—his lucky number—despite the fact that there was a thousand-dollar limit on bets. He was at the Venetian, one of the gaudier casinos, lurid and loud and presumably geared to impress aging rustics, three of whom were at the roulette table beside him.

The three tourists as well as the croupier and the nearest pit boss had all been "spoken to" by Dillon and saw nothing unusual about the fact that the number 32 came up every time . . . despite not actually having come up even once.

The eye in the sky, the constant video surveillance that makes any casino a sort of semi-benign authoritarian state, should have alerted casino security, but Dillon had looked up at the glass hemisphere that concealed the nearest camera and said, "You up there. You see none of this." He'd been lucky: seeing him looking up, they had activated the microphone. And then they, too, saw nothing at all wrong with Dillon's impossible winning streak, or his decidedly reptilian face.

No one did. It wasn't that they didn't see what he was; it was that it did not bother them. Men looked at him and did an unconscious nod of acceptance. Women and some men did a bit more. They found him alluring, which struck Dillon as wonderfully funny. He liked snakes himself and had a two-hour-a-week school-mandated "volunteer" gig with Reptile Rescue. He'd actually gone a few times because the place had been featured on TV shows. But the point was, he'd seen very few women who liked reptiles.

With the possible exception of Miley Cyrus fans. Which had the makings of a joke, but needed work.

The croupier turned the wheel, which rotated as smoothly as if it were levitating, and spun the ball. Dillon enjoyed the sound of the little white ball screeing around in its channel before falling, clattering, to bounce and jump merrily, finally settling in on number 4.

"I won," Dillon said, and the croupier began pushing more chips to him. "You know," Dillon said, "I'm not supposed to be here. Too young. It's tough being young in Las Vegas. I'm not allowed on the casino floor. I'm not twenty-one." He fell into the rhythm of a comedian. "I can walk around the casino floor. I can follow certain passageways through the casino floor. But I cannot touch a card or a pair of dice. See, it's all about protecting our innocence. After all, in Las Vegas, innocence has a cash value. Out at Shari's legal brothel, innocence goes for five hundred bucks a pop." The croupier smiled, but an old woman at the end of the table gave up an actual guffaw.

"It's true," Dillion went on, playing to her now, "the drinking age in Vegas is twenty-one, the gambling age is twenty-one, but once you turn eighteen, you have three short years to adjust to the spiritual emptiness that defines the adult Las Vegan."

The second part hadn't worked as well as the first, which left him feeling a bit deflated. *Like this stupid game,* he thought. Games weren't that much fun when you *knew* you would win.

He stood up abruptly and headed through the vulgar, insistent glitter of slot machines to the Yardbird restaurant, where he strolled through tables of diners until he saw food being delivered. He told the people who had ordered the food to walk away. Only after they had gone did it occur to him that he had placed no limit on how long they should walk. He sincerely hoped they did not end up as piles of bleached bones in the pitiless Nevada desert. He made a mental note to be more specific in the future: no need to create harm unnecessarily. Right?

Unless it's funny.

He sensed that the unseen audience in his head did not approve of his concern. Nor were those unseen watchers pleased with the way he'd spent hours at the roulette table. By means he could not hope to explain, they conveyed impatience. The audience wanted him to *do* something. It was insistent, relentless, and found an easy resonance in Dillon's head.

You want a show, invisible people in my head? Is that it? You want a show?

Dillon ate what he wanted, then ordered a random passerby to bring him a cheesecake from the kitchen. He rolled his eyes as a fight broke out in the kitchen and laughed aloud when the battered, bruised, panting man brought him most of a cheesecake, pursued by knife-wielding chefs.

"Okay," Dillon said, "I really need to try and . . . on the other hand, screw it." He looked up at the battered tourist and said, "That cake's a bit of a mess."

"I'm calling security," the nearest of the angry kitchen workers said.

"Oh, that's not necessary," Dillon said. "You can deal with this yourself. This man needs to be punished."

"Punished?" the cake thief said, sounding baffled.

"Sure. Of course. I mean, in the old days the punishment for stealing was having a hand cut off."

Was it his imagination, or was the unseen audience now leaning forward in anticipation?

"But I am merciful," Dillon said. To the cheesecake thief he said, "This cook is going to cut off your right index finger, and you're going to let him."

Sure enough, the man who had brought the cake sighed and flattened his hand, fingers spread, on the table even as he muttered, "This isn't fair, this isn't right."

The chef grimaced and said, *"Lo siento, lo siento!"* as he raised his fourteen-inch chef's knife and brought it down with a sickening sound.

It took three whacks, by which time blood was everywhere, puddling on the table, sprayed on the faces of both the victim and the chef and indeed on Dillon himself. It was all ignored by everyone within the sound of his voice, but more distant tables screamed and pushed over chairs and shielded their children's eyes.

Dillon lifted the severed finger and gave it to the chef. "You'll want to cook this. It's a sausage."

Come on, audience, laugh!

Had they laughed? Not in any way he could hear, but did they find it funny? Did the dark and invisible audience even have a sense of humor?

Hello, is this microphone on?

He walked back out onto the casino floor as screams of horror and pain rose behind him. He was in a confused and anxious state of mind. On the one hand: power! On the other hand: a very tough audience.

But an audience, just the same.

Dillon was very aware of them and very aware that he had

very little of what comics would call "material." It was as if he'd been suddenly thrust onto the stage at the Comedy Store with a bunch of VIPs in the audience. He felt like he was at some flop-sweat-inducing audition, not sure what to do to keep the audience amused.

He stood between craps tables and blackjack tables and in a loud voice said, "Everyone! Slap yourself in the face! One hard slap!"

He watched the results. Everyone nearby raised a hand and slapped themselves once. But beyond the reach of his voice life went on as normal.

"Yep. Like I thought," Dillon said. "It's all about the voice." He had a vague notion of a joke involving the old TV show *The Voice,* and Adam Levine, but he couldn't quite put it all together. He looked around and saw the main cashier's kiosk. He walked up, told one of the employees there to let him in, which of course they did. He asked where he could find the public address system and was shown a microphone and told how to use it.

"Testing, testing. Dillon Poe radio is on the air, here at the Venetian. How's everyone doing today? Good? All right, then, everyone who can hear me, raise your hands."

It was mid-afternoon, not the busiest time in the casino, but still, between gamblers and employees, there were a couple hundred people. And every single one of them raised their hands. Cocktail waitresses with trays of drinks raised their hands, and beer bottles and cocktail glasses fell, bouncing on carpet.

"Okay, very good," Dillon said. He thought for a moment, then happened to spot a *Walking Dead*–themed slot machine and grinned with sudden inspiration. "You are all flesh-eating zombies. Eat everyone you see!"

Unfortunately, one of the cashiers immediately ran at him, jaws gnashing, and he had to amend that a bit before he started losing body parts.

A craps croupier suddenly grabbed a woman and began gnawing on her nose. A man in a wheelchair was set upon by three people. He yelled feebly for help even as he tried to bite the people biting him. A woman pushing a stroller toward the front desk stopped, pulled her baby from the stroller and, eyes streaming, babbling apologies and desperate pleas for someone to stop her, began to chew on her child.

"No, no," Dillon said. "Not you, lady. There are limits!" He keyed the microphone and amended: "Don't eat children under . . ." He considered an appropriate age, then grinned. Of course. The cutoff in the FAYZ, the age beyond which people had poofed, was fourteen. "Don't eat anyone under the age of fourteen."

The woman returned her bleeding, screeching child to the stroller, at which point she was attacked from behind by an old man biting with feeble jaws into her neck.

Dillon clapped his hands in sheer amazement. He kept doing the impossible, and it kept working!

From everywhere came cries of outrage, screams of pain and anger, shouted apologies as people clawed and bit like . . . well, like zombies. But self-aware zombies. Zombies who knew they were doing terribly wrong things. Tears dribbled down into blood.

It was mayhem. And given that the average age of the Venetian's patrons was *ninety* . . . No. Try again. Given that the average age was *senile* . . . Not quite. Given that the average age was *Jurassic*. Yeah, that was funny. Jurassic. Anyway, given the age of Dillon's zombies, it was wildly funny and, despite the frenzy, not likely to actually get anyone killed.

That will be my rule: funny above all, and no actual killing.

He savored the madness for a while and tried to gauge the reaction of the Dark Watchers. He guessed they were loving it—*yeah, baby*—but also that it wasn't enough. Not enough. He felt harassed by a need to think of the next line, the next wacky move. And he'd had very little sleep. He was tired.

He sauntered out of the casino toward the elevators to the rooms above through a mad melee of people biting and clawing and crying and apologizing as they did it. Despite the TV and movie depictions of zombies, it isn't easy for a human jaw—especially the jaws of the Venetian's septuagenarian patrons—to actually pierce flesh. But he saw an elderly man doing a reasonably good job of biting off a woman's ear as she in turn tried to bite a chunk out of his shoulder.

"Come on," he said, hands outstretched, addressing the Dark Watchers, "you have to admit: *that's* funny."

Security people who'd been beyond the reach of his voice were pouring from concealed doors, unaware that Dillon was the source. He nodded at them as they rushed past, took the elevator to the top floor, and ordered a maid to open the nicest suite. A man was sleeping in one of the beds, and Dillon ordered him to go away. The man, wearing nothing but underpants, left immediately.

Dillon wondered vaguely how the man would interpret the word "away." The English language was not designed for such orders.

Specificity, Dillon, specificity. The best comedy is always specific.

This all might become part of a routine. He could see himself on Fallon, doing a tight five minutes, then schmoozing with Jimmy afterward.

It was gray-on-gray violence, Jimmy. Old people thinking it was the early-bird special! Today's specials: human sushi. And for dessert, ear à la mode! And you know old people: waiter! Oh, waiter! This bicep is cold! Ha, ha, ha, ha.

Biceps? Thigh? Liver?

Liver. Liver was always funny. And it would be a sort of reference to *Silence of the Lambs*. People liked Anthony Hopkins, even when he played a cannibal.

But what about the Dark Watchers? Would they get that kind of reference?

The suite was fabulously gaudy and tasteless in the way only Vegas could be, and Dillon threw himself back on a king-sized bed and looked up at his own reflection in ceiling-mounted mirrors. It was the first time he'd seen himself in this body, and he spent some time admiring what he saw. High school would have been a very different experience if he had looked like this.

He contemplated an amazing fact: he, Dillon Poe, was quite likely the most powerful person on earth. He could do anything, or at least anything he could order another human being to do. He couldn't fly or live forever, but if a human could do it, Dillon could do it.

Amazing!

But after a while of contemplating just how he could use that power, he came back to a couple of realities: he did not have much imagination, and, aside from comedy, he'd never had any sort of life plan or ambition. The dark audience had appreciated his act in the drunk tank, and the impromptu finger-ectomy as well as the old-farts zombie attack. But Dillon knew the difference between a spontaneous bit of fun and a well-thought-out, well-honed act. (Jerry Seinfeld was his uber-hero, and Jerry was a meticulous craftsman.) Random acts of gore? He could do that easily enough, but audiences always wanted more, and he didn't have more. Not yet.

He needed a narrative, a goal. A point of view. He had listened to almost all of Marc Maron's podcasts, and Maron always emphasized specificity in comedy. You had to have a position, an approach, and you had, above all, to be yourself.

Also, as much as he hated to admit it, nothing was much fun unless you had someone to share it with. So he made a call. Strange, he thought, but he was nervous calling Saffron even now. She was a year older and, to his eyes at least, the essence of the sort of girl he could ordinarily never hope to approach.

"Saffron?" he said into the phone, delighted by the suave

confidence that had replaced his more usual thin squeak.

"Who is this?"

"It's Dillon. Dillon Poe, from school. I was just calling to—"

"I'm kinda busy—"

"—tell you to come to the Venetian right now. Steal a car if you have to."

He gave her the suite number and hung up. Two minutes later, the doorbell to the suite rang. He walked back through the huge living room with its floor-to-ceiling windows open to Treasure Island casino across the Strip. He opened the door on a man and a woman, both very fit, both wearing identical blazers with "The Venetian" stitched onto their breast pockets.

"Casino security," the woman said brusquely. "You need to come with us."

"No, I don't."

"You don't need to come with us, but we need to know who you are. Your ID, please."

Dillon shook his head. "You don't need that, either. Go away." He slammed the door on them.

It took Saffron Silverman just fourteen minutes to get there, and when he opened the door on her, he burst out laughing. She'd evidently been lying by her pool. She was in a bikini, her black hair still damp. He focused on a tattoo on her hip—Nemo, the fish from the movie. Saffron's parents were ex-hippie types who had met at a concert, hence the distinctive first name. At school Saffron formed her own clique of nerds and dorks, kids who could get straight As but were too cool to bother. Saffron was the non-nerd queen of nerds, the object of desire for boys and girls who spent too much of their lives writing fan fiction and editing *Star Wars* mash-ups. She was of average height, with Goth-black hair and a determined nose that defined a face more striking and unique than beautiful.

"Hi," Dillon said, unable to stop a blush from creeping up his neck.

Saffron blinked and frowned. "Who are you?"

"Dillon. You know, Dillon Poe, the class clown from world history?" He had phrased it as a question, not an order requiring her to believe him. He felt reluctant to use his power on her. Well, at least now that she was actually right there in his room.

I just made the hottest girl I know come to me.

Saffron shook her head. "No, you're not him. You look . . . not like him." There was an appreciative note in her voice: she liked what she was seeing. Dillon took a second to glance in the nearest mirror. Yes, he was still green. Not vaguely green, but green. And yes, the flesh on the back of his hands and arms and face—and presumably elsewhere—seemed to have etched lines forming scales. And yet, Saffron seemed almost hypnotized.

"Why am I . . . where am I?" Saffron asked, frowning.

"You're at the Venetian," Dillon explained helpfully. "Come in. Let me get you a robe." He found one in a closet and held it open for her, the perfect gentleman snake.

I could . . . he thought. But, no. Not to Saffron, who had occupied more than a few of his daydreams over the last year. This wasn't just about making her do things; he wanted her to *want* to be part of this. Whatever this was. She was smart and she was worldly. And she was a writer who everyone said had a wonderful, dark imagination.

He was the most powerful person in the world, maybe, but he knew enough history to know that ancient kings who had all the power still had wise men advising them. Saffron was to be his wise man. Girl. Woman. He hit upon the perfect example: she would be his Merrill Markoe. Markoe had been both girlfriend and head writer for one of Dillon's comedy gods, David Letterman.

My Merrill Markoe.

"Ever hear the one about Adam in the Garden of Eden?" Dillon asked. "He asks God, 'Why did you make woman so beautiful?' God says, 'So you would love her.' The man asks, 'But God, why did you make her so dumb?' God says, 'So she would love you.'"

Saffron frowned. Not ready to laugh. Especially not ready for a sexist joke.

Wrong joke, Dillon chided himself. *You just blurted that because you're nervous.*

He ogled her hungrily as she passed by, brushing her bare shoulder against his as she shrugged into the robe, sending a physical thrill through him.

"Sit," he said. Then, quickly, "No, on the couch, not the floor." He sat opposite her. "I have to tell you something, Saffron."

"Okay." She was like a person in the first seconds of

waking—confused, aware, but with fresh memories of dreams dragging at the edges of her consciousness.

"The thing is, I can make you do anything I want, Saffron."

She laughed dismissively but not cruelly. "In your dreams," she said.

"Not anymore," Dillon said, smiling inwardly at memories of dreams that involved Saffron. "I can make you do anything. For example, if I told you to put a finger in your nose, you would."

"You're nuts," Saffron said. She started to stand up, shaking her head the way a person does when they can't believe what they themselves have done. "I don't even know why I came here."

"Saffron. Take your right pinkie finger and stick it up your left nostril. Wait! Just to the first knuckle!"

This being a Las Vegas casino suite, there were mirrors everywhere. He turned her head to make her see.

She frowned and said, "What the . . . ?" but she did not remove the finger.

"Tell me what you see."

"I see myself. I have a finger in my nose."

"And do you remember me telling you to do that?"

Her answer came slowly. He could practically see the wheels turning in her mind. Then she said, "I can't pull my finger out. It's stuck."

He shook his head. "No, you can't stop until I tell you to stop. Watch. Saffron? Pull your finger out of your nose. Oh, and you can move—if you like, that's up to you."

For what felt like a very long time she looked at her finger, then up at him. "You're one of *them*. You're a mutant. Like on TV. You're Rockborn!"

"Well," he said with a sort of shy shrug, "I'm not a monster."

"No." She stood up and walked slowly around him. Then she frowned as if concentrating hard and reached a tentative finger to touch his cheek. "Are you. . . green?"

"Only after too many burritos," he said. Then, in a more normal voice, "It seems like I am. But people don't seem freaked out."

"Freaked out? Why would they be? You're . . . gorgeous. I mean, really. I can't stop looking at you."

It was an odd feeling, being inspected this way. He was simultaneously vulnerable and all-powerful. And yet it felt erotic.

"The casino downstairs is full of cops and security and ambulances wheeling people out. I thought there had been some kind of terrorist thing. Was that you?"

He nodded.

"Why?"

He shrugged again, even less comfortable and yet even more excited. "I was testing my power. It seems like anyone who hears my voice has to do what I tell them. No matter what." He did not tell her about the drunk tank or the cheesecake incident. He had the feeling that they made him seem immature.

"How did this happen?"

"Would you like something to eat or drink? I can call room service . . ."

She shook her head slowly, and a long strand of black hair fell forward to bisect her forehead. "Why me?"

"I, uh . . ."

"Is it about sex?"

"No," he lied quickly. "No, I would never make you, you know . . ." He smiled, and she smiled back. And he had not *made* her smile! Of course, he reminded himself, she wasn't smiling at the old Dillon, but at the new and improved Dillon.

"Good," she said, still smiling. "Because then I would have to spend the rest of my life getting my revenge." Her mouth was still smiling, but her voice was not. Then she shifted tone. "So, wow, Dillon. Wow. What are you going to do with this power?"

"Well," he said sheepishly, "I'm not sure. It's mostly why I . . ." He let his thought trail off.

"It's why you brought me here?"

"Kind of."

She let loose a sudden, sharp bark of laughter. "Oh, my God: you want me to be your henchman. I'm a minion! Hah!"

Actually, he'd been thinking "girlfriend," but as soon as the rather old-fashioned word "henchman" was out of her mouth, he echoed her laugh and said, "Yeah!"

"Do you have a name yet?"

"Dillon?"

She shook her head pityingly. "That's not a supervillain

name. Lex Luthor is a supervillain name. Or Ultron or something."

"I'm a supervillain?" He was a bit taken aback by that thought. But he had done some villainous things already; he had to admit that.

"Of course you're a supervillain. Mind control isn't really a hero thing, it's a villain thing." She was nodding now, nodding and looking at him from different angles, considering. "The Dominator? Mastermind?"

"Seriously?" He laughed, getting into it. "Am I going to need a special outfit?"

"'No capes, dahling,'" Saffron said, using a movie line that warmed Dillon's heart. "Definitely no spandex. No, I see you in something"—she waved her hands over him as if trying to conjure an outfit out of the air—"something kind of classy. You're too gorgeous to want your face covered by a mask."

Again she had used that word, "gorgeous," and it sent Dillon into a hazy, happy sort of fugue state. No one—not even his adoring mother—had ever called him gorgeous. He felt the unseen audience growing impatient and almost said, *Give me a break, I'm working on it!*

"Gorgeous, huh?" he said, hoping to get her to repeat it. He doubted he'd ever get tired of hearing it.

"You're what my grandmother would call a real charmer," Saffron said. She snapped her fingers. "That's it! That's your name! The Charmer!"

"The Charmer." He tried it out and liked it. And as soon as he had absorbed the name, he realized Saffron was right:

something kind of classy was called for. "You want to come shopping for an outfit? We can take anything we want, and there's a mall downstairs."

"I don't like shopping, usually," Saffron said. "But in this case?" She plucked the collar of her Venetian robe. "I need something to wear, too."

Dillon had to restrain the urge to dance with pure joy. He had his first henchman, and she was amazing. She'd caught on right away, she had a sense of humor, and she was obviously attracted to him. They could walk through any mall—the Fashion Show Mall, the Bellagio, the one right here in the casino—and take literally *anything*. And he could do it all with Saffron on his arm, like one of those big shots who came to Vegas with a beautiful underwear model on each arm, spending money like water.

Amazing!

"Yeah, let's go shopping," he said. "Then we can . . . well . . ."

Saffron's voice was pitying. "You don't know what to do with it, do you? The power, I mean." She laid a hand on his chest, sending waves of pleasure through him.

"Maybe we could figure it out together?"

"Dude," she said, still pitying. "There's only one thing for a supervillain to do. Take over the world."

That rocked him back on his heels. "Take over the world? What?"

"Take over the world," she said, dreamy now, her vivid imagination overflowing with incredible scenarios.

"Look, I can make people do things, but—"

"Dillon," Saffron said, "it's not just about what you can get people to do. It's what you can get people to *believe*. You can maybe mess with people's minds. You can make them believe things that are not true, whatever you want to put in their heads. Like they were computers and you were writing the software. You could easily be president. If you got on CNN, I mean, if it's true that people have no choice but to obey you? You could literally be king of the world."

Dillon stood stunned. He'd called Saffron because she was hot, and because she was smart and imaginative. And because it was not much fun doing everything alone. But she had ramped things up much further and much faster than he'd expected.

Take over the world?

Sure. Maybe. But why?

"I believe there's a reason for everything that happens, you know? Which means you were given this power for a reason." Saffron looked intently into his eyes. "Things like this don't just happen. This is part of some larger plan. You were meant to have this power, which means you were meant to *use* it."

Dillon nodded along, not quite convinced, and still half thinking he would just tell Saffron to strip off her robe and her bikini and . . . But his thoughts were not alone in his head; the Dark Watchers, his audience, were listening. And they were liking what they were hearing. He could sense their pleasure, their anticipation.

"Well . . . okay," Dillon said with a shrug. "How do we start?"

Saffron smiled. "Let's start with school and work outward."

Dillon winced. "You want me to be a superpowered Dylan

Klebold? I'm not into killing people, I'm just trying to have a few laughs."

"Don't be silly, Dillon. You don't need dead bodies, you need living slaves. And of course one other thing."

"What?"

"A queen, Dillon," she said. "A queen."

Interstice

DEKKA AND SHADE had agreed to communicate only through secure, encrypted WhatsApp.

Shade: D it's Shade. Can you give me info on the ranch?

Dekka: Sending you some notes. If you're going there be very careful. Dangerous place.

Shade: I have a new weapon.

Dekka: Why there and why now?

Shade: I don't trust the government.

Dekka: Who does?

Shade: We can't just wait to be picked off. I have a camera. Going public.

Dekka: Need help?

Shade: No. Take care. SD

Dekka: OK. Sending notes. Good hunting. DT

ASO-6

THE DISAPPEARANCE OF US Coast Guard cutter *Abbie Burgess* mobilized faster ships than the undersea research flotilla. Other Coast Guard cutters steamed to the scene at top speed. They found less than the helicopter had, just a single identifiable piece of wreckage: a wooden box containing an ancient sextant that must have been someone's prized collector's item.

There was no sign of any hostile ship or creature that might have been responsible for the cutter's destruction. But a French satellite captured a fuzzy picture of a creature that looked like some unholy blending of killer whale and crab. The French estimated the length at over two hundred feet, twice the length of a blue whale.

The name given to this creature was "chimera," a mythological blending of different species.

The captain of the USS *Nebraska*, an Ohio-class ballistic-missile submarine, was not warned about mutant sea creatures; his "enemy" was the Russian navy. The *Nebraska* was heading north to take up station in the Norwegian Sea, where it was to spend a month cruising submerged, ready should the need arise, to fire off its twenty-four Trident II missiles, each boasting eight nuclear warheads. In all, the *Nebraska* had the ability to create 192 Hiroshimas—every Russian city from Moscow down to Yeysk, a city smaller and even less significant than Jurupa Valley, California.

The chimera attacked the *Nebraska*, which was cruising at twenty-two knots at a depth of two hundred feet. The chimera's tentacles fouled and froze the ship's screws. It twisted the dive planes and crushed the superstructure and its periscopes and antennae.

The *Nebraska* sank to the ocean floor, but without hull integrity being breached. A hundred fifty-five officers and sailors rattled around like dice in a cup as the chimera, which could hear them, set about getting at them, tearing at the sub's outer skin as if it was an oyster shell protecting juicy tidbits within.

CHAPTER 10
It Takes Six Seconds to Fall Five Hundred Feet

"I THINK SHADE Darby is going after the Ranch," Dekka said, pocketing her phone. Like Shade, she'd been forced to steal phones and switch them out regularly. They were dangerous tracking devices, but on the other hand, they were vital to keeping up with the wider world. And to communicating with Shade.

Armo had taken it upon himself to handle the refilling of the Kawasaki's fuel tank. He tapped off the last drops of gas and replaced the pump handle.

"Did she say why?"

Dekka, leaning back against the Chevron pump, shook her head. "Nope. But I can guess. She's a smart girl. She realizes it's hopeless the way it is, so she's trying to change the game by attacking."

Armo smiled. "Well, you have to kinda like a girl who thinks 'hopeless' means 'attack.'"

Dekka wanted to agree, but it all sounded so much like

Brianna, the Breeze. To hell with the odds—*attack!* But the bigger issue was what she, Dekka, was going to do. She and Armo. They had talked it over with Sam and Astrid and had reached the same conclusion: in the end, they could not survive unless they managed to cause total anarchy. And what kind of victory was that?

Nothing had depressed Dekka more than Sam failing to come up with a clever plan. The master of the last-minute save had nothing. But Astrid had suggested an answer that might be close to what Shade had in mind, in some ways.

"What did you think of Astrid?" Dekka asked Armo.

He shrugged and looked more serious than his usual easygoing smirk. "She's smart. Beautiful, too. Not that I would ever . . . I mean, that Sam dude has a reputation. He's a warrior, and basic warrior code, you don't try to move on a fellow warrior's woman."

Dekka blinked. "Sometimes you're just downright odd, Armo."

"Just sometimes?" He grinned.

"What about her idea?"

Armo screwed the gas cap back on. "You mean go totally public and all? Isn't that what Shade is doing?"

"I assume. What do you think of that?" Dekka had come to like Armo, though she did not have a very high opinion of his intelligence, or his weird obsession with Danes, Vikings, and whatever warrior code he thought he was following. But his answer surprised her.

"I guess it's harder to kill someone you know." He shrugged

and looked away as if expecting to be humiliated for having said something stupid. "I mean, someone says, 'Let's kill all the mutants,' that's one thing; 'Let's kill Dekka and Armo,' that's a whole different thing. You know, if we're real people to them."

"Mutant Lives Matter?" Dekka said wryly. "You've got a country where half the people can't get their heads around black folks or Latinos or gays or trans people being actually human. Now we're going to get them to care about people who turn into freaks? I don't mean to sound cynical, but it comes with being black, female, and lesbian: this country hasn't exactly been kind to people like me."

"Well, some is better than none, right? I mean if even some people don't think we need to be wiped out . . ." Then, shaking his head, he asked in an undertone, "How did my life turn into this?"

Dekka smiled. "I know, an easygoing, cooperative guy like you? Ending up in a shitstorm?"

Armo laughed. "I know, right?"

"Okay. So what do we do? How do we take this public? I can tweet and Instagram like I have a couple times, but there are so many spoof accounts. . . . Some fake Dekka has three times as many followers as I do." She shrugged. "Anyway, the big TV networks and newspapers will be on the government's side. They're all owned by billionaires who just want to make money. We are bad for business, we Rockborn freaks. People don't shop when the world is blowing up."

She swung her leg over the Kawasaki, and Armo climbed on. But Dekka did not fire up the engine. She stood there astride her bike with Armo behind her, lost in thought.

Finally Armo said, "What is it you want to do, Dekka?"

"What do *you* want to do?"

"I asked you first."

"What I want to do is something stupid," Dekka admitted.

"You mean, go give Shade some backup even if she says no?" Armo asked. Dekka's silence was affirmation, so Armo said, "Yeah, me too."

"If we go back up the 5 or the 101, they'll be looking for us. How about a long detour? We could come in from the direction of Yosemite. From out of the east."

"One thing, though," Armo said. "I think it's time for me to get my own bike."

Dekka twisted around and said, "Your own bike?" Then she noticed Armo's gaze fixed on three motorcycle gang members just parking by the gas station's convenience store. Part of her would actually kind of miss having the big goof seated behind her. Not that Armo was much for conversation, but he was good for an occasional sentence or two. But it made good sense: the police BOLO (be on lookout for) would be for two people on one bike, one black female, one white male. Even experienced police tended to see only what they expected to see, and two bikes with one rider each was not one bike with two riders.

"Advice?" Armo asked. "I've never owned a motorcycle before."

Dekka peered at the three motorcycles, all Harley-Davidsons, all customized, all with ape-hanger handlebars. Then she looked past them to a motorcycle mounted on a trailer behind a pickup truck. She pointed with her chin. "If it was me, I'd go for that yellow Yamaha there. Plus, anyone owns a bike that expensive probably has theft insurance on it."

Armo swung off Dekka's bike and sauntered across the lot.

"Need help?" Dekka called after him.

Armo turned, walking backward, and made a face that said, *Me? Need help?* He ignored the bikers, who prudently ignored him back, then hopped up on the back of the trailer. The driver climbed out of his seat and came rushing around, yelling.

And then he stopped running. And froze. And stared slack-jawed at the creature now sitting astride his bike.

"You have theft insurance, right?" Armo asked in a voice twisted by low growls. "I don't want you to suffer. But I need your motorcycle."

The man nodded dully and said, "Are you Berserker Bear?"

"Am I *what*?"

"Berserker Bear. Sir." The man cautiously drew out his phone. "Can I take a picture? Because no way the insurance company believes this . . ."

"WTF is Berserker Bear?" Armo demanded.

"It's what they're calling you on Twitter. I didn't make it up! Don't blame me!"

"You can take a picture, but if you post it, say I do not like the name Berserker Damn Bear. It sounds like something from Build-a-Bear Workshop. I mean, come on, people, I want a cooler name."

"Yes, sir, Mister . . . Mister Bear." The man who was

about to lose his motorcycle clicked a picture of Armo, fully morphed, flexing his arms, and because of the angle and because Armo's morphed face was neither quite human nor quite bear, the photo appeared to be of a leering, bipedal, probably insane polar bear on a yellow Yamaha.

"Berserker Bear," Armo muttered darkly, and powered up the engine. "Gonna have to do better than that." Then he drove the Yamaha right off the back of the trailer, swung into place beside Dekka and said, "Ready."

He revved the engine until his whole body vibrated.

Dekka unleashed a huge and rare grin and did the same.

"Dude called me Berserker Bear," Armo said.

"They call me Lesbokitty."

"Yeah, we gotta get new names."

"You know, Armo," Dekka said. "I was just remembering this quote I heard once. It was from a soldier in World War II. His whole unit was in a trap, surrounded, situation totally hopeless."

"So what'd the guy say?"

"'They've got us surrounded . . . the poor bastards.'"

Armo threw back his head and laughed aloud. "Now that is some hardcore Viking shit! Hah! We're surrounded, Lesbokitty—let's ride!"

It was late afternoon when they spotted the glow on the horizon, evening by the time the glow had become a sparkling jewel chest.

"Ride through town?" Dekka yelled over to Armo.

"Are you seriously asking me whether we should ride down the Vegas Strip looking cool on big motorcycles?"

"So, that would be a yes?"

"It would be a 'duh, of course I'm riding my motorcycle down the Strip.'"

"I kind of thought you might say that."

They glided along, past the mysterious black pyramid of the Luxor on their left and the pastiche of New York-New York, sparkling orange in the setting sun. Lights everywhere, glowing and flashing and swirling, massive billboards ten stories tall, pedestrians shuffling in herds along the strip.

Then, suddenly, Dekka saw a different pattern of lights, one not advertising or enticing gamblers. Police lights. EMT lights.

"Hey," she called to Armo.

"I see them," he said.

"Do we turn back?"

"Maybe it's not about us. I mean, they're all at that one casino. How do you say that word?"

"Venetian," Dekka said.

They motored on toward the flashing lights, keeping to the speed limit, and were soon slowed further by traffic bunching up. They threaded their motorcycles through stopped cars and then they heard a collective *oh, my God!* from a hundred mouths at once, a crowd that stared upward, with hands over mouths in expressions of fear.

Dekka and Armo followed the stares and the pointed fingers and saw what appeared to be a uniformed police officer standing way up high, up on the edge of the Venetian's version of St. Mark's tower. The tower stood nearly five hundred feet tall.

The policeman stood there for a moment and then . . .

Screams!

The drop seemed to take forever. The man fell, feet down, hands by his side, like he was jumping into a swimming pool feet first.

He fell and fell and struck a decorative concrete railing. There was a sickeningly loud sound, a spray of blood, and the body blessedly fell out of view.

Dekka, appalled, looked at Armo. His face was stone. He said, "Yeah," which was all Dekka needed to ride her bike up onto the crowded sidewalk, stick the key in her pocket, and begin to morph.

CHAPTER 11
It's Only Pain

"JEEZ, SHADE, THAT car must be worth a fortune!" Cruz said.

"Well, if we're riding into battle we should ride comfortably," Shade said.

Palm Springs was not far away, and Palm Springs had more than its share of fast cars. The trouble had been finding something fast that would carry the three of them—Shade passed up a number of two-seater Lamborghinis and Ferraris—but that wasn't too much trouble, and Shade had rolled up in a Bentley convertible that was rated at two hundred miles an hour. With Shade driving while in morph, the Bentley could outrun anything the California Highway Patrol had on the road. Though not everything they had in the air, which was one advantage to a convertible: you could see a helicopter overhead.

And the Bentley was very comfortable. Leather as soft as a baby's cheek. It was a 425-mile drive—seven hours according to Google Maps. But Google Maps assumed you were sticking somewhere close to the speed limit.

Unfortunately, the reality of driving two hundred miles an hour for two-plus hours was that the wind utterly defeated the car's clever wind-reducing technology and left Cruz in the front and Malik in the back crouching down low to avoid flapping cheeks and stinging hair.

The CHP picked them up as they passed through Bakersfield, but their cruisers couldn't keep up. So siren-wailing CHP would pick them up briefly on the 5, fall behind, and be replaced by hastily assembled roadblocks, which the Bentley would easily evade by driving onto the dividing strip. A hundred miles north of Bakersfield, the CHP helicopters were on them, but on the long, straight stretches of the world's most boring freeway, even they could barely keep pace.

They turned onto the 198, cutting toward Monterey. This was a two-lane road that wound through dry hills populated only by wind turbines and the occasional cow. Here there were no roadblocks, but as they veered wildly onto the 101 North they encountered the first of the news helicopters coming from Bay Area TV stations.

"Hey!" Cruz yelled against the hurricane. "We've become a high-speed chase." She turned her phone so Shade could see. Sure enough, CNN was cutting between various news choppers and regular folks standing outside Burger Kings or whatever repeating that, yep, they had seen a car go by at NASCAR speeds.

"Like a bat outta hell!"

"Like they was running from the devil himself!"

The chyron at the bottom of the screen read, *Shade Darby en route to . . . ?*

They had become a classic California obsession: the televised high-speed chase. The whole state was watching, which was perfect from Shade's point of view. The more public the better.

The problem was that she had never spent this long in morph, and while she was in that unnatural state the Dark Watchers were present and impossible to dismiss. At first it was the usual sense of being probed, touched, violated by insinuating dark tendrils that somehow passed through time and space to dig through her mind like bargain hunters digging through a yard sale mystery box. Like they were looking for something and not quite sure what. But as minutes stretched to an hour and more, it was less a feeling of being rudely probed and more a sense of losing herself, as if she, too, was a bystander commenting on herself.

She glanced in the rearview mirror at Malik. How many hours had he spent now in the company of those malicious intelligences? Was he still fighting? Could he possibly be? How strong was he?

How long would Malik hold on to his sanity? And what would he do if he lost it?

In that case God help us all.

She felt herself being smothered—by the Dark Watchers, by guilt, by crippling self-doubt that nagged at her, ridiculed her, mocked her pretense of resistance and her no-doubt-futile plan.

In the end . . .

"No," she said aloud, though it was barely a chirp to Cruz or Malik, prisoners as they were of real time. She de-morphed while still driving, slowing to a manageable eighty miles an hour while she was doing so. Breathed hard as she clutched the wheel.

"What are you doing?" Cruz asked sharply, looking back at distant flashing lights now closing the distance.

Shade said, "I just needed a break."

Malik's lidded eyes met hers in the mirror.

She drove in real time, and the CHP vehicles caught up and the helicopters actually had to slow down.

"Stop the car and pull over immediately," came a very authoritative voice through a bullhorn.

In response, Cruz looked up, smiled, and waved. Like they were just some crazy kids driving to Mexico on spring break.

Shade was indescribably relieved to be in her own head alone without company. But she had no time to waste and did not wish to see military-quality helicopters joining the news choppers, so after a few minutes of relative normalcy, she gritted her teeth and morphed again. The Bentley leaped away as she easily threaded through cars going a third of her speed.

Then it was off the freeway and onto what Californians call surface streets. She could blow through red lights, finding the split-second gaps between cars and threading them effortlessly, but there were no more two-hundred-mile-an-hour stretches. It was terrifying to Cruz, who had created permanent divots in the dashboard where her fingertips dug in. It might perhaps be terrifying to Malik, but Malik was silent, looking fixedly ahead, eyes unfocused.

Shade knew where Malik was now. She knew he was locked in battle with *them*. A battle he could escape from only by demorphing into agony.

Nothing you can do, Shade, she told herself. Each time she managed to push away the guilt it came back, though it occurred to her that she felt it far less when she was in morph, just as she had been immune to Malik's blast of pain while she was in morph.

Which meant Malik's power wasn't going to be of much use against other mutants. But against regular humans? Like the regular humans running the Ranch?

Will he do it? Can he do it? Can he control it? Do I have any right to ask it of him?

He's a tool for me to use.

He's a boy who loves me. Or did.

He's a boy I loved. And may still.

It was dark by the time they reached Carmel Valley, what Dekka had said was the entry to the Ranch. Now they drove more slowly still—barely over a hundred and twenty-five—searching for the unmarked road Dekka had described. There were three helicopters overhead, the CHP chopper and two news stations, watching eagerly, seeing the narrowing of the roads and imagining that the long chase must be reaching its end. In that they were correct.

"There," Cruz said, pointing to a road marked with a sign that said *No Thru Traffic.* Of course, Shade had had plenty of time to see the sign, and Cruz's elongated *th-e-e-e-r-r-r* was irrelevant.

They turned onto the road, tires screaming in protest, and within seconds they were confronted by three armored vehicles racing to meet them. Racing to meet them and being easily passed despite their effort to form a roadblock. Armored cars might do as much as fifty miles an hour; the Bentley was still doing almost three times that.

Up and up the winding road through the trees they went, and now a fourth helicopter, faster, sleeker, and far more dangerous, had been added to the chase. But even military helicopters have trouble with a vehicle able to take hairpin turns at a hundred miles an hour and twice that speed on the straightaways.

The dark helicopter, an Army Apache, gave up pursuing and instead dipped its nose and raced ahead, able to take a straight line while the Bentley twisted and turned, and as Shade came tearing around a curve, she found herself face-to-face with the Apache hovering over the road just a dozen feet off the ground like a falcon waiting for a mouse, the blast of its rotors kicking up a whirlwind of dust and debris and bending saplings.

Shade slammed on the brakes, and the car fishtailed madly. She was about to leap from the Bentley to rush the helicopter herself, but at the last second she saw the flash of fire and smoke and yanked the car sharply left as the missile flew past, missing them by inches and exploding in the trees.

The Bentley slewed wildly, and not even Shade's speed

could control it. The car plunged off the side of the road, crashed through a guardrail, and went airborne like some steampunk flying machine, and off the side of a hundred-foot drop. The slope was almost vertical, blanketed in pine trees and punctuated with rock outcroppings.

"Shade!" Cruz screamed in slow motion.

The Bentley was in the air, the heavy engine dragging the nose down, plummeting toward trees and rocks and annihilation. Shade snapped her seat-belt release, stood with one foot on the dashboard and the other on her headrest, bent down, grabbed Cruz under the armpits, and hurled Cruz upward against the force of gravity.

Cruz flew and screamed in what to Shade was comically slow motion, hung in the air for a very long time, then was captured by gravity and began to fall. In that time Shade rolled into the back seat, grabbed Malik under one arm, and launched herself backward as the car fell away from her.

Rising, Shade slammed into Cruz, twisted in midair, snatched her friend, yanked her close, put her free arm around Cruz's chest, and with both her friends in her arms had time to consider how to lessen the impact of the inevitable hard landing.

The car fell, engine lowest, its wheels spinning just a foot away from the jumbled cliff face. It smashed through a small tree, banged into another, twisted and smashed sideways through a third.

The slope of the cliff came out to meet Shade as she fell, and she slid and ran, skidded and hopped on her disturbing insectoid feet, bleeding off speed, dodging trees, absorbing the energy into her inhumanly powerful legs, fighting the mass of herself and her two friends.

The car passed her now, smashed into a tree thick enough to destroy the hood, slammed nose-down into a boulder, flipped end over end, and skidded the rest of the way on its back, trailing a debris cloud of expensive trim in all directions.

Shade, still carrying Malik and Cruz, neared the bottom of the cliff and turned skidding into running across gentler grades and finally slowed enough to drop Cruz and Malik onto the pine needles. Through the trees Shade could make out glimpses of barracks-style buildings ahead and below, just as Dekka had described it.

For Cruz and Malik, it had all taken about seven seconds.

"Jesus H. Christ, Shade!" Cruz erupted once she had patted herself frantically as if she expected to be missing some bits.

Shade slowed her answer, taking forever to say a "sorry" that could be heard and understood by people living in real time.

Where the trees ended was a wide greenbelt perimeter that preceded a double chain-link fence topped with razor wire.

Shade de-morphed, the better to communicate. Back on the road above, the military helicopter was rising to search for its suddenly disappeared prey. One of the news helicopters had captured the whole thing on video, and now the military craft was hovering near the news chopper and a male voice was yelling through a loudspeaker. "You have violated secure air space. Leave the area immediately!"

"Look!" Cruz yelled, pointing at a file of vehicles hastily loaded with armed men and women, some still frantically buttoning uniforms over bulletproof vests. The vehicles were driving into the band of cleared ground between the woods and the compound's fence.

"I'll take care of them," Shade said. "Keep Malik moving!"

"Wait!"

Shade heard him just in time, halfway back to morph. "What?" Malik had been almost mute, like having a zombie along for the ride.

"Let me try," Malik said.

She had not nerved herself up to ask him. She had thought of asking him, but some lingering shred of normal decency had stopped her. The shark's ruthlessness was not for Malik.

"You don't have to do this, Malik," Shade said.

"You're safer if I do it, Shade," Malik said.

Cruz yelled, still very keyed up from having essentially flown through dense forest at speeds that had nearly blown her T-shirt off. "What? What, are you psychic now, Malik?"

Not entirely impossible given the world as it now existed post-rock, Shade had to admit.

Malik looked at Shade, who could not quite bring herself to meet his gaze. "I'm not psychic. I just know how unprepared you are for feelings, Shade. Normal people feel guilt and self-doubt pretty often, but you, Shade? You have no coping mechanism for this. And I'm afraid what you're trying to do now is end it all."

Shade froze. Cruz blinked at Malik, then nodded, understanding.

"I'm not . . . ," Shade said, but found no words to complete
the thought.

"Not consciously," Malik said. "But you're being reckless.
You have a weapon. You have to use it. You do not have my
permission to get yourself killed."

Shade shook her head, but only barely. Her denial would
have carried more conviction had she been able to look at
him, but she kept her eyes aimed away, at the woods, at the
sky, at Cruz, only long enough to see that Cruz agreed with
Malik.

"No, Malik, I can do this. You don't have to—"

Suddenly Malik pushed his face close to Shade's. "It's all
I've got now," he snarled. "It's all I have, all I can do to help.
So shut up and let me do it."

Shade stepped back from his rage. But a part of her was
almost relieved. Open anger was easier than Malik's vacant,
silent suffering.

Shade nodded, not trusting her voice.

Malik closed his eyes and said, "You both need to be
morphed."

CHAPTER 12
Semper Fi

I AM MASTER *Sergeant Matthew Tolliver, United States Marine Corps. Semper Fi!*

The words were silent, in his head alone, because to speak them aloud risked getting a very nasty, very painful shock.

His space was a cell, not small as cells went, but far from the open skies and endless horizons of his Montana childhood. He had served aboard naval vessels, of course, six tours in the Mediterranean, and aboard ship the accommodations were tight to say the least. But on a ship he still had the sea and the sky and a cold breeze on his face.

Now he had a steel box with a bulletproof glass wall on one end looking out on gloom and gray, shadowy distorted lab workers in white coats, private guards in uniform, and from time to time big trucks and earthmovers passing. General DiMarco's "bunker" was up to his left, just a ripple in the glass.

A steel box containing a steel box containing Tolliver, for in addition to losing his freedom and his family and his place

in the world, Tolliver had lost his body. He was no longer
made of flesh and bone and blood, he was a machine with a
human head, a tank with a man's head encased in an armored
steel bell.

*I am Master Sergeant Matthew Tolliver, United States
Marine Corps. Semper Fi.*

After he had suffered a training accident at the Marine
base in Twentynine Palms, HSTF-66 had come for him,
rushing him away to supposedly expert treatment. They had
sliced down his back and pulled out his spine, cutting away
the veins and arteries, the tendons and nerves. His spine and
his head had been removed in a single piece, and then, in a
series of operations—he had lost count—the remaining bio-
logical Tolliver was connected to a maze of wires and servers
and battery packs.

It had taken a month just for him to learn to control the
articulated "arm" on his right side. After that it had taken
only days to master the engine that drove his four big, cleated
wheels. The weapons systems, already optimized for digital
controls, were the easiest. Fully loaded, he was armed with
a cluster of three MANPADS (man-portable air-defense system) capable of shooting down most helicopters; he had six
rocket-propelled grenades; he had a six-barrel mini-gun that
could fire up to six thousand rounds per minute. He could
go three hundred miles on a tank of diesel fuel at speeds of
up to fifty miles an hour. The tank body was small, dense,
and heavily armored, weighing ten tons—about the weight
of three cars.

If there was a weak spot, it was clearly the rounded hump

within which his head still survived on pumped oxygen and nutrient baths. That hump, with a slit for his eyes, sat where the turret would be on a real tank. And that slit was his world now. He was a sardine in a box atop a box inside a box inside a cave.

Tolliver suspected he was losing his mind. Most days he spent doing nothing, nothing at all, but sitting in his cell. Naturally his weapons systems were all unloaded, or he would, without the slightest question, have tried to blast his way out, even if it meant the shock waves would kill him.

He might be a cyborg, he might be a slave with a pain chip in his head, but still . . .

I am Master Sergeant Matthew Tolliver, United States Marine Corps.

Semper Fi. Always faithful, the Marine Corps motto.

But faithful to what? he asked himself bitterly. To the government that had done this to him?

And he knew he wasn't the only one. He was a careful observer, and on testing runs either out in the cave or even out in the open air, he had seen others similar to himself, each a bit different, as if each was a new stage of development.

At least, he told himself, he was better off than the new drones he'd heard referred to by the sickeningly cruel term "baby-go-bang-bangs." These were drones piloted by the brains of infants. The Ranch's researchers had discovered that no computer could identify a human face with anything like the accuracy of a human brain. So infants had been . . . obtained . . . and the unnecessary parts removed, so that what was left was a baby's head and eyes as the "pilot" of a small, quick drone that carried no weapons but its own speed and weight. The brain was trained to respond to a photograph and, once launched, would search for that face, and upon spotting it, would accelerate and ram the target with a hardened steel nose cone. The infant brain was not expected to survive. He'd caught a glimpse of an iKaze, like a quarter-scale Predator with a glass bubble nose, within which rested a small pink brain and the globes of two eyes connected to the brain by a tether of nerves and blood vessels.

So many nightmares he'd seen here. That was the worst.

Semper Fi. Always faithful. To men and women—including military officers like DiMarco—who would do *that*?

I, Matthew Tolliver, do solemnly swear that I will support and defend the Constitution of the United States against all enemies, foreign and domestic; that I will bear true faith and allegiance to the same; and that I will obey the orders of the president of the United States and the orders of the officers appointed over me, according to regulations and the Uniform Code of Military Justice. So help me God.

That was the oath he had taken eighteen years ago when he enlisted at age nineteen.

But back then he'd been fully human. Back then he had trusted. He had been proud to serve. But how to remain faithful when his nation had lost its moral compass? The first part of the oath was to defend the Constitution. It was the *Constitution* he served, not just the people in the chain of command.

He moved his wheels and crept closer to the glass barrier.

Something wasn't right out there. Something was happening. He could barely see, but he was pretty certain that two guards were in serious trouble.

Something was happening. Something unexpected. Something that had his jailers twisting and writhing in apparent pain. He himself was distantly aware of pain, but it did not quite reach him, as if he was standing next to a rushing river, catching the occasional drop but mostly staying dry.

Once, years ago in Afghanistan, he had been on a patrol that had been cut off. Tolliver and three of his marines were in a narrow defile with snipers on high points all around. Their radio wasn't working; they had no way to call for help. It had been hopeless, and they all knew it. And then had come the faint sound of a helicopter, and in the space of three heartbeats he'd gone from grim despair to hope.

This was like that.

His weapons systems were not loaded. He had no bullets or missiles. But he sure knew where to find them. And how to use them.

And who to kill if he got the chance.

I am Master Sergeant Matthew Tolliver, United States Marine Corps. And I will kill these bastards with no more pity than they've shown.

Semper Fi!

CHAPTER 13
Letting the Animals Out of the Zoo

SHADE WAS IN morph, and Cruz joined her, deciding to mimic the appearance of Dekka—first because she admired Dekka, and second because it would confuse HSTF-66 and whoever else was watching. Sadly she would not have Dekka's power, but a Dekka sighting here would perhaps help keep the real Dekka a bit safer. Wherever she was.

"Okay," Cruz said.

"Okay," Malik echoed, eyes still closed. Then he opened them on the view of the Ranch spread out ahead. He formed his hands as if he meant to encompass the Ranch, holding it in a frame of fingers. He breathed deeply.

Cruz felt the invisible blast of pain that came from Malik. It was like someone had suddenly opened a dam and a huge wave was rushing past her. It did not touch her, but Cruz felt its power. And she saw and heard its effects on the men and women down in the greenbelt. Most fell to their knees, on their backs, on their sides. Others ran in wild panic, batting at their bodies as if they were on fire. All screamed.

So many different ways that people expressed agony, Cruz thought. Some high-pitched, some lower register; some a single long ululation, others cursing, and still others making animal noises. One man sounded as if he were barking.

This must be what hell sounds like.

Cruz suddenly realized how calmly she was taking this. Human beings, men and women whose only sin was enlisting and being assigned to the monstrosity that was the Ranch, were crying like babies, writhing like animals, running in panic. And her first thought had not been *Those poor people!* but a distant, chilly *What strange sounds people make when they are in pain.*

Malik nodded. "Now, Shade."

Shade tapped the button on her GoPro and was off like a bolt from a crossbow, blowing past trees, sailing effortlessly over the writhing, desperate security men. She reached a guarded gate and used her momentum to leap over both of the fourteen-foot-tall chain-link fences. A millisecond later she was at the first building. She paused and heard a noise like something from a madman's nightmare: screams and cries from every direction, some muffled by walls, others shrill and near.

She went in, and it was like passing through some modern interpretation of Dante's "Inferno," a bright-lit, neutral-colored office-building hell. Men and women lay in corridors screaming, with tendons standing out in their necks, with eyes bulging, fingers clawing at their own flesh.

She didn't even need her speed. She could have strolled through the place eating an ice-cream cone. But she could feel that Malik had ended his brutal assault. Gradually the effects of Malik's pain blast would lessen; people would wipe their tears and change their soiled underpants and get back to work. But having been briefly exposed to Malik's first assault, she knew it would be some time before people were really functional. What Malik did, the power that he had, was impossible for the human mind to process easily, or easily move past. Even now the sense memory of it was like a wound in her brain, a wound that had only begun to scab over and was a long way yet from healing.

A wound I deserve.

Shade spun back up to full speed and within a minute or so had found an access point from the aboveground Ranch to the underground heart of the place.

She stood there atop a newly repaired scaffolding, vibrating, staring, taking in an impossible sight. It was much as Dekka had described it, but no description could have prepared Shade for the sheer size, the vast space that could have been used as a landfill for half a dozen sports stadiums, with room left over for a scattering of shopping malls.

It was roughly rectangular, with massive, intimidating towers at the corners like something out of a maximum security prison. Cells lined much of the wall space, some only at ground level, others stacked atop each other, most fronted by bulletproof glass so thick that what light escaped from inside those cells was faintly green. Those glass barriers also had the effect of making it impossible to see into a cell without being almost directly in front of it.

The Ranch's hidden underground was a work in progress, with construction equipment and a crane. The crane must have been rotating when Malik had struck—it had smashed into a stone wall, precipitating a small rock slide. She saw the operator in profile. He seemed to be bent over, head between his knees, either crying or throwing up.

Everywhere uniformed guards and white-coated technicians sat or lay stunned, weeping, wiping snot from their faces, reeking of their loosened bowels. None was yet on their feet, but they would be soon.

Shade knew she had limited time, but she could not stop looking—and more importantly, *showing*. She had learned from her earlier experiment with the camera that at full speed it showed little but blur. So she zoomed from cell to cell and paused, counting slowly, keeping the camera fixed for what she calculated was a full second of real time.

It was a video tour of man-made evil. Cell after cell housed monstrosities, horrors, the results of experiments so devoid of human compassion or decency they reminded Shade of what the Nazi monster Dr. Mengele had done in Auschwitz. A one-second take was a long time for the morphed Shade, and at many of the cells she had to close her eyes. There were things she did not want to see.

But interestingly, few of these poor creatures in the cells showed the effects of Malik's pain blast. It seemed the Rock-born were, if not totally immune, at least much less affected by the Malik effect. Good and bad. Good that Shade could

function; bad that Malik would have no power against someone like Dragon or Knightmare.

There had to be a control room. Shade took in the layout
of the place, saw an oblong building perched on a shelf at the
far end of the chamber, presumably a head office. But, she
imagined, controls would be . . . yes, probably in what was
evidently, based on rust weeping from one steel panel, the
oldest of the towers. In a blink she was in the tower, racing
methodically around, coming at last to the uppermost room,
which evoked an airport's control tower, with distorting bulletproof glass all around, framing a podium console with a
touch screen embedded. She tapped it slowly, letting her finger remain in contact.

She was prompted with, *Fingerprint not recognized.*

"Yeah, I figured that," Shade muttered. She grabbed a
woman technician who was sobbing in the corner, dragged
her by the wrist, and placed her finger on the screen, which
obediently opened up.

Still no one had recovered enough to sound an alarm, let
alone form a reaction force. Slowed now only by the process-
ing speed of the computer, Shade clicked through the menu
until she was confident she had what she wanted.

The tiers of cells had to be opened one by one: A Block,
Tier One; A Block, Tier Two; B Block, Tier One—through
eight separate releases. A digital map showed cells turning
from green to red as she unlocked them.

Not all the prisoners were quick to emerge—some had
been human enough to suffer from Malik's pain wave. Some
no longer possessed a body capable of moving on its own.

Something like a great, fat centipede the size of a school bus emerged from one of the cells and instantly chomped into a prostrate guard, leaving his torso looking like an apple with a bite missing.

Was a giant carnivorous centipede really the intended result of these mad scientists' work?

Shade ran up onto the roof of the tower and then leaped slightly upward so that she would fall in real time, which seemed almost comically slow, but which allowed her to take in more detail. She landed atop a big yellow bulldozer's cockpit, then bounced up to balance on the raised steel blade, like a general astride a very unusual horse.

There, she de-morphed and looked down at an audience unlike anything seen in the history of life on Earth—morphs and monsters, cyborgs and Rockborn.

"I'm Shade Darby," she said. "I'm the one who opened your cells."

A creature larger than most and as strange as any, a bizarre, impossible melding of man, robot, and porcupine, spoke in a strained but piercing voice.

"What do you want?"

"I want you to be free," Shade said. "Get away from this place. Spread out. Move. The guards will recover. So, run! Get away while you can."

Many waited no longer but ran. Among them a handsome young man who, as he ran, began to morph, with a long blade growing from his right arm as chitinous armor covered him.

Knightmare!

Well, it was not the time for dealing with that particular

creep; she had bigger fish to fry. She wasn't here to settle scores, she was here to expose the Ranch and liberate its victims.

Hero stuff, she couldn't help but think. *Hero stuff. Finally.*

"Everyone out!" Shade yelled. "They're recovering, and they'll be on us quick!"

"With all due respect, miss, no," a man's gruff voice said. It came from a sort of tank creature with an articulated robot arm and a bristling weapons array that included empty missile-launcher tubes. A human head could be just glimpsed through a visor slit. The placement of the head made it nause-atingly clear that there was no body attached to it.

"No?" Shade demanded. "Why not? And who are you?"

"I'm Master Sergeant Matthew Tolliver, United States Marine Corps."

"Okay, Sergeant, what is it you want to do?"

"Miss, I first want to thank you. Second? Well, miss, sec-ond, I want to take this place apart, brick by goddamn brick, computer by computer, man by man. That's what I would *like* to do."

This was met by sounds of approval ranging from the tim-idly reluctant to the fierce. On the fierce end of the spectrum was the porcupine creature, a body so poorly conceived, so misshapen that he bled from half a dozen punctures he him-self had inadvertently made. He had one human eye, and one mechanical eye that bulged out a bit like a thermostat. His mouth was too wide, as if he was auditioning for a role as the Joker. His teeth, tiny and sharp as needles, made speech diffi-cult. His tongue bled when he moved it over his teeth. Quills like knitting needles stuck out from his forehead.

"I'm Jasper Llewellyn," the monster said, his own blood trickling down his chin. "I speak for no one. But before I run, I'm killing some of these bastards!"

Someone in the crowd hissed the single word "Revenge," and Shade had a sudden, sickening realization that she had done more than free these poor people and expose the Ranch to the world: she had doomed the Ranch's staff.

Disturbed, but with no idea what she should do about it, Shade simply said, "You're free. Do what you want."

Then she stripped off her camera and turned it around on herself. "I'm Shade Darby. This horror show is run by the US government, by a group called Homeland Security Task Force 66. Do you see what they're doing here? Do you see what they're doing supposedly in your name? So who are the bad guys? Us or them?"

Not all the mutant or cyborg denizens of the Ranch were capable of escaping. Some were dependent on exotic chemicals being pumped into their systems. Others were so malformed, so twisted and destroyed by the effects of experiments with DNA and the rock, or such ill-conceived man-machine fusions that they were utterly crippled. But many could escape, and fled into the woods to be pursued by news helicopters filming both the freaks and the military helicopters raining murderous fire down on them.

Others, though, had the means to inflict revenge. And their victims, too, fled for the woods.

Those who lived that long.

CHAPTER 14
Missed Him by That Much

THE VENETIAN CASINO had already seen many strange things, but none stranger than the sight of what looked like a very large, bipedal, tailless, black-furred, snake-haired feline, followed by a towering bipedal, humanish-faced polar bear.

The casino level was a scene of utter chaos. At least four separate groups of EMTs hunched over bloody people, and were surrounded by cordons of police and casino security struggling to hold back what looked like tourists, many elderly, who seemed determined—as astounding as it was—to eat each other, the cops, the EMTs, and the wounded. Indeed, the wounded themselves snapped at the medical techs' hands as they tried to apply bandages. Many of the wounded had been handcuffed for their own safety. Other handcuffed people lay on their sides gnawing at the air, growling and mewling and trying to squirm toward the nearest living person.

And all the while came the moans of those helpless to resist Dillon's cruel orders. *I'm sorry! I can't stop myself! Someone stop me! My God, I can't stop!*

Dekka and Armo shouldered through crowds of people in uniform, the wounded, the mad, and the terrified, demanding to know how they could get to the tower.

Once they were noticed—and Dekka thought it showed just how crazy the scene was that Dekka and Armo were not immediately noticed—a trio of Las Vegas police detached themselves from handcuffing people and advanced with guns leveled and very serious, very angry looks on their faces.

"Freeze or we shoot!" This came from a police sergeant, a Latina with eyes that very definitely meant business.

"Who is doing this?" Dekka demanded.

"Get down on the ground, *now!*"

Armo leaped, swung one big paw, and knocked the sergeant's gun to the ground. He wrapped his powerful arms around her and turned her, helpless as a tantruming toddler, to face Dekka.

"Listen to me, Sergeant, I realize what I look like," Dekka said. "I realize what you probably think of me. But I am here to put a stop to this bullshit, and from the look of it you could use some help."

"Let me go or I will charge you with—"

"Dammit, tell us what's going on! There are cops jumping off the roof!"

Armo released the sergeant but stayed ready.

Dekka moved closer. "Sergeant, I get that you don't know what to do, but the fact is I can kill everyone on this floor—you, your officers, the people, everyone. I can reduce them to bloody McNuggets."

The sergeant wasn't entirely sure one way or the other, so Dekka glanced around, spotted a corner of the floor with a dozen slot machines and no people nearby. She raised her hands as if in benediction, opened her mouth, and let loose a tiger's roar, and the entire area—the slot machines, the railing, the chairs, even the carpet on the floor—became a howling tornado, a shrieking wild chaos.

Dekka lowered her hand, and the shredded remnants fell clattering to the no-longer-carpeted concrete floor.

"See?" she demanded. "Now, what the hell is going on here?"

Over in the sports-betting area the huge screens that usually broadcast horse races now showed the exterior of the Venetian. A second policeman stood on the precipice of the tower.

The second policeman jumped. Just like the first. No hesitation, no drama. Just a step into nothingness and a long, long fall.

"He can make people do anything," the sergeant blurted. "They do whatever he tells them, and they don't stop. We've cut off the phones to the suite he's in, and we've handed out ear coverings to our SWAT guys, but he's surrounded himself with staff and tourists and even some cops and security. We can't get at him without shooting our way past innocent people."

Dekka nodded, as if this was the sort of thing she heard every day: some person with a power misbehaving badly. It was a story she'd heard too many times in the FAYZ.

"Get us ear covering," Dekka said. "And we will take him down." Then she added, "Without having to shoot innocent people."

A policeman, not the sergeant, hastily proffered two sets of shooter's ear coverings.

"Ready?" Dekka asked Armo, who was trying with only limited success to fit the ear coverings over a head that they were definitely not designed for.

"This is total hero stuff, isn't it?" he asked, a bit giddy.

"It is if we win," Dekka said dryly.

They stepped into the elevator, followed by stares ranging from hopeful to skeptical to simply overwhelmed. As they passed the tenth floor they put on their earmuffs. Dekka listened for the dinging of the elevator bell as it rose, but heard nothing. She felt rather than heard their arrival at the top floor.

They exchanged glances.

The door slid open.

The carpet immediately in front of the elevator was soaked with blood. The wallpaper was spattered with it. Two dead police officers and three others not in uniform lay scattered down the hallway. Near the far end of the hallway stood a solid phalanx of men and women, old and young, some in uniform, most not. A few had guns. All stared with eyes blazing with alertness and fury. The instant they saw Dekka and Armo they began yelling, but their words were inaudible.

"Seriously, what the holy . . . ?" Armo began, before realizing Dekka could not hear him.

"Everyone move aside," Dekka ordered.

No one moved aside. Instead perhaps twenty of them began to charge. Not at a walk but at a run, like Dekka and Armo were loose footballs that had to be recovered.

Armo caught Dekka's eye and pointed at himself. Then he advanced on the mob, holding his massive arms wide, his spike claws scraping the walls on either side and shredding the wallpaper. A shot rang out. Armo flinched but sped up. The mob and Armo met, and the front row of attackers went down like bowling pins.

But they jumped right back up, some leaping on Armo, trying to get their arms around his throat, grabbing handfuls of slick white fur, trying to hold on to his ankles. He was very big and very strong, but there were at least a dozen people grabbing at him. He was clearly trying not to hurt them, but the result was that he was immobilized.

Dekka squeezed past Armo, jumped over outstretched arms, knocked a gun out of one man's hands, punched a man in the face, and reached the door at the end, which bore the right number, the number the sergeant downstairs had given her.

She did not knock or use the doorbell. She raised her hands, roared, and the door (and part of the surrounding wall) flew apart. She hurled the shreds of steel and wood at the crowd—not hard enough (she hoped) to permanently injure anyone, but enough to distract some of Armo's army of Lilliputians.

Dekka stepped through the door.

Two people stood there. A pretty girl with wildly excited eyes, dressed expensively and with way too much jewelry around her wrists and neck, and what looked like the Geico gecko wearing an actual tuxedo. Like he thought he was James Bond.

The snake-man spoke. Dekka pointed at her ear coverings and saw a slight recoil.

"You are either going to come willingly and be muzzled, or I'm going to have to hurt you."

He seemed to shout something, but again, she could not hear.

Unfortunately, in the melee in the hall, Armo had lost his earmuffs. Dekka had a split second to see a great beast hurling itself at her. She spun but hesitated and was bowled over by Armo.

Bowled over by Armo going straight at the reptile in the tuxedo, who he hit so hard that the boy flew half the length of the room, smashed into the floor-to-ceiling plate glass, and fell to the carpet, stunned.

Dekka seized the moment and delivered a straight-up sucker punch that caught the girl under her chin, snapped her head back, buckled her knees, and dropped her to the floor as limp as a wet towel.

Armo had the reptilian young man pushed up against a wall, with his long claws poking hard against the creature's throat.

But then, luck intervened. A policeman, bruised, bloodied, his uniform shredded, leveled his service revolver and fired once. Dekka did not know whether he was shooting at Armo or at Dillon, but the result was to shatter the floor-to-ceiling window.

Sudden wind pushed at them, then sucked them toward the opening, toward a fall that not even Armo could hope to survive.

Armo staggered, caught himself, released his hold on Dillon just long enough for Dillon to scream out of the window.

"Kill! Everyone, kill!"

Some of the people below heard it. And one radio reporter had a hot microphone so that Dillon's voice went out over the airwaves to thousands of Las Vegas residents in their cars with the radio on.

Armo scrambled back, tripped, fell on his back and stabbed his claws into the carpet, teetered on the edge with his body from the waist down hanging out of the window. Then he rolled over, got to one knee, and from that position punched Dillon so hard in the stomach Dekka thought it might kill him. She tore off a length of bedspread and wrapped it tightly around Dillon's mouth. Then she used his belt and a bathrobe cord to truss him like a pig, hands and feet behind his back, hands then tied to feet.

Dekka pushed her ear covering back so it rested on her neck.

"Well," she said. "You really, *really* don't take orders, do you?" she asked Armo.

"See? Oppositional Defiant Disorder: it's useful sometimes."

Armo lifted the squirming, furious Dillon by his hair, and Dekka dragged Saffron by one arm down the hallway, kicking and shoving and punching their way through the voice-controlled lunatics in the hallway; they threw the pair into the elevator like two sacks of manure.

"Thank God," Dekka said, relieved. "This guy's power is nuts."

Armo nodded warily. "You ever have that in Perdido Beach?"

"No, thankfully," Dekka said. "Though Penny was close in some ways. We were lucky to stop her."

They emerged from the elevator to a scene of renewed frenzy. Police and EMTs had barricaded the street doors against a dozen or so tourists who beat on the door before turning to attack each other. Gunshots could be heard from the street outside. Dillon's last shout through the broken window had had an effect. Sirens and flashing lights were everywhere, every Las Vegas cop, every casino security team, the local office of the US Marshals, the local FBI, and forces from adjoining towns had all come rushing to help control what was now thousands of Vegas residents and tourists engaged in open-ended mass slaughter.

"Freeze!"

Dekka blinked at a man wearing a suit, who had a 9-millimeter automatic pointed at her. Beside him stood a female version, also with gun leveled.

"Seriously?" Dekka said.

"Dekka Talent and Aristotle Adamo, I'm arresting you under the emergency decree."

Dekka, never the most patient of people, leaped with the

liquid grace and deceptive speed that was part of the gift of cat DNA. She knocked the man's gun aside like it was a child's toy, pushed him roughly into the woman, and Armo was on the two of them like a brick dropped on a daisy.

"What are you idiots doing?" Dekka demanded.

"We're your best bet, Talent," the woman snarled. "There's a KOS out for you."

"A what?"

"Kill on sight," the woman said.

"What are you talking about? I'm an American citizen. You can't just shoot people. What the hell?"

"We can shoot all the animals we want," the man snarled.

"I want to punch him," Armo said, looking back at Dekka.

"Feel free."

So Armo swung his paw, caught the man on the jaw, and left him lying unconscious atop the woman struggling to reach her gun, which had landed a foot beyond her outstretched fingers.

And then, a tingling warning of danger and Dekka turned, already knowing what she would see. During the brief melee Dillon had removed his gag.

"Everyone! Attack them! Kill the mutants! Kill! Kill!"

He danced back as police and EMTs, tourists and staff spun, stared, fixed their aim, and rushed at Dekka and Armo.

"Hah! In fact, you two mutants kill each other. Now! Yeah! Kill each other!"

Dekka took a step back from Armo, and Armo did from

her. But then, neither of them attacked. In fact, neither had any urge to obey.

"Do it!" Dillon roared, as Saffron disentangled herself and ran to his side. "Kill each other!" As Saffron leaped to the attack, Dillon amended quickly. "Not you, Saffron."

But Dekka and Armo both were busy coping with the attacks of the controlled, fending off wild-eyed retirees and moms and even a few kids, trying to do as little damage as possible, but retreating all the while toward the exterior doors.

Madness inside the casino. And no way now to get at the boy with the impossible-to-disobey voice as he retreated behind a phalanx of dozens, maybe a hundred or more maddened zombies.

Madness outside the casino as well. Screams and roars of rage, gunshots, the sounds of fists thudding against flesh, sirens, alarms . . . chaos! All of it bathed in the eerie neon light of millions of bulbs.

Dekka and Armo, punching and kicking through the mob, searched for their motorcycles and found them knocked over, but still where they had left them hastily parked on the sidewalk. They shoved and pushed and, when necessary, pounded people. Then, just as Dekka had managed to fire up her engine, a woman leaped at her, landing sideways across Dekka's gas tank, her face so close Dekka could feel the warmth of her breath. And before Dekka could take her paws from the handlebars to push the woman away, her dreads struck.

Until that moment the effect that happened when she morphed—her dreads turning to agitated snakes—had seemed like nothing more than a bit of a threat display, a bit of theater. But in the blink of an eye, a dozen of the snake-dreads had struck, sinking tiny black fangs into the woman's cheeks and nose and neck.

What happened next forced a scream of horror from Dekka's own lips. Because the woman changed horribly, and with brutal speed. Her skin shriveled, wrinkled, and turned the putty color of an old desktop computer. Her eyes swelled in their sockets, stared at Dekka in uncomprehending horror, then dimmed and, like her flesh, shriveled until they were little more than two white-and-red raisins at the bottoms of empty eye sockets.

Armo, seeing that Dekka was just staring and shouting in terror, reached over, grabbed her shoulder and said, "Ride!"

Dekka shook herself, pushed the dying woman aside, and hit the throttle.

CHAPTER 15
The Bacterium Screams

AS SHADE WAS ripping through the Ranch, Malik lay on his back, looking up at trees. They formed intricate patterns, leaves lower, pine needles higher, black lace doilies against a spread of faint stars, just appearing.

Cruz sat nearby, looking down at the Ranch and feeling a mix of emotions, none of them pleasant. She beat herself up for not being with Shade down there, though she knew she would only slow her friend down. She felt desperately sad for Malik. Malik, eternally morphed. Malik who had not just lost his home and family to Shade's obsession, but now had lost his body, and soon, perhaps, his mind.

And what can you do about it? Cruz asked herself.

Nothing. Nothing but be carried along, one of life's little bits of flotsam and jetsam in the river Shade.

She felt bad sparing even a little energy for self-pity, but it was there just the same. Before she had met Shade, Cruz had just barely begun on her own path to understanding herself.

She had spent most of her lifetime in futile efforts to be what she was not, to please a father who would never love who she really was, and a mother who was cowed and defeated and quiet, like someone out of *The Handmaid's Tale*.

She had been trying to figure out how she could start on hormone treatments. She'd been walking it all through in stages in her mind—do the hormones and see how that felt. Maybe breast surgery and see how that felt. Then, maybe the serious surgery, the one that would make her fully *physically* female. She'd spent ridiculous amounts of time just trying to learn the legalities and had come up against the fact that she was basically stymied until she was eighteen. And then, if she could maybe get a job and maybe get health insurance and maybe this and maybe that . . .

All of that inner turmoil, her fragile hopes, her too-realistic fears, had been papered over by Shade's wild ride, and by Cruz's own decision to take the path of the rock, to become Rockborn. And the rock had messed with her. Nowhere near as bad as what Malik was dealing with, but the rock had messed with her, just the same.

How clever you are, little alien rock. How cleverly cruel.

Now, thanks to the rock, she could appear however she wished. She could be male or female. She could be Dwayne Johnson or Meryl Streep. Big, small, blond, brunette, white, black, Asian . . . and all of it false.

False.

It was margarine rather than butter, carob rather than chocolate. Near beer. An oregano joint. It was looking at photos of the aurora borealis when what you wanted was to lie beneath a real sky glowing with color.

When was she ever going to get back to those earlier dreams? When was she ever going to get a chance to actually experience the physical changes she'd half longed for, half feared?

When do I get to be me?

But self-pity, even justified self-pity, shrank when she looked at Malik. She knew—better than Malik himself—the damage that had been done to him. She'd been in the hospital room when his bandages were changed.

Malik and Cruz, both with their lives irretrievably destroyed.

By Shade.

Yes, by Shade. By her obsession. By her ambition.

And by my choice to follow her.

Malik's eyes closed, shutting out the trees and the sky. He barely felt his own body; his skin was not true skin, his nerves not real nerves. The only true and real thing about him was his mind. It was *his* mind, still, but not his to control entirely. He was still himself, but he was no longer alone in his own skull.

Something Cruz had said came back to him. Something about being able to learn about the Dark Watchers. Like a bacterium on a microscope slide wanting to look up through that microscope and see the eye staring down at him.

He tried to shut out distant screams and gunfire. Tried to

ignore the massacre he knew was taking place just down the hill. He breathed deep and smelled pine needles and heard the rustle of the breeze. But the dark space inside his head spread out, widened and deepened, as if what was inside him was infinitely greater than what was outside. Darkness and more darkness, but somehow that darkness had a structure. A shape. It was real. In that darkness he sensed their gaze. They watched him. They were . . . intrigued.

Why do you watch me?

No answer, of course. No indication that his unspoken question had been heard.

Who are you?

The only response was a chill as an invisible-but-felt tendril curled around him, reached inside him, seemed almost to be leafing through his memories like someone reading a book.

What do you want?

Was that laughter? Were they laughing at him?

He knew he was weak and they were powerful. He knew that they could see what he could not. He thumbed through his own memories—or was it them making him do it? He searched for answers, explanations, theories, Malik being Malik, and he was pleased that even now under the unceasing scrutiny of the Dark Watchers, he still sought answers.

He remembered once reading the Victorian-era story called *Flatland* for physics class. It was a fascinating tale of life lived entirely in two dimensions, with creatures who had left and right, forward and back, but no up and down.

They were as trapped as Mr. and Ms. Pac-Man. But a person in the three-dimensional world could see into those two-dimensional creatures. The 3-D man could, from the 2-D perspective, pass through impassable walls, literally see the insides and outside of a 2-D creature. To the 2-D people, the 3-D man was not visible unless he touched their flat plane, and then all they could see was a 2-D cross-section, appearing as a circle. To the residents of Flatland, the 3-D universe was impossible to imagine, let alone see.

Just as a 3-D man could not grasp, let alone see a 4-D reality.

Yet.

That word hung in Malik's brain. It felt as if it had come *to* him, not from *him*.

Yet?

The sounds of conflict intruded on his thoughts: the sirens that had gone off right after he had hit the Ranch with a blast of pain were still sounding, gunfire, an explosion, unmuffled military engines firing up. Orders were being shouted.

Screams and pleas for mercy.

He knew Shade would be back soon, and that they would once again flee the scene, run away to their next illegal, temporary abode.

Shade. He knew she was trying desperately to make things right. And he knew that she could not.

Sad, he thought, that it had taken his own destruction to teach Shade humility. Humility that might have allowed them in an earlier time to remain together, to be still what they had once been: lovers. The arrogance in Shade, the obsession with the FAYZ, and the seething, impossible-to-satisfy thirst for revenge against the creature that had killed her mother were not gone, but now they were tempered by reality. By the brutal reality of unintended consequences.

Unintended Consequences, Exhibit A: Malik Tenerife.

But his thoughts scattered under a sudden surge of attention from the Dark Watchers. They seemed more intrusive than ever, and his anger rose. Whoever, whatever they were, they had no right! They had no right to torture him this way!

He almost didn't do it. He almost convinced himself it was futile and juvenile and pointless.

He almost did not lash out at the Dark Watchers.

But Malik was controlling himself on multiple fronts all at once, and he was all out of patience.

No answers? Nothing to say to me, Dark ones? Well, I have something to say to you.

He summoned all his will, all his new and unwanted power, and fixed clearly in his mind not the picture of the Dark Watchers, for they had no shape or form, but the *idea* of them, the concept of the Dark Watchers, the emotion they caused in him. He pictured a data wire reaching down from some extra-dimensional space, a segment of USB cable plugged into his brain, down which came the eyeless spies, the invisible burglars of the mind.

Wires, he reasoned, carry current in both directions. They wanted the Malik experience? Fine.

Enjoy, assholes.

Malik fired a massive wave of pain, targeted on *them*. He screamed and raged and roared silently at them, directing every ounce of his agony, his sadness, his despair and rage at them, them, *them*.

"Oh!" Malik cried out. His eyes flew open.

"What?" Cruz asked, knee-walking to him.

"They . . . Oh, my God, Cruz!"

"What? What?"

"I hit them! I sent them pain. And Cruz? I think . . . I think maybe they . . . felt it. It was like, like . . ." He sat up, eyes bright, a weird half smile on his lips. "You know what it's like when you drop a glass in the lunchroom, and suddenly there's total silence because absolutely every eye is staring at you?"

"Okay."

"It was like that, Cruz. They heard me. They felt me. The little bacterium under their microscope just gave them the finger."

Shade was ready to go. She had done what she came to do. She would upload her videos, show the world what was happening at the Ranch.

But her eye was drawn to that imposing rectangular office above her, perched on the side of the cavern.

No one could stop her. The Ranch was finished. She could see that. The guards might eventually organize some kind of resistance, but how many of them would survive that long?

She spotted a metal staircase and was up it in a blink. There was a heavy steel door to the office. Locked. And not likely to be opened any time soon. She leaped to the roof, then leaned over the edge to see the single long window. It was bulletproof glass, able to withstand a high-powered rifle shot.

But bulletproof was one thing, and Shade-proof was a very different matter.

She pried a large rock from the cavern wall, leaned again over the edge of the roof, and smashed the rock into the glass.

Nothing much.

Then, using the strength her morph gave her, as well as the speed, she smashed the rock into the glass a hundred times in a few seconds. The glass starred and cracked. A small hole, about big enough to push a pencil through.

Given time, she could smash her way in. But was it worth it?

She had to use one hand to shield the reflective light and peer inside. A woman in army uniform was just rising shakily to her feet. That uniform was askew, and her hair was plastered down with sweat. Her face was ashen.

Shade tapped the rock again, using the *dum-pa-da-dum-dum . . . dum-dum* rhythm.

The woman turned slowly, cringing. Her eyes widened as she saw Shade's upside-down face.

"Hey!" Shade said.

The woman's face twisted in rage and she shouted something that Shade did not hear but could guess at. The woman was white with fury, spittle hanging at the corners of her mouth.

Shade said, "Can't hear you, but I have a message."

At which point Shade raised a middle finger and held it for long enough that it would be easily visible—and she hoped very memorable—to the officer.

Then she was away, running across the cavern floor, a battlefield, dodging man and machine and things in between. She zoomed up the stairs, through the corridors, and emerged with a sigh of relief into the open air.

She found Cruz and Malik where she had left them, blurred to a stop, and de-morphed.

"What happened?" Cruz asked eagerly. "Are you okay?"

Shade said, "Look," and pointed down the hill to the Ranch. A woman in a white coat ran from a monster made of needles. She tripped and the creature rolled over her, stabbing her a hundred times, leaving human Salisbury steak behind.

All around the compound, men and women fled before avenging beasts and racing cyborgs beneath the pitiless lights. Smoke rose from one building. An explosion rocked another, blowing out windows. Machine guns chattered. And all the while the news helicopters swept over and back, sending pictures to the world.

"Let's get out of here," Shade said.

"They're tearing that man apart!" Cruz cried, pointing.

Shade grabbed her shoulder. "What do you think that man did to deserve it?"

But Cruz could not stop looking. It was a scene out of a horror movie, monsters versus humans, a massacre without heroism or nobility. Slaughter. Bloody, remorseless slaughter.

"My God, Shade," Cruz said in a whisper. "This is our future, isn't it? This is the world now!"

Malik, eyes barely open, said one word. "War."

CHAPTER 16
Everything's Coming Up Dekka

FRANCIS SPECTER KNEW nothing of what was happening in Las Vegas when she saw the road sign for Las Vegas, grinned beneath her dark plexiglass visor, and turned her motorcycle north toward the distantly glowing city. She figured the outskirts of Vegas would be a good place to find a motel and spend the night.

It occurred to her that she could easily use her power to enter any room she liked, but the truth was that a simple motel would be more luxury and normalcy than she had known since early childhood. Anyway, she was squeamish about continuing to commit crimes. She had escaped the gang—permanently, judging by the size of the explosion from the Predator's missile—and she fervently hoped that she had also escaped that whole criminal life of drugs and drunken fights and stealing. She was on a quest for normalcy. She would have gladly traded her Rockborn power for a life as an anonymous high school kid with nothing to worry about but grades.

She had been a long time in the wilderness.

But now as she drew near the city she saw a seemingly endless flow of cars and trucks heading out of town. It was night, and yet it almost looked as if people were fleeing. In fact the traffic soon spilled out of its own lanes and invaded extra lanes so that anyone going toward the city had to thread their way through oncoming cars.

She pulled off the highway to get a bottle of water at a convenience store, but as she was taking off her helmet she saw something even stranger than the mad rush of cars leaving Las Vegas. She saw two motorcycles, driven by what were either two people in amazingly convincing cosplay costumes . . . or were mutants in morph.

She stuck her helmet back on and went in pursuit.

General DiMarco strode stiff-legged through the wreckage of the Ranch. A drained and traumatized Atwell whispered in her ear from time to time, giving an update on what was coming in from the damage assessment team, as well as what was happening in the media, and he reminded her of calls pending from the Pentagon, the Department of Homeland Security, and more.

Two things were clear to DiMarco. One: The Ranch might be finished, done for, unless something happened to move public opinion sharply against the mutants.

And two: Something like that had just happened in Las Vegas.

"Coverage is forty percent Vegas, sixty percent the Ranch,"

Atwell said as DiMarco nodded curt acknowledgment at a
bleeding staff doctor being loaded onto a gurney, his body a
mass of blood-soaked gauze.

"The full Shade Darby tape is up on YouTube, and the hit
counter is going crazy."

"Show me," DiMarco said.

The two of them stood in the blood of slaughtered scientists and techs and security men and watched Atwell's phone.

DiMarco's eye twitched. Her mouth was a snarl. She
watched the brief videos of the cells. Followed by Shade's
opening of same. The speech by Tolliver. And Shade Darby's
final, arrogant speech to the camera.

*"I'm Shade Darby. This horror show is run by the US gov-
ernment, by a group called Homeland Security Task Force 66.
Do you see what they're doing here? Do you see what they're
doing supposedly in your name? So who are the bad guys? Us
or them?"*

DiMarco and Atwell stood near the spot where Shade had
addressed the recently liberated. They were at the center of
the great cavern, and now DiMarco turned slowly, taking
in the fires, the shattered glass, the twisted steel, the smoke,
the bodies. The parts of bodies. It had been a surprisingly
deliberate, complete, and disciplined act of annihilation, led
by that goddamned marine who had broken into the armory
and wreaked the kind of purposeful havoc that only a professional soldier could create. (The bulldozer Shade had leaped
atop had been later blown apart by one of Tolliver's missiles.)
DiMarco had barely a handful of uninjured staff still present.

"We are now at twenty-two confirmed dead, ninety-six seriously wounded, another eighty with less serious wounds."

"That's half of them," DiMarco snapped. "Where are the rest?"

Atwell hesitated a revealing few seconds before saying, "Many are chasing the mutants down in the woods."

DiMarco snorted. "Sure they are. Some. But most are running for their lives from our creatures!"

Suddenly, Atwell noted bitterly, it wasn't *my* creatures but *ours.*

No, you vile woman, they are yours, and the results are yours as well. Though, he knew, his career was now bound to hers. His time in the US Army—which he had expected to serve for thirty years—was just about over.

I'll go work for Janet's father rehabbing old homes in Kansas City. I'll never speak of this to anyone. Ever.

"Well, Mike, we are screwed good and proper," the general said. She'd been able to change into a clean uniform. Atwell had not had a spare uniform, and the urine stain on the front of his trousers had only just begun to dry.

"We can rebuild . . . start at least some of the programs again . . ." Atwell shrugged.

DiMarco was silent, looking around, feeling her career sliding off the edge of a cliff. She had to act quickly and she knew it. The secretary of defense was not calling to congratulate her.

"How far is it from Fort Irwin to Vegas?" she asked.

He Google-Mapped it. "Three hours, give or take."

"Okay. Put me through to the commander at Irwin. I'm not relieved of duty yet. And I still have the authority."

"May I ask what you want from Fort Irwin?"

DiMarco laughed, a short, bitter sound. "What do I want from the national tank training facility? What do you think I want? Tanks. That's what I want: tanks! And one other thing."

"Yes, ma'am?"

"Darby was briefed. Had to have been. She's in contact with Dekka Talent. That's the heart of this: Tom Peaks's misguided experiment: Dekka. Shade is smart, but Dekka is a leader. She just moved to the number-one spot. I don't care what it takes, what we have to do, but that . . . young woman . . . needs to die."

It had been a very close call for Dillon and Saffron. The ease with which Dekka and Armo had taken him down had left him fearful. He had power, amazing power, but it did not seem to work on either of them. Which meant it was likely that his power could not affect any mutant in morph.

Which was very, very bad news.

"I shouldn't have killed those cops," Dillon muttered. "I thought it would kind of get a laugh. . . . Now they're just all going to be focused on getting rid of me."

"They tried to arrest you," Saffron said sullenly.

It had been her suggestion that Dillon send a strong warning of his power. That warning had turned into an order to two policemen to leap from the tower to their deaths. So much for his briefly held determination not to kill. Hey, if people wanted to kill him, what was he supposed to do?

Saffron was pale and trembling with either fear or fury or some combination of both, but she did not argue as Dillon announced that it was time to get the hell away from the Venetian. It was not good to be a target and sit in a known location, waiting. The two Rockborn who'd come after him could come back.

They pushed through rampaging tourists and overwhelmed cops who did not yet know what either of them looked like. The Strip was a scene of panic, cars driving up onto sidewalks to get around stalled cars or bodies lying in the street. From time to time the angry, concussive noise of gunfire erupted. A billboard truck advertising a strip-tease show swerved madly and toppled onto its side in a spray of sparks.

"We have to keep moving," Dillon said, grabbing Saffron's hand and pulling her along.

"Earmuffs," Saffron sobbed. "That's all it takes to stop you!"

Earmuffs and the Rockborn, Dillon corrected silently. He flashed on the old Verizon ads: *Can you hear me now?* Probably something there . . . should make a note in his comedy notebook . . . later.

"We have to get out of here, find some new place, some place to hide, to . . . to rest . . . to think," Dillon said.

"Think?" Saffron snarled. "Every minute that goes by they'll be more ready. My God, I can't believe all of this is happening!"

An army, that was what Dillon needed, an army. Not the

ancient relics who pulled the slot-machine crank handles at the Venetian, but younger, fitter, more capable people.

"You were right about one thing you said," Dillon said to Saffron as they pushed through the killing crowds using Dillon's voice to part the waters. "I need an army. An army of voice slaves. But, who? Where am I going to find them?"

Saffron was completely unprepared for the level of insanity in the street. She cowered and flinched and said, "That crazy man back there almost stabbed me!"

Then Dillon spotted something. A woman wearing a San Jose State jersey. He grabbed her as she tried to bite his arm. "Stop attacking me. Answer me: Why are you here?"

The woman blinked. "I . . . I came because we had tickets for the game, but they turned out to be forgeries. I couldn't get in."

"This game, it was *tonight*?"

The woman—who seconds before had been desperately searching for someone to kill—shrugged. "It's still going on, I guess."

Dillon and Saffron exchanged glances. A man filled with a Dillon-enraged need to kill, kill, kill, ran his Jeep into a gaggle of frantic pedestrians, throwing broken bodies left and right before stalling out atop a pile of squirming, screaming victims.

"Get out," Dillon ordered the man, who was weeping and apologizing and whimpering that he couldn't help himself, couldn't stop. Dillon jumped in behind the wheel, leaned over to open the passenger door for Saffron, and saw her dragged back by a large bald man.

"Hey, you, baldy! Leave her alone!"

The bald man instantly released Saffron, and she grabbed the headrest and tried to pull herself into the car when a man raced up, swung a meat cleaver, and cut into the back of her neck and through her spinal cord. Dillon saw her eyes go from alert to alarmed to wounded, like she couldn't believe the unfairness . . . before going blank. She was dead before she slumped to the ground.

Dillon whinnied in terror, pushed the gear shift into reverse and jammed on the gas, running over more people, swerved wildly, and then fishtailed out onto the Strip before being blocked by traffic.

"Get out of my way!" he yelled out of the window, but other drivers had their windows rolled up for safety and heard nothing. So he rammed the space between the nearest two cars, and looking back in his rearview mirror saw Saffron's body, her head at an impossible angle.

The mass lunacy Dillon had created now enveloped Dillon's stolen car so that he advanced at a snail's pace. He sat fuming, weeping, begging the audience of watchers in his head to show him a way.

But that wasn't how it was going to work, Dillon realized. If the Dark Watchers had any affection for him, they'd have warned him about that Dekka creature and her furry white friend.

No, they only watched, he realized bitterly. They really were just an audience, but like a cynical New York audience, they were just as pleased to see him flop.

"I'm on my own," Dillon said to the steering wheel. "Everyone is against me."

It was, he told himself, unfair.

"Jesus!" Cruz erupted as Shade drove her and Malik away down dimly lit, serpentine mountain roads in a purloined BMW previously owned by a Ranch geneticist who was currently dragging his bleeding body through the woods. Cruz was staring at her phone.

"What?" Shade snapped.

"Something . . . It's nuts, I mean nuts. Crazy. Las Vegas! There's some kind of full-on battle taking place, thousands of people under some kind of mind control. Dead people everywhere!"

"Mind control?" Shade asked. "Are you kidding me now?"

Cruz leaned forward, holding her phone for Shade to see. Shade was no longer in morph, so driving at normal human speed since they had spotted no pursuit, which she slowed to a crawl as she watched the video.

"Scroll back," Malik instructed, speaking for the first time in a while. "There! Stop!"

The freeze-frame was blurry, but it showed what looked like some terrifying combination of feline and human, pushing through a crowd. It was only the briefest glimpse.

"Dekka," Malik said. "She's there. In Vegas."

"And now," Shade said, "we have a destination."

ASO-6

SUBMARINES ARE HOT dogs inside of buns. The bun is the outer hull, shaped to move quietly and efficiently through the water. The hot dog is the pressure hull, a cylinder built to withstand crushing pressures.

It was the bun that the chimera shredded as it dragged the *Nebraska* along the ocean floor.

Inside the sub the crew were like beans in a baby's rattle. Mostly the chimera just lugged it across sand and the occasional rock. Sometimes the sub was right side up. Other times it was on its side, or upside down. The seemingly random starts and stops threw crew against steel bulkheads, smashing muscle and bone.

Other times the chimera raised the sub to near vertical, and crewmen rolled and slid and fell through the air to crash against pressure hatches. Each section of the hull was sealed off, lest a hull breach in one area drown them all.

During one particularly hellish episode, the chimera had

slammed the sub again and again until there was no member of the crew without lacerations, bruises, broken bones, or a split scalp. The ship's doctor had stopped trying to treat anyone when his arm suffered a compound fracture.

That episode had at least led to the remaining coherent crew coming to a tentative conclusion: whatever impossibly big and powerful creature was out there, they may have become stuck to it somehow. Maybe the prop had been wedged between . . . well, between whatever limbs the chimera had. Because it certainly seemed like the beast had tried to shake them loose.

Only emergency lights were on in the *Nebraska*. All communications, all sensors were dead. They had no way to see outside—there are no portholes in a pressure hull. No one could do anything but lash themselves into a bunk and grit their teeth.

And try very hard not to think about the fact that among the things being brutally shaken were enough nuclear warheads to kill billions.

CHAPTER 17
The Cheerios of War

"GET OUT OF my way," Dillon snapped. "Step aside!"

It was called the Shark Tank, though the official name was the Thomas & Mack Center. It held 17,923 people in its basketball configuration, but as Dillon arrived at the venue on foot, shaking visibly from the aftereffects of stress, especially the sudden, shocking death of Saffron, which kept playing over and over in his head, he saw people streaming out, despite the fact that the game was not over, despite the fact that the UNLV Runnin' Rebels were playing their nemesis, San Jose State.

Obviously the news had reached the fans via their cell phones. But the slowness with which the crowd moved showed the arena still held thousands.

"Sir, you can't—" a guard began.

"Shut up and get out of my way!"

He was pushing against the crowd and would never have made progress but for his ability to order people out of his way and have them comply immediately. He was a salmon swimming upstream, but a salmon who could command the waters to part.

He grabbed the next security guard he saw and said, "Take me to the control booth. Now!"

The guard muttered something about authorizations, but he obeyed without hesitation and led Dillon through an unmarked door, down a series of long corridors, to a set of stairs that opened onto another corridor. And then through a door into a wide booth festooned with glowing monitors and a half dozen men and women all fixated on those monitors.

Beyond the monitors and desks was a long open window looking out over the arena.

"Listen up! I want a mike that everyone in the place can hear!"

Three people practically fought for the chance to bring him a handheld microphone.

"This is on?"

It was.

"Everyone stop moving and listen to me." His voice boomed and echoed pleasingly. He could see that everyone in the arena stopped.

"Who knows how to estimate a crowd?" Dillon demanded of the people in the booth. "How many people are still inside?"

There came a babble of voices throwing out different numbers, but the consensus seemed to be that at least seven thousand people were still present and listening to the sound of his voice.

Dillon walked to the edge of the booth, right up to the window. "Put a spotlight on me." Into the microphone he said, "You are all my slaves. You are my slave army. You will obey me. Say it. Say you will obey me!"

Thousands of puzzled faces looked up at him. And with one voice, they thundered, "We will obey you!"

"I am the Charmer! I have come to lead you. Rejoice!"

Where the hell he got the word "rejoice," he would never know. It was some distant holdover from Sunday school. But it pleased him, seemed to give him some new reserve of strength. A sea of faces gazed up at him, most showing UNLV red and black, others in San Jose's blue and gold, all began yelling happily, as though their team had won.

Rejoicing! Hah!

Incredible. An incredible thing to see, Dillon thought. *Too bad Saffron* . . . He shrugged off that sad thought—he'd liked her, he'd have liked to sleep with her, but she was replaceable. In fact, he could see several young ladies down below who could replace her.

"So, let me ask you," Dillon said, his voice echoing off the polished wood floor and bouncing around the high steel rafters, "what's the difference between a dollar and the San Jose Spartans?" Pause. "You can still get four quarters out of a dollar."

Roughly a half dozen laughs. Well, it was an old joke, just slightly reworked. And this was a tough audience, scared and confused as they were.

"Anyway, you are my slaves, and I have a job for you. I

want you to leave this place and—"

The mob started moving.

"Not yet! Damn! Let me finish my sentence." He sighed. This whole voice-of-God thing had a steep learning curve. "I want you to leave here, drive or walk to the Strip, and attack anyone you see in uniform. Kill them all. Police, security, anyone in a uniform."

And with that he dismissed the rest of his "funny but not deadly" vow. Even he couldn't quite see the humor in the situation, but what was he supposed to do? Just wait to be exterminated?

Thousands of puzzled, troubled faces, all waited.

"Now!" Dillon cried. "Now, my slave army! Go! Kill! Kill!"

Then, reminded of something interesting, he added, "All except the cheerleaders. You stay where you are and I'll be right down."

The cheerleaders were seven young women and two young men, college kids dressed in black spandex shorts and tight red tops with the letters UNLV across the front.

Reaching the floor, Dillon winked at them. "You nine are my private personal guard. The Charmers Cheerers." No, that wasn't quite right. "The Charmers cheer squad. Never mind. Security!" Three nearby campus cops came at a run. "Give these people your gun belts. Don't worry, we'll find enough for everyone!"

"You nine follow me wherever I go, and do whatever I say. Now, let's get out of here, because a serious shitstorm is about to start."

The murderous crowd had almost emptied out of the arena, and it occurred to Dillon that he didn't need to follow them. They had their orders, and if past history was any judge, they'd keep attacking and killing anyone in uniform until Las Vegas was cleansed of cops and casino security.

"I am the king of Las Vegas," he said, and laughed. *Pity about Saffron, but look at me now,* he thought. *My own squad of hot college girls.* Well, and the two guys. He could get rid of them, but he didn't want to look sexist. Anyway, maybe he'd get them all to do a special cheer for him and do the whole pyramid thing, and he assumed the guys were helpful for that.

The Charmer's Chatterers?
The Charmer's Chaplains?
The Charmer's Cheerios?

That might be okay. Yeah. He'd try it out with audiences, see if it worked.

With thousands of helpless slaves and with nine cheerleaders, Dillon was starting to recover his confidence. But he had been shaken by Saffron's murder, and more shaken by Dekka and Armo. But, he told himself, he would never again be caught off guard. The two Rockborn meddlers would have their hands full coping with his thousands of ready killers.

"Someone show me the way to the best VIP box," Dillon said, clapping his hands. "We are going to party like it's the end of the world!"

Malik closed his eyes in the back seat, blocking out the wind, blocking out the fear, pushing everything away.

Like meditating.

Like meditating while teetering on the edge of disaster.

Malik had never been proud of his intellect. He considered it a gift from his DNA, like being dealt a pair of aces in a hand of poker. He hadn't done anything to deserve it, it was not the result of effort, so he wasn't proud. But he was grateful.

What about you, Dark ones? Do you feel pride?

Till now Malik had used his brain primarily to get good grades. High school had required very little effort, and even his all-too-brief start at Northwestern had not felt very challenging.

But now . . . well, now he needed every last IQ point and wished he had more. He had Cruz's phone and from time to time would scan articles on topics that were at the limits of his mental capacity. Physics. Quantum physics. Multiple universe theories, of which there were several versions. The fanciful theory that our universe is a simulation. One giant game of the Sims.

Easy for you, isn't it? You're the top of the food chain and I'm what? An insect trying to understand you?

Many had speculated on multiple universes and sims, especially since the Perdido Beach Anomaly, the FAYZ. But physicists and sci-fi authors and the like had long played with the notion that our universe might not be the only one; that the big bang might have thrown off many, many universes.

Some thought universes were like foam, like a handful of soap bubbles scooped from a bath, each bubble pressed against and deformed by others. Others preferred flat universes, piled up like a ream of paper.

Do you know the answers? Or are you still figuring it out?

When speculation turned to simulations, the questions centered on whether the sim was like a wind-up toy, going along all on its own. Others imagined the sim universe as a game, something being actively *played*. It was very like a belief in God—not the benign God of Judaism, Christianity, and Islam, but something closer to the ancient Greek gods: capricious, emotional, needy.

All these ideas had long been dismissed for one simple reason: there was no proof. None. Until . . .

Until the FAYZ had proven that the laws of physics, the supposedly unbreakable laws of the one and only universe, had been broken. Broken, shattered, and stomped upon.

That shouldn't have been possible.

And yet . . . Am I right, you invisible intruders? Would you tell me?

For four years many physicists had hidden their heads in the sand, stuck their fingers in their ears, and yelled *la la la la,* so as to shut out the seemingly impossible. Others had rushed to concoct theories that treated the PBA as a strange, localized warping of space-time. But now that, too, was a dead end, because now the whole world was the FAYZ.

Still, the vast majority of people, even many scientists, could not come to grips with the new reality. Fear was a big part of it. But also the limits of the human brain, a brain that could not visualize a universe that had forward, back, left, right, up and down, past and future, but no *elsewhere*.

Is that built into the sim? Did you design us to be blind to other dimensions?

Malik liked questioning *them.* They never answered, of course, and they never let him alone, but somehow demanding answers of them gave him a sense of control. An illusion, perhaps. A bit of self-deception, perhaps.

Yet, when he questioned, he felt that they heard him. Just as he was convinced his blast of pain had reached them in some form.

I can't see or hear you. I can't even imagine you. But I can demand answers from you.

"Little solace," Malik muttered.

Cruz looked at him. "What's little solace?"

Malik sighed. "Nothing," he said. Then silently added, *yet.*

CHAPTER 18
Tanks for the Memories

"WHAT THE HOLY hell . . . ?" Brigadier General Maxwell Fullalove put the landline phone back in its cradle. He had a full colonel and two majors with him in his HQ, along with various enlisted folks and junior officers. None could quite grasp the nature of their orders.

"We're driving an ABCT into Vegas?" the colonel sputtered. An ABCT, armored brigade combat team, consisted of roughly 4,700 soldiers, ninety Bradley infantry fighting vehicles equipped to carry six armed soldiers, a 25-millimeter chain gun, a 7.62-millimeter machine gun, and two TOW anti-tank missiles. There were also over a hundred armored personnel carriers. But the real punch came from ninety M1A2 Abrams tanks, which carried machine guns, missiles, and either 105- or 120-millimeter cannons. "Bradleys and Abrams on the Vegas Strip? If nothing else, it'll play hell with the road surface . . ."

Fort Irwin, California, was in a desperately isolated area

of desert and more desert. It was the National Training Center, specializing in preparing combat brigades for the real thing. At present it had two serious forces, its own OPFOR—opposition force, which acted as "the enemy" in training operations—and the visiting Iron Brigade, whose insignia was a blue-red-and-gold pyramid badge with the slogan *Strike Hard!*

The emergency order from a General DiMarco—backed up, to the surprise of Fullalove, by the Pentagon and the national security advisor—had thrown the base into a controlled panic of activity.

"Get to work," Fullalove snapped. He was no more happy about this lunatic order than his officers were, but this was the army, not debate club. "I want hourly status updates."

Fullalove figured he could field most of a scratch brigade, taking from his own OPFOR as well as the visiting Iron Brigade.

The big problem as always was logistics, starting with the loading of live ordnance, thousands of tank rounds, hundreds of thousands of rounds of machine-gun and chain-gun ammunition, not to mention the issue of fuel. Then they would need to refuel en route, which meant sending fuel trucks, of which he had far too few. Moving at speed right down the interstates with no regard for traffic or road surfaces, and moving at tank speed—he had neither time nor enough flatbeds to truck the tanks to the scene—they could be in Vegas five hours after they set out. But even with top-priority, all-hands-on-deck measures it would be ten hours before they could start. Ten hours to prepare, five hours to drive, and it was now after three a.m. That would have them arriving in the city at sunset the next day.

And then?

His orders went no further than, "Engage enemy mutants and restore order." Nuts! A tank brigade in the middle of an American city? He had seen the news; he knew Las Vegas was experiencing an emergency, but the solution to civil unrest was not supposed to be tanks, for God's sake. These were not Special Forces; they weren't even infantry, though they would have some foot soldiers with them. These soldiers were not trained for civil unrest. One modern ABCT could have taken on and defeated the entire German army of World War II. The destructive power was shocking. And he'd been assured he would have support from the air as well, though what in hell the Pentagon thought they could accomplish with F-18s over a major city was terrifying to contemplate.

He considered taking personal command of the operation, but this whole thing had career suicide written all over it. Congressional investigations, maybe even a court-martial. He had two experienced colonels he could task with the job, the OPFOR commander, Andrea Mataconis, who was a protégé, and the visiting unit's colonel, Frank "Frankenstein" Poole. The nickname came from the colonel's unusually high forehead, and from junior officers who whispered that he was a monster if you pissed him off.

Fullalove summoned Poole, who arrived in crisp uniform and polished boots, his oblong face alight with excitement.

"Poole, I'm giving you this scratch brigade. You will take command and advance at speed to Las Vegas to deal with the . . . the situation."

Poole was a gung-ho, hard-charging officer, but he wasn't crazy, so he said, "General, I assume there will be *written* orders?"

Fullalove nodded, already imagining himself before a Senate investigating committee of smug, stupid senators. "I'm having them cut right now. But Frank, you're going to have a lot of autonomy on this. We don't exactly have battle plans for this sort of thing. You'll develop rules of engagement as we get new info."

"Understood, sir."

Frankenstein Poole received his written orders—vague and clearly rushed—and practically levitated down the steps to his waiting staff car. He'd served fifteen years and had yet to fire a shot in anger. Now he was to ride into Vegas like George freaking Patton, with every camera on earth watching.

"Hell, yeah," he said, and laughed.

The Las Vegas Metropolitan Police Department had 2,600 sworn police officers. The casinos hired many times that number of security officers of varying levels of professionalism. All wore uniforms.

The first police officer to die at the hands of Dillon's slave army was officer Carla Sanchez, exhausted from the already bloody day. She and her partner had pulled into a 7-Eleven to get coffee when a half dozen civilians charged them and beat her to the ground before she could draw her weapon. Her partner fired off a full clip of 9-millimeter, killing two and wounding one, before the rushing mob swept over him as well, oblivious to the danger.

Officer Sanchez's last conscious thought was that it was strange, very, very strange, to die from tire-iron blows delivered by a middle-aged woman who kept apologizing.

Nevada State Troopers rushed to the city. Cops and EMTs and firefighters from towns and cities as far away as Bakersfield were on the way, but blocked by panicky people who jammed all lanes of traffic on both sides of every road. Vegas was doing its best to empty out, but with a population of six hundred thousand, not to mention at least a hundred thousand tourists, it would take hours. Days.

Meanwhile police and security were being rushed by mobs that could not be stopped by anything short of death. But the mobs also attacked and murdered shift workers at McDonald's and In-N-Out, as well as doormen and valets, sanitation workers, and even cocktail waitresses and blackjack dealers.

It took four hours before the police chief realized that the mobs were focusing on *uniforms*. Any uniform. Mostly cops and guards, but when they couldn't find anyone in those categories, the mob would pour into casinos and bite, beat, strangle, stab, and shoot anyone wearing what could be described as a uniform.

The PC ordered all police to remove their uniforms immediately, with the result that now there were cops in underwear who were safe from attack, but too disorganized to even begin to formulate a strategy. The PC did his best to alert the casino security teams, but communications were overwhelmed, and it wasn't as if anyone was pausing to check their texts or emails.

By three a.m., Las Vegas was in lockdown. The casino doors were locked and barricaded with piles of slot machines. Guests still in the casinos were not allowed out, and no one but no one was getting in.

At least at first.

In the early morning hours the mob—now minus close to five hundred dead who lay scattered all up and down the Strip alongside hundreds of their victims—began to commandeer the early morning garbage trucks and used them to ram the doors of Treasure Island casino. The Venetian was already in flames; Treasure Island soon followed.

Tom Peaks had finished Drake's half bottle of vodka. He stepped outside of Drake's cave. Peaks did not have a weak stomach, but that place was the heart of evil, and he was sickened by it.

He fired up his phone. It was a risk, he knew it was a risk. He had swapped out SIM cards, but still, the US government had serious skills when it came to electronic surveillance.

But he needed contact with reality.

He tried to check his wife's Facebook page. She'd shut it down. That hurt. It was not hard to guess at the social media abuse his poor wife had endured. God only knew what his kids were going through. He'd always taught them to be honest and straightforward, to stand up to bullies, but what was the honest and straightforward way to counter, *Your dad is a monster!* Or, *Your dad killed people!*

He considered taking his own life. Drake surely had a gun lying around. A knife or a razor would do the trick as well. Or he could just climb up this very hill, this pile of rocks, take a last look at the stars, and jump.

Then he came across Shade Darby's uploaded video of the annihilation of the Ranch.

That brought some grim satisfaction. DiMarco must be crapping herself. But then, too, many people Peaks had worked with, had hired, had nurtured as employees, were dead. The Ranch—his creation—would never recover.

The US government was very far from finished, but they would not have their mutant army. They would not have cyborgs. They would have to prevail by more conventional means.

He was about to shut off his phone when by habit he clicked on the *Washington Post* and saw the screaming headlines about Las Vegas. And there, in blurry video, his nemesis, his failure: Dekka Talent.

It did not take a man of Peaks's intellect and education to see that Vegas would be the center of an epic battle. Government versus mutant versus mutant.

With DiMarco humiliated, maybe the Pentagon would see that they'd made a mistake casting Peaks aside. Maybe they'd start to see that he was the only one who could lead the fight against the Dekkas and Shades and Knightmares of the world.

Especially if he turned the tide of battle in favor of the government. But not, he realized, if he was still involved with Drake. People who crucified people in caves were never going to be popular, whereas Dragon . . . well, who didn't kinda sorta like dragons? And with time he could spin the massacre at the Port of LA as just a case of him trying to stop what's-his-name, Vincent Vu.

He had a stolen SUV. And he had . . . he checked his wallet . . . twenty-seven dollars, which should buy him enough gas to make the three-and-a-half-hour drive.

Dillon had spent a delirious night in the huge, posh VIP box looking out over the now-empty stadium. He still had his Cheerios, all fully armed, though not at all good at actually shooting, as he had discovered when he had them target shoot in the arena, aiming at basketballs he rolled for them. He'd enjoyed himself to the point of exhaustion, with CNN on in the background, the pictures shifting from dramatic overhead chopper shots to wild-eyed street reporters to surveillance cameras inside casinos to gray-faced, worried "experts."

Experts, he'd sneered. *There was no such thing as an expert in what was happening.*

His only regret was that the news cut away to what was apparently video uploaded to YouTube by the Shade Darby person.

He watched that over and over again, fascinated by the horrors that had been created there. Fascinated as well by the slaughter. And strangely a bit jealous of Shade. Media coverage should be totally on him, the Charmer, not divided with the creepy girl with the sleek, Plasticine head and the bug legs.

He slept for a few hours and had himself bathed in the giant whirlpool tub. He tried calling for pizza delivery, but his landline was dead. A cell phone worked, but the phone just rang and rang. No one in Las Vegas was delivering pizza.

He sent two of the Cheerios down to find food in the hot dog and beer stands, but they never came back. He had ordered them to get food and return, so either the orders were too vague, or impossible to carry out, or . . . or someone had taken out two of his Cheerios.

Dekka? The bear? Or was Shade Darby here now?

No need to be afraid, he reassured himself. He had the greatest of all powers. And he had an audience to impress.

"Now what?" he wondered, and went back to the TV, to exhausted-looking news anchors and . . . *Breaking News*. The news that was breaking involved amateur video of a tank column. An actual army tank column! It was like something out of the Iraq war.

"Wow," Dillon said. "I stirred something up here, didn't I?"

One of the cheerleaders, the Asian woman who said her name was Kate, answered. "Yes, you did. A lot of people are going to die."

He shot her a look and almost ordered her to bite her tongue off. "If I want criticism, I'll ask for it. So shut up."

But she wasn't wrong. The UNLV mob had formed into three subgroups, one very large mob of maybe five thousand, and two smaller groups, all wandering up and down the Strip looking for anyone in uniform.

The Strip itself, and the various walkways between casinos, were all studded with bodies, most dead, some crawling along leaving blood trails on bare concrete.

"Tanks, huh?" Dillon said, then sang a bit of a ditty— *"Tanks for the memories"*—which earned a nervous smile from Kate and made him like her a little. He was glad he hadn't made her mutilate herself. "Two goldfish are in a tank. One says to the other, 'Hey, how do you drive this thing?'" That got an honest titter.

Her laughter warmed him, but he was still worried. He had taken on the cops and won. He'd taken on Dekka and Armo and at least survived. But tanks? Yeah, that was going to be tough.

What he needed, he realized, was to get on nationwide TV, like Saffron had said. Just ten seconds of airtime and he would be able to create millions of obedient slaves.

"No, Dillon," he said suddenly, snapping his fingers. "I don't need TV."

He had a Facebook page with seventy-eight "friends." That would be a start.

"Hey, Kate. Take my phone. You know how to film video?"

In the bowels of the National Security Agency, the reigning world champions at electronic surveillance, now, in the emergency, allowed to spy openly on what they called "US persons," a computer pinged.

An analyst known as Captain Crunch for the box of sugary cereal he kept close at hand turned in his chair in his cubicle and said to the guy in the next cubicle, "Hey, I've got a hit on Subject 19."

It took twenty minutes of verification and double-checking, by which time half a dozen senior NSA supervisors were huddled around Captain Crunch's cubicle, and many more eyes watched via computer link.

It took another hour for the news to make its way up the chain of command. And thirty minutes for orders to reach the Creech Air Force Base just outside Las Vegas.

From there it took another half hour to arm and launch the drone, and another hour to reach the target. Men and women in dark, air-conditioned trailers parked in the desert sat in padded armchairs facing monitors. They searched high and low for signs of life in the target area. Nothing.

Good enough.

A Hellfire missile was launched, coincidentally just as Drake Merwin emerged from his hideout, wondering where the hell Tom Peaks had got to.

The missile blew Drake into the rocks. Or at least pieces of him. Chunks of Drake—many burning—fell between crevices or splatted against stone. His head was torn in half, with most of his brain, his right eye, and nose a jellied, slow-burning wad of goo.

The remainder of his head, comprised of his left eye, a bit of nose cartilage, and his mouth, fell, somewhat intact, onto a cactus, where it sat like some demented bird's nest.

"Damn," Drake's mouth said. "This again?"

CHAPTER 19
Ruthlessness: Not Just for Sharks Anymore

DEKKA AND ARMO managed to catch some sleep and some food in a suite at the barricaded Caesars Palace resort—classier than the Venetian, but still wonderfully gaudy, with facsimiles of Roman architecture and statuary. Though the excellent, life-sized copy of Michelangelo's *David* was actually from Renaissance Florence, not Caesar's Rome, but hey, what was a millennium or two?

Some bright person at Caesars named Wilkes—newly promoted by virtue of her former boss's death at Caesars—had recognized the wisdom in giving the two Rockborn a place to crash.

Dekka woke first and stumbled to draw the curtains open on blazing sunlight. The room faced north, her view encompassing the Linq and Mirage casinos. And across the strip from the Mirage, the Venetian, which burned, with smoke billowing from shattered windows.

The Strip was almost devoid of cars, aside from those that

had crashed or been overturned. Some cars and trucks still smoldered. Bodies were everywhere, little rag dolls dropped in the street, on sidewalks, in fountains.

An empty police car was still flashing red and blue. Through the thick glass Dekka heard sirens and alarms trilling endlessly.

Weariness swept through her. Not sleepiness, though she felt that, too, but bone weariness. The bed she had just left called to her. Armo was still asleep on his bed, facedown, so big that he managed to hang over the foot of the bed and both sides simultaneously.

Dekka found the remote control and turned the TV on.

A state of barely controlled panic had seized the country, with the news split about evenly between what Shade had done at the Ranch and the growing madness of Las Vegas.

But, the anchor said, tanks were on the way. Like that was going to be a good thing.

She opened her phone and WhatsApp, struck by the fact that she was using the favorite app of terrorists.

Dekka: Shade?

Shade: Yes?

Dekka: Coming to Vegas?

Shade: Yep.

Dekka: I thought you might be. Come to Caesars Palace. Text when you get here and I'll have them let you in.

Shade: Malik says "Avengers assemble?"

Dekka: Something like that.

Dekka met Shade, Cruz, and Malik downstairs. "Glad you came," Dekka said, shaking their hands. "Armo and I were on our way to back you up—which you obviously did not need—and got sidelined here."

"Thanks for the thought," Shade said wearily. "It's been a rough day."

"The days are all rough now," Cruz said.

Dekka made eye contact with Shade and subtly inclined her head toward the hallway leading to the bathrooms.

Shade said, "I have to duck into the ladies'."

"I'll go with you," Dekka said. "Armo, you mind taking Cruz and Malik up to the room?"

"My pleasure."

Dekka intercepted a look between Malik and Cruz. Neither of them had missed that Dekka wanted to talk to Shade alone. But neither wanted to interfere, either, so they followed Armo toward the elevators.

Dekka led Shade to an alcove housing landlines and an ATM.

"What's up?" Shade asked, unable to conceal a deep weariness identical to Dekka's own bone-deep exhaustion.

"You know about the FAYZ? You read the books, saw the movie?"

Shade nodded.

"So you know who I mean when I say that Drake is alive. Or what passes as life where he's concerned."

"Whip Hand," Shade said, suddenly more alert.

"Whatever you think you know, the reality is worse. Much worse. He's been living out in the desert, but Tom Peaks brought him to LA. Don't know where he is now, hopefully back in the far reaches of the Mojave. But even if he is . . ." She exhaled a shaky breath. "He's obsessed with her."

"Astrid Ellison."

Dekka nodded. "Sooner or later he'll go for her. And Sam won't be able to stop him." She took a long pause, knowing the gravity of what she was about to ask. "No normal human being will be able to stop him."

Shade looked at the floor. "Dekka . . . I . . ." She made a small, bitter laugh. "I'm not real impressed by my own decision making lately, you know? Especially when it comes to the rock. Malik . . . You don't know what's happened to him, what he's become."

"It's a risk, a terrible risk," Dekka agreed. "But you do have some?"

Shade nodded so slightly it might almost not have been intentional. But after a moment she spoke. "Yes, Dekka. I have some."

Armo was fast asleep by the time Dekka led Shade into the room. Dekka and Shade had picked up some coffee and pastries downstairs, and Dekka now set them out on the coffee table, like she was catering a business meeting.

But first Cruz and then Shade and then Malik used the shower, and by the time that was done, Armo had yawned and woken up. He sat wearing only boxers, blissfully unaware that Cruz was eyeing him like he was the last donut.

At six feet in a world that still felt women should be shorter than men, Cruz had few options. But Armo? Armo was massive.

In a good way.

"So," Dekka said.

"So," Shade agreed.

They sipped coffee, each seeming to Cruz to be waiting for the other to announce a plan.

"Tanks will be here by sundown. And as far as I know that Dillon person is still free," Dekka said. With an apologetic look, she added, "Sorry. We almost had him."

"It's all over the news, obviously," Shade said. "It's shaping up as some kind of showdown. I won't be surprised if more Rockborn show up. A lot of the . . . people . . . we cut loose at the Ranch . . . I saw Knightmare running for it. God only knows what that starfish kid, whatever he calls himself—"

"Abaddon," Cruz supplied. "Vincent Vu."

"Yeah. Him. Last seen in LA."

"How fast can a giant starfish crawl?" Cruz asked drolly, and was rewarded by a grin from Armo. No surprise, he had perfect teeth and a gorgeous smile.

"What do we *do*? That's the question," Dekka said, looking at Shade. Then everyone looked at Shade.

Shade shook her head. "Don't ask me." She lowered her gaze and seemed to shrink a bit.

Dekka let go a snort. "Who are we supposed to ask, then? Look, honey, I've seen a lot about you online, and you're supposed to be smart as hell."

"Yeah, well, guess what? IQ is not the same thing as wisdom. Anyway, you've got the experience," Shade said. "And you didn't . . ." Her eyes went to Malik. Malik sat, silent, eyes half closed as they often were. Looking just like Malik . . . only not.

Dekka, irritated, turned to Armo. "What have you got, dude?"

"I got half a croissant left if anyone wants it."

Whether he was dead serious or joking, no one was quite sure. But Cruz smiled.

Not really the time for that, Cruz chided herself. But she'd only briefly met Armo in the midst of a raging battle, and he'd been rather furry at that point. Cruz had never been even in the same room with someone like Armo. Cruz was transgender, but hetero in her preferences, and it would take a seriously picky straight girl or gay boy not to react to six feet, five inches of smooth, muscular gorgeousness. He might even be better-looking than Malik, for whom she could no longer feel anything but pity and sadness and a sort of sibling love.

Okay, enough! Once again, she was standing back from decisions that would shape her life. Or end it.

"I don't even know who we're fighting," Cruz blurted. "Are we fighting this Charmer person, this thought-control Rockborn? Or are we fighting the actual United States freaking Army?"

"We're fighting the Dark Watchers," Malik said, breaking a long silence.

Every face turned to him.

"I believe . . . ," he said, before breaking off and frowning. He shook his head slightly, bedeviled by those very Dark Watchers. "What they want, the Watchers, is to watch. I think we are entertainment. In some ways we are like characters in a movie. I don't know whether they meant this to be entertainment or it just kind of happened. I don't know . . . well, anything; it's all just . . . Look, maybe they were just flipping channels and there we were, visible to them because of some long-forgotten experiment with the rock. I don't guess it matters. But now that they're watching, they want the show to be entertaining. And their taste in entertainment runs to the dark, the gruesome."

Shade, still a muted shadow of herself, said, "Are you saying we have no free will in this?"

Malik shrugged. "In Philosophy 101, you get into the debate over whether free will exists or whether it's just an illusion. The result is inevitable: it doesn't matter. Either we have free will or we don't, but we are not capable of acting as though we don't. So, effectively, we do."

Shade's smile was genuine and wistful. "College boy."

Cruz saw that her friend was in agony waiting to see whether Malik took this as a good-natured jibe or not. When Malik managed a small quirk of his lips, Shade seemed on the edge of tears of relief.

"That's all fine," Dekka said, "but what about freaks and tanks?"

"It comes down to who is going to win in the end," Malik said.

"Not who is right?" Cruz asked.

"That's always important," Malik acknowledged. "But here's the thing. If the government wins, they will inevitably hunt us down and wipe us out. Which may be the best solution—would be—if not for . . ." He shrugged.

"If not for it meaning we all have to die?" Armo snarked.

"The Ranch," Shade said. "The Ranch proves the government will use the rock to create its own mutants. Do we trust a government that would do that? To its own citizens?"

Suddenly there was another person in the room. Armo leaped to his feet, fists clenched and white fur sprouting.

"Whoa! Whoa!" Francis Specter said, holding up empty palms and shaking her head no. "I'm one of the good guys!"

"How the hell did you get in here?" Dekka demanded, rushing to check that the door was locked.

"It's this thing I can do," Francis said. "I'm one of you. I have a . . . you know . . . a power."

Introductions and explanations followed.

"You're just a kid," Dekka said.

"So were you, Dekka," Shade said. "So were Sam Temple and Astrid Ellison and the rest." In response to Dekka's raised eyebrow she added, "I told you: I've read all the books."

"She really has," Cruz confirmed.

"I'm here because I saw you on TV," Francis said, dipping her head shyly toward Dekka.

"Me? Oh, man," Dekka said. "Great. I'm the Pied Piper now. Well, you're here, and it looks like you're bringing some serious capability. So welcome. I guess."

Dekka extended a hand, and Francis shook it, abashed and with eyes downcast, like a personal assistant looking to be hired by a movie star.

Shade summarized. "Okay. I have speed and a fair bit of strength as well. Francis says she can basically go through solid objects, and given the fact she just walked through a locked door, I guess she can. Cruz can alter her appearance or disappear completely. Dekka can shred anything. Malik can send out a blast of unbearable pain. Armo can bring some serious brute force." At this Armo flexed his biceps and made his pecs dance, which Cruz found ridiculous and yet did not hate watching. She had her Moleskine on her lap and idly sketched a bit of his shoulder.

"All of which is amazing," Shade continued. "We have powers. Serious powers. But we still don't have a plan."

"I have an idea." The words were out of Cruz's mouth before she could stop them. Any other time the look of skepticism on Shade's face would have wounded her, but Cruz understood. Understood and agreed that she was very unlikely, based on past experience, to have a useful suggestion.

"Go ahead," Dekka said, leaning forward from the edge of her bed.

"It's just something stupid," Cruz said. "Because I was thinking about writing and stories and . . ."

"Spit it," Dekka snapped. "Our resident geniuses and our experienced fighters aren't coming up with anything."

"Well . . . okay. It's what Malik was saying, about this being entertainment. Like a TV show or a book. And I started thinking about it as if it was a story, you know? Like a comic book or a movie? Well, what do superheroes do? They save the day."

"So, that's it? That's the plan? Save the day?" said Shade, looking almost pitying.

"No, no, I mean, yes, but . . ." Cruz felt a flush rising in her cheeks. "I just mean, it's about *when*, isn't it? Timing. Basically we have two bad guys—the government, and the Charmer and people like him, evil Rockborn. We all know we can't let some sadistic creep with mind-control powers win. I mean, that's the end of *everything*. Which leaves the government. In the end, we kind of need *them* to win, but not unless they decide they need us alive. So, we can't ever help the Charmer, but we can maybe help the government. But only if they're really desperate."

"So . . ."

"So, if this is a story, an *entertainment*, when do the super-heroes show up to save the day?"

Malik smiled at her. "When all hope is lost."

"Cruz, that means standing by while people die," Dekka said. "Doing nothing until we're sure the time is right."

"Yes," Cruz said heavily. And as she said it she had an image in her mind of the shark within Shade Darby, suddenly migrating to take up residency within Cruz.

Two minutes earlier she'd been ogling Armo. Now she had blurted out a plan that might cost—very likely would cost—innocent lives.

Two of the people in the room understood clearly, down to

the depths of their souls, the burden she had just placed on herself. Cruz had just come off the bench to join the game, opened her mouth and made herself complicit in whatever followed.

Shade and Dekka looked at her, mirror images of pity.

Interstice

FBI—Washington

URGENT

Note: The following transcript was prepared using a voice-to-text program.

Transcript of Dillon Poe Facebook video:

Hello, world, this is Dillon Po [sic] coming at you from beautiful downtown Las Vegas.

I'm going to give you an order and your [sic] going to follow it.

I command all who hear this to do two things.

First, you will forward this video by all social media to all of your contracts. [sic]

Second, once you have done that, you will come by the most direct means available, to Las Vegas. Once you are in Las Vegas you will defend the city against all government forces, killing any soldier or police officer you find, as well as any person helping them.

You will follow this order for twenty-four hours after arriving in Las Vegas. Then you will await further orders.

If you don't get further orders from me, you will stop, stand in place, and refuse to eat or drink.

Thanks for listening, thanks for obeying, and don't forget to tip your waiters!

THE WHITE HOUSE
Office of the Press Secretary
FOR IMMEDIATE RELEASE
Operating under the emergency provisions enacted yesterday, the President has ordered the immediate shutdown of all social media, to include Twitter, Instagram, Facebook, and similar services, as well as YouTube and any other peer-to-peer means of broadcasting or rebroadcasting of video or voice.

Any individual, company, or group knowingly broadcasting, rebroadcasting, or in any way aiding the person identified as Dillon Poe will be arrested and face severe punishment, to include ten years in federal prison and the forfeiture of all assets.

Classified: Top Secret
DEPARTMENT OF HOMELAND SECURITY
Director of Homeland Security
Under the powers granted by the emergency decree, you are ordered to immediately make available any and all "backdoors" to your WhatsApp application.

Failure to comply will result in the immediate seizure of your business and the termination of any and all ownership claims, whether by you or by stockholders and investors.

This same letter will be sent to all developers of similar encrypted messaging applications.

Expedia regrets that at this time we are unable to accept reservations for flights or hotels in the greater Las Vegas area.

47 U.S. Code § 606—War powers of President

(d)Suspension or amendment of rules and regulations applicable to wire communications; closing of facilities; Government use of facilities.

Upon proclamation by the President that there exists a state or threat of war involving the United States, the President, if he deems it necessary in the interest of the national security and defense, may, during a period ending not later than six months after the termination of such state or threat of war and not later than such earlier date as the Congress by concurrent resolution may designate, (1) suspend or amend the rules and regulations applicable to any or all facilities or stations for wire communication within the jurisdiction of the United States as prescribed by the Commission, (2) cause the closing of any facility or station for wire communication and the removal therefrom of its apparatus and equipment, or (3) authorize the use or control of any such facility or station and its apparatus and equipment by any department of the Government under such regulations as he may prescribe, upon just compensation to the owners.

SUBSUNK ALERT
Classified: Top Secret
DEPARTMENT OF DEFENSE
Chief of Staff, US Navy

Be advised that we have lost all contact with USS Nebraska *last position within twelve miles of USCG cutter:* **Abbie Burgess.**

NSRS (NATO Submarine Rescue System) is en route via C-5 aircraft from HM Naval Base Clyde (Scotland). Scheduled to arrive on-scene in nine hours.

F-15 aircraft from the 104th Fighter Wing (104 FW— Massachusetts Air National Guard) to provide air cap.

CHAPTER 20
Monster Surplus

THE FIRST ATTACK came on I-15, just north of the intersection with state highway 127.

Colonel Frank "Frankenstein" Poole was riding in a JLTV—Joint Light Tactical Vehicle—the replacement for the venerable Humvee.

Within the truck was a miniaturized combat control center, a mass of computers, radar, and communications equipment meant to give Poole total command of the battlefield. The JLTV monitored video from drones flying overhead, and above them jets, and above them satellites.

Frank Poole was riding shotgun, up front, occasionally glancing in the rearview mirror to admire the long column of gray-green or sand-colored tanks, armored personnel carriers, and trucks stretching for almost two miles behind him.

It was sheer, naked, destructive power, that column: death on tracks and wheels. Death from helicopters and fighter jets. Death from machine guns and cannon, from missiles and bombs. It was Poole's greatest moment as a soldier, though he was exceedingly worried about blowback: the rules of engagement were not at all clear, and the whole world was watching.

"Colonel?" the driver, a sergeant, said. He nodded ahead.

Poole saw a tan Lexus crossing the highway dividing strip, bottoming out and sending up a spray of sand, but plowing through.

Poole had a brief glimpse of children in the back seat pounding on the seat before them, screaming silently, ignored by the determined-faced man at the wheel.

"What the . . . ?" Poole said.

And at that the car escaped the sand, wobbled as its tires bit concrete, then accelerated to smash into the side of an M1A2 Abrams tank. The tank weighed nearly seventy tons; the car weighed less than two. The car's front smashed, the rear end jumped off the ground, and the Abrams didn't even vibrate. The tank plowed on, crushing the front end of the car, squeezing it off the road, and moving on as if nothing had happened.

Poole turned in his chair to speak to his adjutant. "Transmit new rules of engagement. Anbar rules: Any vehicle appearing to try and ram the column should be taken out. And detail an ambulance to see about the people in the car."

They were at the Nevada state line when the second attack came. This time it was a minivan that came up from behind and smashed into an armored personnel carrier, slightly wounding one soldier.

No shots were fired, and it began to occur to Poole that his soldiers had been trained to kill enemy forces, not their fellow Americans. This could be trouble. He'd had no time to fully brief officers or GIs on this new reality.

The third attack was more serious: a loaded ore truck pulled onto the freeway ahead of them, then managed a long, awkward U-turn to come racing right toward Poole's JLTV.

"Engage!" Poole shouted, and after a moment's hesitation, the gunner opened up with his .50 caliber. But he was firing warning shots, tearing up the road. The trucker did not slow, let alone stop.

"Fire for effect, goddammit!" Poole shouted as the massive truck closed the distance with shocking speed.

This time the chattering gun blew apart the truck's engine and made hamburger of the driver.

The JLTV went around the steaming wreck, and the first tank in line shoved it off the road.

As Poole looked back, he saw one of his own ambulances pull off, medical techs rushing to see if the driver could be saved.

Poole sighed. The US Army had not knowingly fired on an American citizen since the Civil War. It was a glorious fact that the US military had never participated in a coup or interfered directly in politics. Poole would not have wanted to lead a force that enjoyed killing American civilians.

But, he thought grimly, *they're going to have to learn.*

Tom Peaks was trapped driving behind Poole's column. He had driven past the annihilated ore truck and had a pretty good sense that trying to pass the column might end badly, so he stuck carefully to the forty-five-mile-an-hour speed of the column.

The sky was darkening, and in the distance he could see the garish lights of the city—somewhat diminished, as it had occurred to at least some of the casino operators that they were not, currently, looking to entice gamblers.

And he saw as well a massive pillar of smoke that rose high before spreading out to form a hanging gray veil.

Then he spotted flashing lights on the road ahead and realized the Nevada Highway Patrol had set up a roadblock that the army column would blow right through, but that he, in a stolen minivan, would not. He had no way to fool the highway patrol—his name and photo were on every law enforcement database in the country, with flashing arrows and exclamation points.

So he pulled off the freeway and drove into the desert.

Tom Peaks could not reach Vegas.

Dragon could.

Vincent Vu had watched television coverage of the attack on the Ranch, and the madness of Las Vegas, which MSNBC's chyron called *Crisis: Las Vegas*, and CNN called *Battle for Las Vegas*, and Fox News labeled *Sin City Apocalypse!*

The decision to go to Las Vegas was a combination of factors. One: There wasn't much on TV but news. Two: He had run out of Pepperidge Farm Montauk cookies—his favorite. Three: He had always wanted to see Las Vegas.

And then there were the voices in his head.

Vincent suffered from a cluster of serious mental illnesses, the most terrifying of which was schizophrenia. He knew he was schizophrenic. He knew the voices he heard were not real, that the voices often lied. But when they berated him for laziness, cowardice, uselessness, and alternately reminded him that he was the avenging angel Abaddon, it was very hard to ignore them. Especially when he hadn't taken his meds in weeks.

And, by the way, he could actually become a nightmarish monster. That was not a figment. That was not a hallucination. And once you accepted the fact that you could actually *become* a giant starfish-human mash-up, well, the things the voices suggested seemed less crazy. Watching the last twenty-four hours of television—the Ranch, Las Vegas—notions of sane and insane had become rather . . . mixed up.

The only time the Schizos—his name for his usual voices—receded was when he turned into the creature, into Abaddon. Then he faced new voices, different voices that spoke not in words but in urges, and those voices, the Dark Watchers, reduced the Schizos to a background murmur.

He rose from the couch in the house he'd taken by killing the previous inhabitants. (Reason #4 for leaving: The bodies were starting to stink.) He found a handgun in the night-stand of the master bedroom, and car keys in the dead wife's purse. He had never driven a car before—he was too young—but he'd seen it done plenty of times. And he knew how to enter a destination in the GPS.

L-A-S V-E-G-A-S.

Anyway, it looked like the cops had bigger problems than arresting underage drivers. As he drove down surface streets through the greater Los Angeles metro, he saw the signs of destruction and decay, not from what he'd done down at the port, not from any freak. This was looting and vandalism, burned-out cars, shop windows covered with plywood, uncollected trash bags burst open, glass on the street, fire hydrants open and gushing water. Streetlights flashed on their emergency settings. Cars and trucks passed by, loaded with household goods. Refugees. Going where? he wondered.

A billboard for an upcoming movie had been spray-painted over with just one word in dripping red paint: *REPENT*. A graffito on a real estate office wall used blue paint to say, *KAM*, the abbreviation for *KILL ALL MUTANTS*. There were swastikas and obscenities, hatred of this or that group.

Few people walked the streets, mostly just homeless folks pushing Ralphs grocery shopping carts loaded with the typical rags and cans, but topped now with pilfered TVs and computers and fur coats. The few others out in public walked in pairs or small groups with at least one gun prominently displayed.

The world was a gingerbread house, and it was being eaten away, bite by bite.

I came as Abaddon the Destroyer, Vincent thought. *Gaze upon my work and bow down before me!*

But he did not yell this from the windows. This was not the time or place. That would come.

Justin DeVeere, aka Knightmare, had escaped the Ranch and kept moving as fast as he could, tumbling down hillsides, scraping against tree trunks, stumbling over fallen branches.

It was a simple, straightforward, run-for-your-life moment. For approximately a millisecond he had considered helping the uprising, using his power to help wipe out the Ranch. . . .

But he got past that very, very quickly.

Being Justin, he accompanied his gasping panic with a self-justifying narrative. "Not my problem . . . outta there! Screw all of them . . . not standing around trying to be Captain Courageous . . . every man for himself . . . situation like this . . . one of the most important young artists . . . any kind of artist, to hell with young . . . not cannon fodder, I'm Justin DeVeere!"

Of course, he was Justin DeVeere with a control chip in the back of his neck, right where a tap on an app could send waves of pain through him. Yeah, that was an issue. If DiMarco survived—and somehow he expected that, like a cockroach, she would survive—she could still activate the chip any time she wanted.

Well, depending on what kind of transmitter she had. Did it work from satellites? That would be bad.

Suddenly he burst from the woods onto a nicely paved two-lane road.

"No!" he cried. He had been running in what he hoped was a straight line, but it was apparently just an arc, because he was back at the main road, but still not at the front gate.

His sense of direction was poor, but he was in luck, because coming from the Ranch was a flatbed truck, followed by an assortment of official vehicles and private cars. It was like something out of a Mad Max movie. It was monsters on parade.

The flatbed truck pulled to a stop, and Justin gaped at the cyborg monster occupying most of the cargo area.

And gaped harder when the creature swiveled a hideously deadly-looking chain gun toward him.

"You staff or prisoner?" the cyborg demanded.

"Me? I'm . . . I'm like you," Justin stammered. "I mean, not a cyborg, but a rock guy. You know, Rockborn. A mutant."

"Yeah, you're too young to be staff." This judgment was rendered by the human eyes behind a tank-like slit. "I'm Master Sergeant Matthew Tolliver. You coming with us?"

"Where are you going?" Justin asked.

"Las Vegas."

Justin could have asked why. He should have asked why. But at the moment he had an invitation to Vegas from a terrifying cyborg with machine guns and rockets.

So, Vegas. Yeah, that would be perfect. He would be able to disappear into a crowd of tourists. And if he couldn't parlay his good looks and artsy bullshit into finding a sugar momma in Vegas, well . . .

"Vegas it is," Justin said.

"Vegas and Valhalla!" Tolliver said grimly. "Semper Fi!"

Justin knew what Valhalla meant. It was the Norse heaven, the Viking heaven, where any Norse warrior who had died with a sword in his hand would sit at Odin's table surrounded by other honored dead warriors and drink ale.

It made Justin think of ale.

It made Justin think of doing a series of mythology-inspired paintings. Someday.

It did not make Justin wonder why a Marine Corps master sergeant turned into an NRA wet dream of a cyborg would be referencing the celestial home of men who died in battle.

So Justin said, "Yeah!" with all the enthusiasm he could muster, and hauled himself up onto the flatbed, a young man thinking he'd just been handed a free pass out of trouble by an older man who saw his best future being a righteous death.

CHAPTER 21
With Great Power Comes Pure Malice

DILLON POE STOOD in the doorway of Triunfo, a tall, gold pillar of a hotel, now entirely under his control thanks to his voice and to the battering power of a Coors beer truck his Cheerios had used to smash in the doors.

He was furious that Facebook, Twitter, and Instagram had been taken down. Even YouTube! How was a desperate nation going to get its Jenna Marbles and PewDiePie fixes?

The major media were dumb but, sadly, they weren't dumb enough to broadcast his video. The video would certainly have already reached a lot of people anyway—it had been two hours before Facebook had taken it down, and three hours before some bright person in the government had ordered a shutdown of all social media. But he knew without active social media he would reach only thousands, not millions.

The battle was coming, and he needed an army of his own. But Nevada was a small state in population, and as a practical matter the only large population center close enough to provide the huge numbers he wanted that was near enough to be useful was Los Angeles. How many Angelenos would hear his call in time? People coming from Kansas two days from now were not going to save his ass.

It amused Dillon to realize that at least some people overseas would have seen his video and were now desperately trying to catch a flight to Las Vegas. Well, good luck with that—the airport was closed. He imagined various Dutch or Japanese or Kenyan people spending the rest of their lives trying to follow his order.

Funny. Dark funny, like The Onion, *or Frankie Boyle, but funny.*

If only he could speak directly to the soldiers rolling up from the south, followed by news cameras and breathless news anchors as adoring as if the column was Jesus, Jehovah, and Mohammed all coming together to save the day. But how? He could grab a bullhorn, and maybe reach some of the troops, but they'd be in loud, armored vehicles, many wearing headphones . . . Yeah, that wasn't a solution. Anyway, he wasn't crazy about exposing himself physically to a column of tanks: he was all-powerful, but he was not bulletproof.

The Strip was largely unpopulated now aside from earlier iterations of his slaves still trying to carry out his old orders. There must still be lots of people in the greater Las Vegas metro area. But how could he reach them? Fear rose inside him like a sickness.

How did all this happen? Just because I got myself thrown into the drunk tank?

Notebook: Something about tanks and drunk tanks. Explosive vomiting like cannon?

He had moved from the stadium to the Triunfo, a hotel without a casino, on the theory that hotel security was less prepared, less trained than casino security. That had proved correct—the Triunfo's security had ear coverings, but the staff and tourists milling like frightened sheep in the lobby had not been protected. They had made short work of the security team.

But even the relatively easy conquering of the Triunfo had left him rattled. One of his mind-controlled slaves had badly injured one of his Cheerios, and he'd had to leave him behind to be torn apart by the mobs Dillon had created. His mobs were greatly diminished in number, either because they'd been shot by police, or because they'd killed each other—it was very hard to speak orders that guarded against friendly fire, the killing *of* your people *by* your people. So, his army was diminished in number, but still comprised thousands, scattered up and down the Strip. Sadly, it was an army he could no longer reach with his voice, so some were insistent on eating any person they came across, while others were following his later order to attack anyone in uniform. They were disruptive and destructive, but cops in street clothes were mostly safe and had gotten quite used to shooting to kill any attacker, and Dillon did not try to fool himself into believing his forces could prevail.

After smashing the front door with the beer truck, he'd been able to get to the intercom at the hotel, and now all the staff and all the remaining tourists were under his control (or dead), but that wasn't nearly enough.

He needed live bodies. Not in some other country, not even in Chicago or New York. He needed them here, now.

Here! Now!

"Who knew taking over the world would be so hard?" he muttered. "I'm the most powerful person in the world, and I can't get anything done!"

After giving Kate and some of the other Cheerios orders, Dillon took the elevator to the three-bedroom penthouse suite he'd appropriated. The suite was complete with three bathrooms, a kitchen, and a great view. He still had six—or was it five?—Cheerios. And in his suite he had TVs everywhere, in every room, tuned to the cable news channels.

"This is very, very important," some fool was babbling, "That you not look at any—any—new or unfamiliar video."

"Not helpful," Dillon muttered. He tried a work-around, dialing the CNN newsroom.

"This is Dillon Poe. Put me through to whoever is in charge." The person answering had no choice but to obey.

Too late he realized he had given them his name, so when the person who'd answered announced to her superior that she had to take a call from Dillon Poe, well . . . *click.*

Local radio proved less well prepared, and in mere seconds he was on the air with some DJ named Ferris.

"Ferris, first things first: do not hang up on me, no matter who tries to stop you. Second, put me on air."

Ferris did as he was ordered.

"Anyone who can hear me, listen and obey! I am Kodos, your new insect overlord." *Simpsons* references were timeless, Dillon figured. "You will immediately come to the Strip and attack any soldier or police person you see!" As an afterthought he added, "Whether they're in uniform or not. Use your best judgment on that."

What Dillon did not know, and Ferris did not mention, was that the station's chief engineer was already halfway to Salt Lake City, having had the good sense to grab his family and flee hours earlier. So transmission was not all it might have been, and the order came out garbled.

". . . immediately . . . Strip and attack any soldier or police . . . see!"

Dillon did not hear the broadcast—he was on the phone. But he ordered Ferris to continue replaying his order forever.

He heard frantic noises on Ferris's end of the line, a loud banging, a rending of wood.

"Hey, I'm on air here!" Ferris yelled at unknown people.

"Not another f—king word!" a male voice yelled.

"Hey, this is my show, asshole!" Ferris yelled back. "I'm going to loop that and play it as long as I'm on the—"

The next loud bang was undeniably a gunshot.

Half an hour later came the first video from a news helicopter of a scattering of people standing stark naked outside their homes, many carrying guns, and glancing like metronomes up and down the street.

"Dammit!" Dillon cried. He really missed Saffron now. She'd had a good imagination, that girl. And in some ways she was more ruthless than he was. It had been her idea to make the two cops jump off the Venetian tower. Sadly, none of the Cheerios seemed half as bright, or half as ruthless. It was, he reflected, the downside of turning people into slaves: they only obeyed, they did not counsel or advise or suggest.

On MSNBC Rachel Maddow was warning that Dillon Poe had tried to get on air with a radio station. "I am sorry to even say this, but if you work at a radio station or broadcast TV station, you must not answer your phone unless caller ID gives you a number you know—absolutely *know*—is safe."

"Oh, I'm going to hurt you, Rachel," Dillon vowed.

How to assemble the mighty slave army he needed?

Old school? He could just sit and start randomly dialing Las Vegas numbers. But when he tried to get a line out of the hotel he just got the rapid busy signal.

He had a cell phone, but he'd sent the owner off to kill himself before getting his security code, so all he could dial was . . .

Dillon's face split into a smile. He grabbed the cell, and yep, there it was, security code or no: 911.

911 was busy. Very busy. It took sixteen tries, followed by a very long time on hold. Then:

"911, state your emergency." The voice was ragged with exhaustion.

"Do not hang up. Listen only to me. Tell me: Do you have access to an intercom?"

"Yes."

"Something everyone there at the emergency center will hear?"

"Yes."

"Can you connect me to that intercom?"

"I . . . I think so . . . maybe . . ."

"Do it," Dillon snapped.

He listened to keys being tapped, and the operator's muttered thoughts. "Don't know . . . shouldn't do this . . . maybe this will work . . . Hmmm . . . Okay, sir, I think I can do it."

Deep breath. Get it right, Dillon, get it right.

"Attention, everyone in the emergency center. I am going to give you an order. You will broadcast this order over police radio."

He could hear the hollow echo of his voice coming through the public address system at the emergency center.

"This is the statement you will send out to every cop—"

"Excuse me, sir," the operator said.

Dillon was taken aback. "What?"

"Well, just to LVMPD? What about private security?"

Dillon's voice was silky. "Wait . . . are you saying you can reach out to casino security people?"

"Well, sir, some, yes. We have an emergency communication system called—"

"I don't care what it's called!" Dillon said, and did a little dance around. His reptile form was a much better dancer than his old human form. "Here goes the message: All people who hear this message will first do all they can to spread it by any means available. They will take two hours doing that. And then, they will assemble on the Strip, near, um . . . what's a central casino?"

"Caesars Palace? The Cosmopolitan?"

"Okay. Take two: All people who hear this message will first do all they can to spread it by any means available. They will spend two hours doing that. And then, they will assemble on the Strip, near Caesars Palace. There they will wait until the military column arrives and then they will attack the military, killing everyone. Without mercy."

The "without mercy" was irrelevant, but Dillon was pleased by the note of grim determination it added. Part of his mind noted the comic possibilities in the phrase "without mercy." What was the alternative? With mercy?

"That's the message you want us to put out there?" the operator said.

"You and everyone at the center. Oh, and, what's your name?"

"My name? Dot Perkins."

"Well, Dot Perkins, as soon as you've spent two hours spreading this message, I want you to hop in your car and drive to, let's say, Dallas. You should be safe there. You helped me out with a timely suggestion, and the Charmer rewards his friends."

"Dallas?"

"Don't worry, Dot, they'll be hiring a whole lot of emergency operators there, too, soon enough."

CHAPTER 22
World War Vegas

FRANK POOLE STOOD up in the JLTV, squeezing up through the same hatch occupied by the machine gunner, and scanned the road ahead.

Cars stalled or burned out. Bodies lying in the road. The air stinking of smoke. It looked like they'd started the war without him.

He drove on past the Mandalay Bay, passing a looted liquor store on the right, and a McDonald's, which gave him a pang of hunger despite the nausea of anticipation.

Next came the black pyramid of the Luxor casino, with its Sphinx replica out front.

So far, so good.

Maybe this wouldn't be so bad.

Excalibur, with its Disneyesque Knights of the Round Table theme.

A person came out of nowhere, an elderly man dressed in sweatpants with neither shirt nor shoes. He was clearly unarmed.

"Hold your fire," Poole said to the gunner.

The old man ran at the JLTV, kept running, slammed into it, and fell straight back, knocked cold.

They came to the state road 593 overpass and suddenly:

Bam! Bam!

Poole dropped down into his seat as rifle rounds pinged and bounced off the JLTV's armor.

"Take him out."

"Roger that, sir."

Poole peered up through the windshield and watched as his gunner's big .50 shredded the man with the rifle.

Now it was the New York-New York casino with its half-size replica of the Statue of Liberty and its faux New York skyline. A pedestrian walkway crossed the Strip from New York-New York to the MGM Grand. Poole saw three people on the walkway. And he saw the silhouettes of guns.

"Don't fire unless we are—" Pool ordered. At which point the three on the walkway opened fire with handguns and a shotgun, none of which would have any effect on the JLTV, let alone the tanks.

"Okay," Poole said, and the .50 opened up again, showering spent brass down the windshield and killing the civilians.

If they knew what a .50 caliber does to flesh and bone . . . Poole thought.

Thirty-five miles an hour now, slowly past the Monte Carlo, slowly past the Aria. An electronic billboard advertised Celine Dion, who, Poole was pretty sure, was going to have to cancel her show.

Another pedestrian walkway. More gunmen firing. More

gunmen with big holes in their bodies and chunks of themselves sent flying through the air.

Civilians. American civilians.

He would go down in history as the first commander to
open fire on American civilians. He felt sick. But at another
level, relieved, because so far the only firing done had been
by his own JLTV. So far this hardly called for a whole tank
attack force.

But then he saw the crowd. In the street, just standing there.
Thousands of people, a silent mob in front of Caesars Palace.
They stretched from the casino doors down the semicircular
driveway, then a quarter mile of them on the Strip itself. He
raised his binoculars and gazed into faces that might have
been any random cross-section of American citizens, with no
doubt some foreign tourists mixed in. He saw weapons—lots
of weapons, including military ordnance—assault rifles, grenades, shoulder-carried missiles. Someone had broken into
the National Guard arsenal. Poole could only hope no one
knew how to use the anti-tank weapons, because if they did,
and if they used them, then he was going to have to order a
massacre.

Poole stood up in the hatch again. An observant corpo-
ral handed him a set of shooter's earmuffs. He asked for
the microphone—the JLTV had an onboard public-address
system.

"Under the emergency decree passed by Congress and
signed by the president, I order you to disperse immediately."

The crowd just stared.

"We have already been forced to open fire. We do not wish to harm you, but you must disperse."

A woman toward the front of the crowd was saying something, looking very earnest. Poole pushed his earmuffs back from one ear.

". . . not trying to get killed but we can't disobey!" the woman said. "Don't you understand? We have to attack you and kill you! Without mercy!"

Lowering the bullhorn, Poole said, "If you fail to disperse we—"

And suddenly a mellifluous, compelling voice spoke into a handheld bullhorn. The voice said, "Soldiers! I order you to blow this town apart! You, boss man! Order your soldiers to annihilate this town!"

At which point Poole keyed his microphone and said, "Attention to orders. You will immediately begin firing on any and all buildings."

One tank—the one immediately behind Poole, whose commander had heard Dillon on the loudspeaker, swiveled his cannon, aimed it at the largest target at hand: the faux Eiffel Tower of the Paris casino.

Ka-BOOM!

A round of high explosive blew up as it struck the restaurant level about a third of the way up. Bits of steel strap and rivets and a shower of glass went flying.

"Sir!" Poole's driver yelled. Having headphones on, he had not heard Dillon's voice.

"You heard my order!" Poole shouted.

"Sir, no sir, we can't just start blowing shit up!"

Poole drew his service revolver and pressed it against the man's head. "I said fire!"

"I'm the driver, not a weapons operator!" Poole's brain screamed *NO!* but he fired once. The driver's brains decorated the inside of the windshield and side window.

The JLTV swerved left, bumped against a light pole, and stalled. Poole, afire with desperate need, leaped out and ran down the line of his column yelling, "Fire on all buildings! Fire on all buildings!"

He was tackled by a second lieutenant, still raving and punching. More soldiers ran and surrounded their commander, lifting him as well as they could given his hysteria, and hauled him toward the ambulances in the rear.

At that moment a pickup truck, its bed full of barrels, came roaring out of the Paris driveway and smashed straight into the number-one tank. The barrels, filled with gasoline, split on impact, spraying fuel over the tank. The tank's commander stared stupidly, still yelling orders to his crew to *fire! Fire! Fire on that casino!* Gasoline found the hot engine block and burst into flames as the crew bailed out of their hatches. The fleeing tankers were immediately set upon by the waiting, sinister crowd and were beaten and battered to death.

The tank's commander yelled, "Fire! Fire!" until smoke from the literal fire choked his throat and then rose to consume him.

"Irony," Dillon muttered, shaking his head in mock concern. He had snuck away from the Triunfo to directly supervise his mob on the Strip, confident that his control meant he could return when necessary. But then, trying to find a place to hole up, he had been beaten back by determined (ear-covered) resistance at the Flamingo and at the Linq, the two casinos across the Strip from Caesars. But he'd been able to take control of a restaurant called Margaritaville, and now stood on the second floor, looking out through a window he'd had Kate shoot out so he could hear—and speak—as well as see.

He still had five Cheerios with him, as well as three ex-military who claimed to know how to use the missiles Dillon's forces had seized in a raid on the National Guard armory. One of them had, when forced to do so, made some recommendations, among them that Dillon should divide his forces into battalions.

On the plus side, Dillon thought: *I have a very nice margarita here, with extra salt.* He had never tasted a margarita before, and he quite liked it. But after his earlier experience he made a mental note not to drink more.

On the negative side, he could not get the Jimmy Buffet song out of his head. Which was far from the most annoying thing in his head, because all the while the Dark Watchers were whispering their silent whispers and seeming—at least to Dillon—to be watching with the enjoyment of professional sports fans on Super Bowl Sunday.

And on the still more negative side, one tank round through the front of Margaritaville . . .

Dillon glanced at his ex-soldiers. "Yeah, we can't have you guys shooting from here, you'll draw fire. Go out, walk south, and take a shot when you find a good target."

One tank was burning. The lead vehicle, the command JLTV, had been driven off the road. But a shocking amount of death-dealing armor was slowly but inexorably advancing, now less than fifty yards from the first line of Dillon's slave army.

Dillon took a long pull from his margarita, raised his bullhorn, and yelled, "First battalion! *Attack!*"

Words I never expected to say . . .

With a will, a thousand or more people, people of all ages, from elderly down to small children, ran down both sides of the column, firing guns. As they ran they lit the Molotov cocktails Dillon had thoughtfully provided after having his Cheerios hijack a Chevron fuel truck. These they smashed against tanks and trucks and armored personnel carriers.

Half a dozen vehicles were on fire before the temporarily leaderless men and women in the column reached their own conclusions and opened return fire; .30-caliber and .50-caliber machine guns roared. Tracer rounds lanced here and there like bright lasers.

B-r-r-r-r-t!

B-r-r-r-r-t!

Civilians ran at the tanks and fell, heads blown open like dropped watermelons. They ran as parts of them—hands, ears, shoulders—were crudely dissected by slugs the size of a man's fingertip flying at a devastating 2,910 feet per second.

But they did not stop. They screamed, they shouted apologies, they begged to be spared, but they did not turn tail. They were helplessly fearless, running down the column, throwing their gasoline bombs, firing at any exposed soldier. But it was flesh-and-blood amateurs versus professional soldiers, and the slaughter was horrifying.

"You like that, don't you?" Dillon asked the unseen audience. "Yeah, you love that shit."

The second tank in line swerved past the first, past the crashed JLTV, gunned its engine and drove right into the remaining crowd, machine guns blazing.

"So much louder in real life," Dillon muttered. "You! Get me another margarita. Extra salt!"

The tank treads crunched bone and squashed flesh, but none of Dillon's voice slaves ran.

None moved aside.

They stood and were crushed. Or, if they were in the first battalion, attacked and were gunned down. Dozens had fallen already. Blood in slick pools reflected the Las Vegas lights.

The machine guns tore big red holes in legs and chests, in stomachs and groins and faces. In men and women. Young and old. And as they fell to the guns they were crushed beneath the M1A2's seventy tons.

Woosh . . . *BAM!*

The first of the missiles was fired at the fifth tank back. The tank erupted in flame. Leaning eagerly out of the window with his drink in hand, Dillon saw the tank's tread spool off. Crewmen bailed and were shot or stabbed or mauled.

Maybe, Dillon thought, his true calling was as a military leader. He was doing pretty well, it seemed to him. But could you be a great leader and still be a comic?

The army column was still advancing, but slowly, at a crawl. "Time for round two," Dillon said. "Let's play Civilian Crush." He yelled through his bullhorn, "Battalion two! Do it *now*!"

Approximately a thousand people dropped to the ground. They scooted around, getting into position until they formed a human chain of prostrate bodies across the Strip. It was a wide street, so his human chain was only four people deep, and he'd have liked to have more, but still, he figured he had presented the army commander with an insoluble problem. Would the tanks roll over passive, unarmed civilians just lying in the street?

At first he thought it had worked. As he watched, the tank column suddenly executed a crisp left turn onto Flamingo Road, treads gouging concrete, machine gunners picking off attackers.

"Shit!" Dillon yelled. "You know what they're doing?" he demanded of Kate, currently wearing her cheerleader outfit crisscrossed by heavy ammo belts. "They're going around!"

"Yes," Kate said. It was just about the only safe word to use around Dillon. Kate, like the other Cheerios, was bound to the power of Dillon's voice and had no choice but to obey. But that did not mean she liked it. In fact, she was straining her last nerve to get herself to draw her gun and shoot the monster.

"Maybe stick with comedy after all," Dillon muttered. But his audience—the Dark Watchers—sustained him. To Dillon, they were a demanding but fair audience. Not easy to please, but not impossible, either. They seemed glued to the action. On the other hand, he'd never sensed them laughing at any of his jokes.

"Battalion two, get up and run after them! Throw yourselves in front of them!"

He glanced up at the news helicopter that was defying the army's no-fly order. The camera up there recorded a dozen or more people, including one in a wheelchair, literally throwing themselves in front of vehicles that remorselessly rolled on over them.

Dillon shook his head. "Not enough." Raising his bullhorn, Dillon said, "Battalions three and four, run to the Triunfo! Run! And Kate? Drive the fuel truck back there."

CHAPTER 23
Rough Beasts, No Bethlehem

"SURE, I DID a tour in Afghanistan," Master Sergeant Matthew Tolliver said. "Iraq, too. None of that was good. But hey, one thing you can say about floating around on Navy ships, the squids keep a nice mess. Steak once a week. Fried chicken . . ."

Justin DeVeere was torn. Should he stay on the flatbed with the deranged marine? The truck of misfit toys? He had quickly grown bored with the old marine's war stories and reminiscences. But as an artist, this trip down the two-lane 95 through the utter wasteland of the Nevada desert was a field day.

I'm on a truck with an entire bestiary of monsters. And the sunset is gorgeous.

". . . ice cream. It's boring, but the Navy will definitely feed a man."

"Are you hungry, Tolliver?" Justin smirked.

"No," Tolliver replied. "I don't have a stomach anymore."

This was said without rancor, just a fact of life: *I don't have a stomach.*

What the hell lunatic asylum am I in?

He could jump off the truck at any point; no one was keeping him prisoner. But A) there was nothing but rock, sand, and scruffy plant life. And B) when would he ever get a chance to see a woman who could morph into an abomination that was half turtle, including a faintly purple shell?

But mostly it was A): it was a long, long, dry walk to anywhere. They were heading toward Las Vegas, and as it happened, Las Vegas was the nearest human habitation worth going to.

He slept for a while and dreamed of his long-lost patron and girlfriend, Erin O'Day. She had been killed.

He woke to a night sky and dropping temperatures made colder by the wind that buffeted the open truck bed. And tears on his cheeks. He wiped them away angrily.

He hadn't loved Erin, but he'd liked her. And she was rich and could have done amazing things for his career.

Career. As what? As a promising young art prodigy? Or as the monster who destroyed the Golden Gate Bridge?

Justin knew the answer. Even if he created art to rival DaVinci, Van Gogh, and Picasso it would never wipe away the image the world had of him. Never.

His stomach turned and his mouth twisted, and he wallowed for a while in self-pity. The phrase "not my fault that . . ." kept coming up, followed by various specifics. *Not my fault what happened on the plane at La Guardia; not my fault what happened on the bridge; not my fault that Erin was blown to pieces and died beneath an obscure lighthouse.*

In a world gone mad, how could anyone blame Justin DeVeere? Hadn't he told them all that Knightmare wasn't him but a whole separate person? Most of Justin knew this was nonsense, but enough of him was willing to at least pretend to believe it—when the lie was necessary. When accepting responsibility would leave him naked and defenseless in attempting to justify his actions.

"I have to believe in me even if no one else does."

"Eh?" Tolliver asked. The tank man had better-than-human hearing.

"Nothing," Justin said. "I was just—unh! Oh! Oh, shit!"

Justin had been on his rear end, sitting cross-legged, but now he writhed and rolled onto his side and slapped impotently at the pain chip still embedded in his neck, with wires tied directly to his spine.

"Pain chip?" Tolliver asked.

"Just a tap, not a . . . Ah! Dammit!"

"DiMarco," Tolliver snarled. "Or whoever took over for her. A little reminder from the Ranch that you're still their property."

"I need to find a doctor to get it out of me," Justin said. "It must work by satellite!"

The turtle woman—currently just a woman—said, "No, it's the cell towers. Their system uses cell-phone signals, wi-fi, direct radio. You need to find a place where there's no coverage."

"Not far now," Tolliver said. He pointed with his articulated mechanical arm.

Justin shook off the pain, which had been, as Tolliver suggested, just a quick tap, a reminder. He looked ahead and saw the glow of Las Vegas. There would be doctors in Vegas. There would be rich, lonely women looking for a handsome young . . . monster? No, no, artist. Artist.

Monster.

One of the truck passengers, a slight teenaged boy who'd been forced to take the rock along with a dose of hawk DNA, began to morph. The result was extraordinary, even with so little light. He had wings, which he kept folded. He was covered in feathers that ruffled in the stiff breeze. His face was still human, but dominated by oversized yellow eyes.

It was those hawk's eyes he trained on the city ahead. In a hushed, awestruck voice he said, "There are things burning. Big fires, at least two."

"Looks like they started the battle without us," Tolliver said.

But Justin's eye was looking elsewhere. At the moon, halfway up the sky in the east. A big yellow gibbous moon.

And the small, swift shadow that crossed it.

"Christ," Dekka said. It was all taking place a few hundred feet below them, illuminated by Las Vegas's eerie neon glow. Unbelievable scenes of innocent civilians crushed by tanks that had no other choice. Scenes of civilians tearing soldiers apart. In the middle of an American city.

Dekka saw Armo draw back, too sickened to watch.

Cruz watched it all, perhaps, Dekka thought, as a sort of grim penance for having come up with the idea of waiting to intervene. The smart move, but also the ruthless move, and Cruz had never struck Dekka as that kind of person. Sam had been that kind of person, as had Caine. The two great powers of the FAYZ had used that gift of ruthlessness in very different ways, but they had each been decisive. Cruz looked like she was shrinking into herself, wanting to be somewhere else, anywhere else. Dekka wondered if there was anything she could say to ease Cruz's pain. But anything she said would sound condescending and false. That was the damned thing about making life and death decisions: they could eat you up inside, and no one could really do much to help.

Francis Specter watched quietly. She was the new kid, the untested one. Dekka wondered how her peculiar power would even be useful when they finally got into the battle.

Whenever that was.

Only Shade avoided the window and watched the TV coverage from the news helicopter, supplemented by dozens of unenslaved tourists aiming iPhones through hotel windows. All video shown on TV was sound-off as a precaution, so the gruesome pictures had as soundtrack only the horrified exclamations of TV anchors.

"They're going around," Shade called, wincing and closing her eyes as what looked like a child emerged from beneath tank treads, roadkill in a pink, spangled Disneyland T-shirt.

Shade opened her phone, clicked on the maps, and held it

up for Dekka. "They'll most likely come back around Treasure Island," she reported. "That's, like, a mile north."

The same thought had obviously occurred to Dillon Poe,
because the mass of his own army was now running north.
The news said the Triunfo was under his control. It was north,
and his victims would have to run fast to get there before the
army turned back toward the Strip and cut them off.

"Did you drop this?" Cruz asked Dekka, holding up a
crumpled yellow Post-it note.

Dekka's eyes went wide. She practically snatched the paper
from Cruz and stuffed it deep in her pocket. "Thanks. Must
be an old shopping list."

Cruz nodded, a bit disappointed to discover Dekka lying.
The paper had not been a shopping list; it had borne six words.

If it has to be: me.

Cruz wondered if this had something to do with Dekka's
little tête-à-tête with Shade. She could ask, but now was not
the time.

Dekka watched and calculated and waited. She knew that
despite Cruz's strategic decision, she, Dekka, would be the
one to give the actual order to attack.

Possibilities:

One. Cut off Dillon's mob. But how? If they ignored tanks,
they'd ignore her. She would be left to use her power to
slaughter innocent people.

Two. Go after the Charmer. But where was he? On the
Strip or at the Triunfo? Some third place?

Three. Try to stop the tanks to avoid further massacres?

And leave the Charmer in charge of the city?

Her internal mental struggle must have been evident on her face because Cruz, Francis, and Armo were looking at her intently.

"Not yet," Dekka said.

Abaddon the Destroyer—Vincent Vu—was sort of excited to see the column of tanks charging straight at him down the freeway like single-file cavalry.

The disease he bore in his morph, the starfish densovirus, had already caused two of his limbs to break free, trailing viscera and goo. Now he sent them tube-crawling forward, his own slow-moving cavalry as his limbs grew to replace them.

"*Da da da da!*" Vincent sang a trumpet fanfare. "*Da! Dada da dada da daaaa!*"

There were two explosions. The smaller explosion—more a sound like a tornado's rushing wind—the round being fired; and a split second later . . .

BAM!

The first tank round hit one of Vincent's mini-me's and turned it into sushi confetti.

"Wow!" Vincent exclaimed. It was exciting! Much louder than he'd expected. He had two layers of voices in his head now, the silent ones urging him on, and his own schizophrenic hallucinations surprisingly urging a cautious retreat.

Well, he knew better than to trust *those* voices.

"I am Abaddon the Destroyer!" he cried in his thin voice.

At which a second round was fired, and this one hit one of his legs, exploded, and showered him with bloody bits of shredded starfish. He wiped the goo from his face.

The starfish would regenerate. *No problem,* he told himself, and believed it for as long as it took the second tank in line to peel left, swing its turret toward him, and fire.

The explosion was smaller, and Vincent taunted. "You cannot defeat Abaddon!"

But something was wrong. This round did not blow up and shower him with his own viscera, it just burned. It sat lodged in the thickest part of one of his limbs, all too near to the human part of him, and burned and burned, a furious fire, like a living thing, like some rabid beast.

The fire hurt, but in a distant sort of way. Yet there was no denying that it was consuming him. The moist starfish flesh bubbled and melted and oozed away from the fire. Furious white smoke rose and swirled around him, stinging his eyes.

"Wait!" Vincent yelled. "That's not fair, I can't see!"

He couldn't see, but now yes, yes, he was definitely feeling not the mind-shattering agony he'd have felt if he was fully human, but pain nevertheless; pain as the unquenchable fire burned his starfish flesh, eating its way up to where he was a shirtless kid who . . .

. . . who now, suddenly, felt the heat much more directly on his remaining human flesh. Unbearable heat. Unbearable pain.

My God! Oh, my God!

He tried to scream, only to gag on the billows of smoke.

Help me! Someone help me! I am Abaddon! he cried inwardly.

The Dark Watchers seemed rapt. Fascinated. Indifferent

to his agony as the fire curled and ashed his waist whips. His starfish body was half melted, a bubbling cauldron of magma, and he was sinking into it, sinking down helplessly.

He screamed soundlessly, his flesh melting, his mind a wild merry-go-round swirl of panic and self-righteous anger and now-intolerable pain.

"No!" he tried to cry, but his last word was a choking sound.

Vincent Vu, Abaddon the Destroyer, was reduced to a mound of flaming goo, like someone had dropped a marshmallow in a campfire.

Abaddon would destroy no more.

The tanks swerved around the fire and clanked on. They had lost just five minutes in destroying Vincent. A consequential five minutes.

CHAPTER 24
We Are the Chimpions

DRAKE MERWIN WAS now most of a face—he had a mouth, one eye, and one ear. He could see and he could hear. And because he was smashed against a boulder in a fairly upright position, he could watch the reassembly of his body.

This was not his first comeback from destruction. Brianna had used her machete and her super-speed to chop him to bits and scatter the bits far and wide in the FAYZ. It had taken him a while to come back from that.

He had been almost complete when he'd faced Sam the final time. In the breakdown of the FAYZ system, he had been weakened, and that weakening had resulted in his being burned to ashes.

For a long time there was no Drake Merwin.

And when he started to regrow, it was not from the ashes, but from one of Brianna's chunks. She had taken the time to bury some parts of him, and other parts she had hurled into the ocean. Ninety-plus percent of those bits and pieces had slithered together to create the Drake that Sam had destroyed, but one piece had not been part of that doomed Drake iteration precisely because Brianna had tossed it into the ocean.

That chunk of Drake had been eaten by a swordfish, who then swam out to sea. The resulting swordfish turd had been all that was left of Drake, so his regrowth had not had the benefit of being able to use existing bits and pieces; no, the turd had had to grow a whole new Drake. And that Drake, the Drake who'd been splattered everywhere by the missile, had only acquired eyes very late in the process, when he was already a mangled mass of pink flesh crawling blindly up onto the beach.

Months, that's how long it had taken him to regrow. In fact, it had been a full year before he was entirely, 100 percent himself. Well, himself plus Brittany.

But now he watched himself regrow much more quickly. The bits of him, the human shrapnel of him, crawled out of the rocks like shell-less snails and fitted themselves in place like so many puzzle pieces.

Some bits were completely unsalvageable—the right side of his face, his right eye—but to his great pleasure, his whip hand was already half regrown. He'd even managed to move it.

He was annoyed at Peaks for running off, annoyed even more that he'd somehow managed either to attract, or deliberately cause, the missile attack. And eventually that annoyance would result in Peaks being nailed to the wall of Drake's cave. He would extend Peaks's suffering, he would make Peaks pay, but it was more out of a sense of duty than the prospect of pleasure. Drake couldn't let Peaks get away with it, and he would absolutely reduce the man to a shattered, mutilated creature who would beg for death, but Drake knew he wouldn't enjoy it. Torturing Peaks wouldn't be fun. Not really.

Drake knew what would be fun. He knew *who* would be fun.

"Old hate is the best hate," Drake's mouth whispered.

And no hate was older than his hatred of Astrid. Astrid Ellison. Astrid the Genius. It was funny to Drake that so many in the FAYZ had disliked her, because he had to admit, she had been a formidable enemy. The kids had all—well, almost all—loved Sammy. Surfin' Sam, the reluctant hero. But if Sam was the Captain Kirk of the FAYZ, Astrid had been his Spock and Edilio his Riker and Albert his Scotty the engineer.

"Don't forget Dekka," Drake muttered to a passing horned toad. "His Sulu. His Worf."

Drake hated Dekka and Edilio and Albert and . . . well, pretty much everyone. But his dreams were of Astrid. She would be fun. She would try to engage him intellectually. She would play word games with him, desperately trying to trick him. He would let her beg and plead. And then he would whip the skin from her. But Astrid was tough, and oh, she would put up an excellent fight.

The joy would be knowing that she would be so aware of her own slow disintegration. Stupid people, weak people, they collapsed quickly and ended up just screaming and begging. Astrid would end up there, too, in the end, and she would hate him, but she would hate herself even more for being weak.

The only thing better would be to have Sam nailed to the opposite wall, forced to watch it all. To see Astrid degraded as Sam watched? He could not imagine anything better.

Why had he not gone after her already? Because she was in a major city and watched/guarded by cops. That was not a situation that lent itself to long, lazy days and nights of torture. He could easily get past whatever security was around her, but he would only be able to kill her before all hell came crashing down on him. The next time he was destroyed, someone might do a thorough job of it, and it might take him years to reassemble and regrow. Astrid might be an old woman by the time he was able to go after her.

"You don't want to rush your pleasures," he informed the toad, who cocked one bulbous eye at him and rudely snapped up and ate a small slithering chunk of Drake. He moved his stunted whip hand and the toad ran off.

Yes, it had not been possible to realize his fondest dream—not with cops and FBI and a whole metro area in his way. But Peaks had given him new hope. Peaks seemed to think the whole world was coming down around their ears. And if that was true . . .

Drake glanced down and saw a steel wire protruding from his chest. Ah, good old Brittany Pig, as immortal as he was. They would soon be back together. His body would complete itself. His whip would return.

And in a world that was falling apart, who could stop him from finding and taking Astrid?

"Not winning!" Dillon said with angry emphasis. "Not losing, but not winning, either."

One of his Cheerios had driven him back to the Triunfo in a shot-up Nissan Altima with two flat tires.

Not exactly a snow-white charger, he thought. And then, *Why is it always a snow-white charger? Is that racist? Can there be horse racism?*

He pulled out his notebook and scribbled, *horse racism?*

Dillon's surviving army of voice slaves had been sent running down Flamingo Road, then turned north on Frank Sinatra Drive, which fed into Sammy Davis Jr Drive.

Only in Vegas would directions include Frank Sinatra and Sammy Davis Jr. That could be a bit.

In the heat of the day, his instruction to run the whole way would probably have left 10 percent of his mob passed out or dead from heart attacks, but the night was cooling rapidly.

The enemy would of course translate the running mob as panic. They would follow, but they wouldn't want to stop them running . . . until they realized they were all going the same place.

I'm not winning, but I'm really pretty good at this.

"I think I'm getting good at this general thing," he said aloud.

To which Kate said, "Yes," and glared fear and hatred at him.

This next bit would be sketchy, hard to manage, Dillon

knew. As the Cheerio had driven him to the Triunfo, he'd put his mind to assembling a list of demands. He would voluntarily leave the city and the whole country, for that matter, if they gave him what he wanted. Taking over the world had become much less of a priority since the army had rolled into town; it was starting to look as if survival was the main goal.

Taking over the world to mere survival in what, a day?

He would need a helicopter, of course. Then a jet, a big one that could go a long way, fueled up and ready at the airport. And a hundred million dollars. That shouldn't be a problem in a place like Vegas, which was awash with cash.

Destination?

That was complicated. His power rested on being heard and understood, so ideally he wanted an English-speaking country. But Canada was well tied in to the US media, and they'd be more than ready by the time he reached . . . what was a Canadian city? Was Seattle in Canada? And England was such a long flight, they'd be even more ready. Might even shoot him down over the Atlantic.

Dillon had an image of himself in an inflatable raft yelling orders to passing whales. It was not reassuring or funny. Not really.

His mind passed wistfully over the idea of some remote Pacific island, but islands were traps.

Mexico. He would fly to Mexico. There he would make contact with a drug gang, take it over, and build a real army, an army of millions. Hah! Assuming enough people there spoke English.

He reached the Triunfo seconds ahead of the first runners,

sauntered in projecting all the arrogant control he could manage, spotted a Triunfo cocktail waitress, and yelled, "Get me a margarita. Extra salt!"

It would be his fourth drink, but stress and excitement— he would not allow the word "fear"—had kept him feeling all too sober. He opened a map app, typed in "Mexico," and tried to decide the best place to go. Wasn't Machu Picchu in Mexico? He Googled it: no. After some more Googling he came up with Culiacán, in Sinaloa, where the most notorious gang hung out.

Yeah, that'll work.

He pictured himself landing in his jet. Local dignitaries might meet him. Or Mexican cops. But even if they had ear coverings on, he'd be able to show them millions of dollars, and wasn't Mexico super corrupt? Eventually he'd be able to speak, and he would order them to take him to the drug gang's headquarters.

As more and more of his minions arrived, gasping and wheezing to form up in front of Triunfo, he got to work thumbing in an email.

Dear Former Powers That Be:
I am the Charmer. You've seen a small part of what I can do.

He paused to Google a scene from the movie *Tropic Thunder*, in which Tom Cruise screams threats into a phone.

So, if I were you, I'd take a big step back and literally f-ck your own face!

He wondered if he should include attribution. It was fatal to any comedy career to be called out for stealing a joke. Dillon had few morals—fewer with each passing hour—but he did not want to be accused of joke stealing. So he retyped:

> If I may paraphrase the brilliant Tropic Thunder . . . if I were you, I'd take a big step back and literally f-ck your own face!

That should do it.

> But I weary of conflict. I am not a bad person, but I will not be disrespected. So if you want me out of Las Vegas, I'm ready to go. All I ask for is sun, a beach, and plenty of margaritas. If you leave me alone, I'll leave you alone.
> So here's the deal:
> A helicopter on the roof of the Triunfo. The pilot will not wear ear covering.
> A fully gassed-up jet minimum size like an A-320. Pilot and flight attendants without ear covering.
> One hundred million dollars in cash.
> A guaranteed spot on Fallon, Colbert, or Kimmel. I'll do a tight five, maybe seven minutes. And I'll pretape it so you can check to make sure I don't, you know . . . say anything I shouldn't.
> A one-hour Netflix special.
> Give me all that, and I will happily live my life and not bother you anymore.
> Respectfully,
> The Charmer (Dillon Poe)

He emailed this to the three news networks. His control over the Triunfo staff was not absolute; there were still staff who had not heard his voice, but most of the employees were safely under control, and his Cheerios had orders to shoot anyone they thought was even slightly a threat.

His people, his army, his voice slaves were clustering in ever greater numbers in the circular driveway of the Triunfo. The Fashion Show Mall was across the street, Nordstrom a stone's throw away.

He nodded approvingly. Good. The street was much narrower here, and the hotel's entrance was relatively modest, which would make it harder for tanks to maneuver around.

Kate, the head Cheerio, arrived with the Chevron truck. It was too tall to fit beneath the hotel's overhang, so she parked it on the street, blocking the driveway entrance.

More and more gasping, staggering zombies . . . *No, wait,* Dillon thought, *that's a generic term.* He had his Cheerios, he needed a name for his army. Dillon's Danger Squad? That was funny. Kind of. Dillbots? That sounded a bit too trivial. Besides, he wasn't just Dillon Poe, he was the Charmer.

The Charmer's Champions? That could work. Wasn't at all funny, though. The Charmer's Chimps? The Charmer's Cholaborators?

"Wait . . . Chimpions! Hah! That's good." Using his bullhorn, he said, "You are all now honored, respected members of the Charmer's Chimpions. With an 'i' instead of an 'a.'"

The swelling mass of people did not know how to react. So they mostly just stared in a dazed way.

"Hey, come on, that was worth a laugh. Laugh!"

He had privately sworn never to use his power to get laughs, but this was different . . . in some way he couldn't quantify. And the sound of what was now more than a thousand people trying to laugh despite panting and wheezing with exhaustion was hysterically funny.

"Okay, that's enough. Stop laughing. Kate. Kate!" He yelled to be heard over the fading laughter. "Kate! Start . . . wait, you'll need help. You and you." He pointed at what he guessed were working guys, guys with muscles, anyway. "Go help Kate. Kate? Time to hose down my brave and loyal Chimpions."

He retreated inside as Kate and the two men labored to unlimber the fuel truck's hose.

ASO-6

AFTER MORE THAN twenty-four hours of battering and dragging, the *Nebraska*'s crew had been reduced by sixty-four deaths. The bodies could not be moved; they could only be tied down. Tied to pipes, to equipment that was no longer relevant. Bodies hung like effigies, like gruesome warnings.

It was very cold aboard the *Nebraska*. Very cold. Oxygen was not yet a problem, in part because so many fewer people were breathing it. Crewmen did not walk, they crawled, with cushions and life jackets tied to their heads like makeshift helmets. Survivors did their best to move food and water up and down the length of the boat, tapping on pressure hatches to signal that they had bread or a piece of sausage to share.

The emergency lights were fading.

A few crewmen still clung to hope. Most had given up. And many had lost their minds entirely under the assault. One of those was a petty officer named Debbie Forte, who had been locked up in the missile bay since the start. She was the only living person in the missile bay. She had tried to tie down the six men and woman beaten to death by the shaking, but it had been impossible, so bodies would tumble past when the chimera shook the boat. Her friends. Her people. People she had trained.

Forte was sure that the chimera was dragging them deeper and deeper. The boat would never float again, it no longer had even the theoretical ability to float again. Which meant they were all dead. It was just a matter of time.

But Forte knew what to do. It wouldn't even be a real act of self-sacrifice, not really, because she was a dead woman walking.

And she'd be damned if she let some monster do this to her boat, her people, and her. She knew what would kill the chimera.

She had access to weapons that would kill anything.

CHAPTER 25
Random Chance

"WHY DO YOU just play solitaire?"

Malik looked up slowly. A girl. Did he know her? Sure. Sure, Shade or someone had introduced her.

"It's a very . . . philosophical game," Malik said.

"It is?" Francis asked.

Malik nodded. "Yes. Each game reflects the reality of human life. I bring the intelligence DNA gave me. I use my experience. I apply my free will. And the cards are sorted by random chance. In fact, the odds of any hand of solitaire ever having been played are trillions to one. Each hand is a completely new set of possibilities. DNA, environment, free will, and . . . chance."

Is it like that for you, too, Dark ones? Do you have DNA? Are you shaped by experience?

All the while he played on. His 2,309th game. He held the phone in both hands, almost at arm's length, thumbs tapping. He had a streak going, six winning games.

"Ah, okay," Francis Specter said, and nodded.

Are you bored watching me play game after game?

"I'm Francis."

Malik saw her hand extended. It hovered in the air. He looked at it, trying to figure out what it meant. Then it came to him, almost as muscle memory, and he reached out and shook the hand.

"Malik Tenerife," he said.

"Cruz said that you can . . ."

"Cause pain," Malik said quickly. "Yes."

Your gift to me, eh? A life of living under your eyes, with you in my head, and the only escape is into agony and death.

"Yeah. This is all so weird, isn't it?"

Malik said nothing.

"The thing I can do . . . you know, my power—which just sounds crazy, doesn't it? My *power*?"

You don't like her, do you? You don't want me talking to her.

"What is your power?" Malik asked. He wasn't feeling especially curious. More he was curious about this vague feeling that *they* didn't like Francis.

Francis shrugged and looked at the seat beside Malik. Malik looked at the seat beside him as well, slowly trying to guess the significance and . . . Oh, of course. "Want to sit?"

She did.

"I've never been in a real fight before," she said. She twisted her fingers. She was afraid.

"I was," Malik said. Then, with a hint of his old, dry humor, added, "It didn't go well for me."

"Cruz told me."

Malik said nothing.

"I don't know what to call the thing I do," Francis went on. "I can go sort of . . . around things. Through things." She shrugged. "It's hard to explain. Normal words don't work."

Words don't work so well in describing you, either.

Malik turned to look at her. She was just a kid. Kind of tough-looking. Dirty, secondhand clothes, but with some style, some panache.

"Try," he said.

"Well, it's like . . ." She took her time thinking about it. "Okay, it's like if you'd never seen blue and I was trying to describe it. Only this isn't colors, it's shapes. Things that should be solid aren't. Things that should be square, like a wall, are kind of . . . flat. That's kind of it. It's like I'm still me, but everything else is flat. And I can see inside things. It's kind of gross, actually. I mean, when I see a person I see everything at once, their face, their eyes, but also their lungs and their guts and, well, everything."

Malik stared hard, his game forgotten. "You see inside people?"

"Inside, outside, all at once. I know they're people, I see their faces, but at the same time it's like they've been turned inside out."

No, Malik, no excitement, not yet. No hope. Nothing . . . yet.

Malik said, "Cruz. Can I borrow your Moleskine?"

Cruz hoped someday to write. She did at times, bits of this and that, which she noted in neat handwriting in her purple Moleskine.

"Don't read my stuff," Cruz warned, handing over the

Moleskine open to a blank page.

Malik drew a square. He drew two eyes on the edge of the square. "His name is Frank. Flat Frank."

"Okay," Francis said cautiously, like maybe Malik was nuts.

"Frank is two-dimensional. He can't see us because we are 'up' and he doesn't have an 'up.' But we can see all of him at once. His edges *and* his inside."

"Right."

"Real people are three-dimensional. But a four-dimensional person would see inside of us as easily as we see inside of Frank. A 4-D person would see your face and your brain, your body and your heart."

"Ah. Okay. So . . . when I do the thing I do, I'm like a 4-D person?"

Malik looked at her.

No, Dark ones, I won't push her away.

"When you morph, how do they feel to you?" Malik asked.

"They?"

Malik felt something. Hard to name it. It was like the feeling of a jigsaw puzzle piece snapping into place. The feeling of something fitting.

"The Dark Watchers," Malik said. "When you morph."

"I don't . . ." She frowned, half convinced he was teasing her.

"When you morph, when you change, when you are able to go through solid objects, do you feel like you're being watched? Like there's someone in your head that isn't you?"

The old Pink Floyd lyric came to him. *There's someone in my head, but it's not me.*

Francis shook her head and her frown deepened.

Malik felt his heart skip, flutter, then settle. *Don't get ahead of yourself, Malik.*

Are you hearing this? Of course you are. I know you felt the wave of pain I sent you.

Malik said, "Cruz."

Cruz came over and stuck out her hand for her Moleskine. "You done?"

Malik met her gaze. "Francis doesn't feel the Dark Watchers."

"Lucky her," Cruz said, took the notebook, and returned to her vigil at the window.

"Lucky," Malik said, and smiled. "When you do your thing, Francis . . . this will sound wrong, but, anyway, do you keep your clothing? I mean, you can do this with your clothes on?"

Francis shifted a bit farther away on the couch. Malik couldn't blame her.

"It's not a creepy question, there's a reason," Malik said.

"Yeah, of course I keep my clothes on."

Well, well.

Well, well, well, well, well.

"Of course you do," Malik said, nodding. There was a change in his voice. He was still dreamy and distant, almost without affect. But something with sharper edges was taking shape in his mind. "Of course you do."

"Why?"

"Because you may be more powerful than you can imagine," Malik said. "You may even be *too* powerful."

Francis, completely perplexed, just nodded and said, "Okay, I'll be careful then. I'd better . . ." She nodded toward the group at the window, got up, and left.

I don't know if you have DNA, Dark ones, don't know whether experience shapes your lives, but you have free will. And you have random chance, don't you? Oh, hell yes, you do. And I think maybe it will bite you in the ass.

"But are you watching, or are you playing?" Malik muttered under his breath. "That's the mystery. Is this a show? Or is it a game?"

Tom Peaks had much the same problem as Dekka: it was hard to plan a battle when you didn't know who you were fighting. But it seemed to him that the safe bet was still to back the military. They would see his usefulness, his power, and if not welcome him back, at least not try and kill him.

Maybe.

In a perfect world, he would sneak into Vegas unnoticed, spy out the situation, and get the lay of the land before revealing himself. But given what he'd gleaned from the car radio, the situation was chaotic, violent, and completely unpredictable.

The one thing Peaks was pretty sure of was that in the end, the superpowered villain, Dillon Poe, would be taken out by the awesome might of the military.

It still amazed him how painless it was to morph. It seemed impossible that a human body could grow horned, armored skin and rise to fifty feet, let alone have a belly full of liquid fire, and yet feel only a certain . . . itchiness. But he supposed the alien virus engineers had realized that the powers wouldn't be much use if the pain killed you in the process.

From fifty feet up, his view of the city was much improved, his morphed eyes shifted all colors toward green. His ability to travel without a road was even more improved. Each step was twenty feet, and Dragon could move quickly when he chose.

Fwoo-WHUMP! Fwoo-WHUMP! Fwoo-WHUMP!

Each step was a rush of air and an impact that shook the ground. He loped through the dark desert, crushing desperate shrubs and badger burrows, startling jackrabbits into sudden flight, shaking the ground as his many tons of weight landed on feet that were more like talons.

No news helicopter spotted him. No drone popped off a Hellfire in his direction. The highway was off to the right, a row of streetlights, flashing emergency lights, flashlights, interior car lights. Ahead the much more enticing lights of the city.

It was glorious stomping through emptiness, feeling his huge muscles contract and release, feeling within him the killing fire.

Who could stop Dragon? I am mighty! I may be the mightiest creature ever to walk the earth!

Peaks knew these kinds of thoughts were absurd, but when he was *Dragon* he felt such a power high it was hard not to revel in it. Let them all come at him, Dekka, Shade, Knightmare, what did he care? He would destroy them. He took particular pleasure in constructing an imaginary con-frontation where he faced Dekka and burned her to ashes.

Of course, the eyeless eyes were on him, inside him, above and behind and through him. Their attention tempered his giddiness. They were a constant reminder that human power, even Rockborn human power, was a product of some far superior intelligence.

What did they want, those Dark Watchers? What did they gain from this? Was it all some needlessly elaborate ruse to destroy humanity? But if that was the goal, surely they could have engineered the rock virus to simply wipe people out.

Drake had said it was all TV. But Drake, while clever enough in his own vile way, did not even have a high school diploma, let alone an advanced degree. Of course Drake would seize on a simplistic analogy.

Well, he would make short work of Dillon Poe, save the day, then humbly offer his services to the army. The army might now be more open to a giant fire-breathing reptile than the contemptible DiMarco—if she had even survived the attack on the Ranch.

And then? Return to his family?

That thought stabbed him in the heart. He had barely thought of his wife or kids because, well, he'd been . . . what? He'd been sitting in a torture chamber with Drake Merwin?

He had avoided thinking of his family, Peaks knew, because it hurt. For all the—in his mind necessary—ruthlessness he'd shown in building the Ranch, for all the violence he had committed as Dragon, he did still love his kids.

Tom Peaks, fifty feet tall and breathing fire, still conjured up images of kissing his kids good night. Right about now they would be in bed. Had they brushed their teeth? Had they done their homework?

Was there anything he could do, *ever*, that would allow him to see his family again?

Saving the day. Being a hero. Redeeming himself. Somehow. *Somehow.*

Here I come to save the day, Tom Peaks thought as he marched toward the lights.

They could no longer see the action from the window of the suite at Caesars. What they had now was just what came from the news chopper, and whatever video the networks picked up. Jerky, choppy videos that might be minutes old.

"This isn't good," Dekka said.

"No," Shade agreed.

Cruz was not so sure. She was relieved to have the horror farther away. If she never saw another human being crushed beneath a tank, it would be too soon. She was sickened by it all, sickened by the violence and the pure malice that must fill the mind of Dillon Poe. What kind of a human being did this? What kind of human being thought he had a right to take over people's lives, to use them like puppets? To send them to their own deaths with murder on their consciences and innocent blood on their hands?

"We need eyes closer up," Dekka said. Cruz glanced at her and felt something off. Dekka was carefully not looking at her. Too carefully. Shade, too, did not look at Cruz. The two of them let the silence stretch.

"Oh," Cruz said.

Now they turned sad eyes on her.

Cruz nodded slowly. "Oh," she said again. Feeling like she was announcing her own death sentence, she said, "I can do it." The words weighed tons. She had to push them out.

Neither Dekka nor Shade wasted time pretending to disagree.

"How should I . . . how should I look?" Cruz asked, wishing she didn't sound so scared. But, dammit, who wouldn't be scared?

"Like anyone but yourself," Shade said. "But not someone famous, that might get his attention. But, come to think of it, why be visible at all?"

Cruz nodded, too fast, a nervous gesture that went on for too long.

"You'll be fine, Cruz," Shade said gently. "You were amazing at the hospital. You can do this." She took Cruz's hand and squeezed it. Shade had once felt an almost parental affection for Cruz, automatically seeing herself as the leader and Cruz as the led. Malik had changed all that. Malik was the living, breathing, unmistakable proof that Shade was not as clever as she'd thought. Malik's existence was a big finger of doubt pointed straight at her. With the arrival of Dekka, Shade had felt herself willingly assuming a subordinate role. It was a relief not making every decision.

A part of Cruz—a big part—appreciated Shade's kind words. But another part was silently screaming, *You got me into this, you crazy, obsessed head case!*

"Okay, so . . . now?" Cruz asked.

"Listen," Shade said. "You're going to have your phone connected to me, all right? I'll be downstairs, and I'll be ready.
Anything goes wrong and I'm on you in a heartbeat."

Cruz nodded again. "Yep."

Can you outrun a bullet, Shade?

"I guess I'll go invisible." She tried for a joke. "I'm too nervous to think of looking like anyone."

"I'd go with you, Cruz, but I guess I'd be kind of notice-
able." Armo made a sad smile. "But look, if anything goes
wrong, I won't be as fast as Shade, but I'll get there."

Cruz nodded, not trusting her voice. Armo didn't really
know her, might not even know quite what she was. But she
believed he would try to save her.

On stiff legs she walked from the room, with Shade for
once walking behind her. The casino staff—many bandaged,
with torn uniforms and haggard looks—nodded respectfully
as they passed. Strange, Cruz thought, how quickly people
could adjust to the impossible, when they had motive enough.

"I live in a world where lots of people hate me for not being
what they want me to be," Cruz said as they rode down in
the elevator. "But now they're tipping their hats to a pair of
Rockborn monstrosities."

"Mmmm," Shade said. "I don't mean to disillusion you,
Cruz, but there are a lot of idiots in the world."

"Two of them in this elevator."

Shade blew out a breath. "It's hard to argue with that." She leaned forward and pushed the stop elevator button.

"What?" Cruz asked.

"You don't have to do this, Cruz. You don't have to play hero; that's not what you signed up for."

"No, I signed up to be a sidekick," Cruz replied, trying and failing to make it a joke.

"Well, Robin, I think you picked the wrong damn Batman."

A few minutes one way or the other, and we would never have met. A roll of the dice.

Perfect for Las Vegas.

Their eyes met. *It's different now,* Cruz thought. *Something is different.* When life was more normal, Shade and I would talk like friends, like equals, but there was always something in Shade's gaze that marked her as dominant. In charge. After the rock, that became even more pronounced. Shade almost craved battle, each confrontation a rehearsal for the revenge she could never achieve against a creature long dead.

And there had always been something in Cruz's own eyes, no doubt, that signaled her submission. Her willing, even eager submission. Shade was smarter. Shade was stronger willed. Shade was a "real" girl. So defined, so definite.

So different from me.

What am I? What the hell am I? Even my power is about concealment—proof that the alien rock had a sense of humor?

Yet, when she looked in Shade's eyes, she saw herself reflected now as an equal.

Suddenly Cruz laughed. "Malik's list. His, what do you call it?"

"His superhero taxonomy?" Shade said, and curled her lip.

"Monster, villain, hero," Cruz said. "There's no category called 'sidekick.'"

"Well," Shade said almost tenderly, "you are not a monster, Cruz. And you are definitely not a villain."

Cruz pushed the emergency stop button and the elevator began to descend once again.

"I'm scared to death to go out there," Cruz said, fighting back tears. "But I'm doing this."

"Kind of the definition of a hero, isn't it?" Shade said. "Scared to death; doing it anyway."

CHAPTER 26
The Hero Thing

CRUZ WAS USHERED past casino security and stepped out into the world.

Cruz disappeared. Completely.

The first thing she focused on was a dead body.

Since being swept up in the madness, Cruz had seen more violence and death than she had in her previous seventeen years of life, by a factor of a thousand times. But she was not inured. The body was a middle-aged woman. Her clothing was twisted, her blouse exposing white belly. Her mouth was twisted into a look of horror and pain. Someone had stabbed her in both eyes, then left the knife sticking from the side of her neck.

Cruz stepped around her. Down the long driveway past other dead. Past wounded who still crawled and snapped at the air, still trying to obey the Charmer, even as blood loss and now thirst and hunger dragged them to the arms of the Grim Reaper.

It was a long walk to the Triunfo. Cruz stuck to the sidewalk. A man bumped into her, spun, blinked, and seeing nothing, shrugged it off.

People are all about vision. They will dismiss touch, smell, scent, hearing unless their sight confirms.

She walked quickly when she focused, slowed when she did not. Once or twice she broke into a trot, but her limbs were leaden with dread and she couldn't keep it up.

And the oppressive attention of the Dark Watchers was on her. She had dealt with them during her protracted time at the hospital, but it had made her less, not more, immune to them. It felt wrong, unjust, for them to be watching from safety. It felt somehow sacrilegious that they enjoyed slaughter and pain and fear, and Cruz was convinced that's what they were doing: enjoying.

She considered calling her mother. Talking to her. Telling her . . . what, exactly? That Cruz loved her? She did, but love was only a part of what she felt. That generous emotion was mixed with feelings of betrayal, of resentment.

Hi, Mom, I'm probably about to die, but I love you. Just one thing: Why did you never defend me from Dad?

Explain that, Mom. You knew how scared I was. You knew how vulnerable I was. And you watched him bully and sneer and belittle, and you said nothing.

When she considered calling her father, she quickly dismissed the notion. He would be glad she was gone. He might not want her dead, but gone? Gone would be just fine with him.

And that, she realized, was the whole list of people she cared anything about, aside from Shade. And Malik. And increasingly, Dekka.

And Armo, though that was in a slightly different category.

She laughed silently at her own absurd nascent crush on him. Yes, he was gorgeous. And, despite what Cruz had seen of him in the heat of battle, in calmer times he was . . . well, kind of sweet. Centered. Funny, sometimes. But he was also a white, cis-male, presumably hetero dude who would be horrified by the notion of anything more than friendship. He would think she was creepy. A freak of nature. Delusional.

Behind her back he might laugh at her. Call her a tranny. Cruz forced herself to see that, to recognize her own foolishness.

People like me don't get happy endings.

Once, long ago . . . well, not so long ago really, it only felt that way . . . Once Shade had said that hope was the best form of torture.

Maybe. But how the hell could you live without it?

She knew deep down in her soul that her life would not somehow end with her happily with someone like Armo. Not that there could possibly be anyone *like* Armo; he was . . . unique. More an ideal than a real boy, Cruz told herself. A fantasy, not a reality. A fantasy even if it had been smart, beautiful, confident Shade setting her sights on him.

Let alone me.

Cruz heard gunfire and flinched. Invisibility did not make

her invulnerable. She was still a body, she was just an invisible one.

She slowly rounded a curve in the Strip and saw the Triunfo rising behind the mall. The casinos to her right were still bright by normal standards, but muted for Las Vegas. The Triunfo still blazed gold.

She wished she'd brought water. She was finding it hard to swallow.

The army column had finally, after the delay in dealing with Vincent Vu, made its way back to the Strip. They'd been too late to cut off Dillon's voice slaves. The army column was coming up slowly, cautiously behind her now, and for the life of her Cruz couldn't tell whether that was a good thing or bad.

A crazed man burst from the Nieman Marcus store at the mall and ran screaming toward her. Cruz recoiled before realizing he could not see her. He ran on into the street.

The air stank of the burning Venetian and Treasure Island.

A left. It was here she had to turn. And here she saw the mob in front of the Triunfo. She crossed herself and wished she had a rosary. This was a mob completely under control of Dillon Poe. A mob that could be turned into howling murderers with a few words from the Charmer.

A mob ahead; a column of tanks coming up behind.

Cruz raised her phone, still connected to Shade, who had her phone on mute in case a sound gave Cruz away. Everyone in the group was in morph lest they overhear some command of Dillon's. Cruz whispered, "I'm here."

She slowed and narrated. "I'm at Triunfo. There's a big

crowd, like maybe a thousand people. The front doors are smashed in. A Chevron truck is blocking the driveway. I see people up on the overhang, you know the thing that sticks out over the driveway? The windows up there are broken out."

Cruz reached the edge of the mob and stopped talking. She searched for, then found, Dillon Poe. He was atop the overhang, walking back and forth and seeming to talk to himself. As she watched, Dillon grinned, pulled out a notebook, and scribbled.

The gesture was so like herself when she would have an idea and pull out her Moleskine. She pushed the thought away: she had nothing in common with this monster.

Then she saw the the cheerleader awkwardly unlimbering a hose on the Chevron truck.

Behind her, the army tanks *clank-clank-clank*ed their way along, closing the distance.

Cruz looked up at Dillon. Objectively he was terrifying, bizarre, a green-scaled reptile in a tattered tuxedo. But for some reason people did not see him that way. And, Cruz supposed, if she was de-morphed, she might see him the way they apparently did. But she was in morph, so his charm did not touch her.

Suddenly a bullhorn crackled and screeched to life. Dillon said, "Okay, show 'em the first sign!"

Two people peeled off from the crowd and ran toward the lead tank holding a piece of poster board, on which was written, *Stop right there: I am ready to negotiate.*

The tanks did not stop.

"Kate!" Dillon yelled. "Time to spray!"

To Cruz's utter horror, the cheerleader on the truck turned a valve and liquid first spit and sputtered and then flowed. The smell was instantly recognizable as gasoline. The cheerleader played the hose over the mob like a suburban mom playing with her kids in the backyard. Tears ran down her face; she was sobbing like a heartbroken child, but she did not stop.

"Hey, what's going on?" people asked. But did not move.

"That's gas!" another said. And likewise did not move.

Then Dillon called to another cheerleader, who ran from the second-story window that had been broken out to allow access to the overhang. And she carried something small in her hands.

"Careful with that," Dillon ordered. "That's a collector's item!"

Dillon took the object in his hands, held it up as if for inspection, then began earnestly winding a key. Only then did Cruz recognize the object as a wind-up toy. A little car or truck, a piece of junk from a souvenir shop.

What? Why?

But then, as the Charmer walked to the edge of his platform and held out his hand, she understood. The gas fumes were overpowering. If the Charmer held a lit match up above in the rising fumes it might ignite the fuel. But a sparking wind-up toy? If he dropped it, it would fall to the ground below, crisscrossed by rivulets of gas. He would have perhaps a second or two . . .

"Second sign, go!" Dillon ordered.

Two more of his mob, hair limp from gasoline, ran with a piece of poster board whose ink was smearing.

All it takes is a spark. If I drop it, they all burn.

"No," Cruz whispered. Then, forgetting about concealment, she yelled into the phone. "Shade! *Now! NOW!*"

Dillon, hearing Cruz's voice looked sharply at . . . at nothing. And at that moment a shot rang out from an army sniper on the roof of the mall.

Crack!

It was night. It was a long shot to make. And rising gas fumes distorted the light.

"Aaaarrrgh!"

The bullet meant for Dillon's heart flew and hit his left collarbone. He twisted as if punched by a strong man. He dropped to one knee. His wind-up toy dropped to the overhang and fired off multicolored sparks as it scurried around.

For a moment the toy was lost to view. And then, suddenly, it flew over the edge of the overhang and spiraled down, still sparking.

The mob, unable to move, screamed.

The word "now" seemed to take a long time to Shade.

She was out of the casino doors, down the driveway and turning onto the Strip before the "w" was done resonating.

She had run fast before. But this was Cruz.

She felt her clothing flap and shred. She felt the way her Plasticine body reshaped itself to use the wind to push her down, to keep her from flying off wildly into the air like some out-of-control race car.

Her legs were a blur. Her hands moved so fast she felt the heat of friction.

The Strip blew past. Bodies were blurs.

She skidded into a turn and there were the tanks. She ran past them, a whirlwind, a sudden gust of wind like a tractor trailer passing at a thousand miles an hour.

In a split second she saw it: the gas truck. The immobilized mob. The sparking toy twirling slowly down and down.

At any second the gas fumes would . . .

No time!

She kicked off, leaped into the air going the speed of sound, bounced off a man's shoulders, stretched out her hand . . .

With her accelerated vision she saw the very moment a spark caught the vapor. Saw the spark become a flame, a slow-motion fire rose unfolding in midair.

Shade snatched the toy in midflight, closing her fist around it to stop it sparking.

The wind of her passing sucked the oxygen away, and the flame . . . died.

Shade landed at the far edge of the mob, but it was an uncontrolled landing, and she plowed into three people, a hundred pounds of armored girl moving at eight hundred miles an hour, killing two instantly, spinning the other like a top.

Shade rolled away her momentum, stood, and threw the toy as far as she could. It landed on the roof of the mall.

Atop the overhang, a bloody, roaring Dillon was being half carried by his cheerleaders, trying to get back through the broken window to relative safety.

Shade shut her eyes to the destruction her landing had caused—no time for that now. She ran, leaped, and landed on the overhang. Dillon was being dragged down the hallway, yelling, cursing. Shade would have him in seconds. But now she heard the slow, slow sound of Cruz's voice in the phone.

"S-h-a-d-e!"

At the same moment she felt a vibration. That, too, was slowed down, which just made it all the more puzzling. She glanced back. And froze.

Dragon had arrived.

CHAPTER 27
Dragon and Gasoline

DILLON WAS CRYING. The pain was incredible. It came in waves, wave upon wave, faster and faster. His shirt was soaked with blood, soaked as if he'd been caught in a sudden rain shower of blood.

"Get me to my room!" he bellowed.

His Cheerios hauled him to a room, and as he entered he saw himself in the full-length mirror. He almost fainted. The front of his shoulder was red around a single round hole. But the back of his shoulder was a crater. The bullet had done what it was designed to do—to tumble and twist its way through flesh at incredible speed. The result was an exit wound six inches across, tattered flesh and bits of shattered bone, the pulsing worms of arteries and veins.

"Oh, God, I'm going to die! I'm going to die!"

The aspiring comic in him saw nothing funny in this.

The Cheerios laid him on the bed, groaning and weeping.

"Get me a doctor! Get me a doctor!"

The women all obeyed instantly and raced from the room.

Too late it occurred to Dillon that he was now alone. Alone, in agony, and bleeding onto the bedspread.

"Peaks!" Dekka yelled.

The TV cameras were all on the massive lizard creature people called Dragon. But she knew the monster was her old nemesis, Tom Peaks.

"Okay," Dekka said to Armo, Malik, and Francis. "The situation is clear enough now. That is Tom Peaks, the man who created the Ranch. Some things might still be confused, but one thing is crystal clear: that asshole needs to die!"

She strode purposefully to the door and opened it. Casino security was outside. "I need a car. Now!"

Jody Wilkes, head of casino security, had entirely accepted Dekka's authority in dealing with anything not actually inside the casino.

"SUV?" Wilkes asked.

"Yeah."

"You want some volunteers to go with you?"

Dekka shook her head. "The creep, Dillon, isn't dead yet, and his voice might still reach anyone you send. We've got this. But thanks."

She went back inside. "Okay, we're getting in an SUV—in morph—and we're going after Peaks."

Malik nodded slightly, and seemed distracted. Francis just gulped and nodded.

Armo said, "OK." He grinned at Dekka. "See? I am totally doing what you want."

"Only because you can't wait to get into it," Dekka said.

"Well . . . yeah. Duh."

They rode the elevator down. The elevator music was play-ing "Maybe I'm Amazed," which would not have been her first choice for a theme song as they went into battle.

Dekka looked Francis over. She was both beautiful and disturbing. Her shape had not changed, nor her size, and she was dressed in the clothes she'd come in. But every exposed part of her—face, hands, neck, even her hair—was a bright, swirling rainbow. Like someone slowly spinning a color wheel. There were reds bleeding into violet, greens turning blue, bright orange and yellow whorls. And there was some-thing else, something Dekka couldn't put a name to. It was a depth of field, a sense that the colors were not on the surface but extended into Francis, like her skin was just the surface layer of a lake of colors.

Francis's eyes were stunning to look at, infinite pools of deepest violet and red, shifting highlights of gold and green. They were hypnotic, surreal.

"I think we have your superhero name," Dekka said.

"What?"

"Rainbow," Dekka said.

Malik leaned back against the mirrored wall. "Francis. Do you feel them now?"

Francis shrugged. "Feel what?"

Dekka frowned and met Malik's gaze. "She doesn't feel them," Malik said. "There's something about—"

He did not finish, for the elevator had reached the ground floor. Two civilians who'd been drafted into casino security stood pointing guns at them.

"It's us," Dekka said.

It was a long walk to the front door of the casino, a walk through slot machines, some of which had been broken off their stands and dragged to the door to form part of an impressively weird barricade. The barricade was lined with casino security and cocktail waitresses and more drafted tourists, all looking grim.

They pushed past, went out, and saw a black SUV waiting, engine running, doors open. Wilkes was there.

"Last chance," Wilkes said.

"Yeah," Dekka said. "But no. And thanks, Wilkes."

Wilkes nodded and from the door a voice yelled, "Kick some ass, Lesbokitty!"

Dekka's grin was feline, baring too-sharp teeth. "Lesbokitty, Berserker Bear, and Rainbow. We just need a ridiculous name for Malik and we'll be a damn *Sesame Street* spin-off."

Dekka climbed behind the wheel. Armo took shotgun. Francis sat in the back beside Malik. "I'm not sure how to use your powers, Francis," Dekka said, making eye contact in the rearview mirror. "So . . . improvise."

Tom Peaks was one of the few people in the world who could correctly interpret a flash of fire, a rush of wind, and random people brutally knocked to the ground.

"Well, if it isn't Shade Darby," he said in a voice that matched his size.

The situation was straightforward to Peaks: the speed demon had to die. There was a mob of civilians, all damp for some reason, presumably innocent people fleeing the violence. Between him and the mob and Darby, a hundred yards of open street.

He saw her for a split second as she hesitated atop the overhang. He saw her, and she saw him.

In a heartbeat she would be on him. He opened his mouth and vomited fire, aiming it at the ground that separated them, so that if she came at him she'd have to pass through magma first.

But Shade was already there! He felt the rush of wind, heard a sonic boom, felt a faint impact on his shoulder, and there she was, her streamlined face vibrating inches from his.

He heard a buzzing sound like an angry wasp.

The gout of fire cleared his mouth.

Then, like a buzz being slowed down so that it was just barely understandable, he heard, "No. Fire. *Gas!*"

By the time she'd spoken, and he'd deciphered and begun to puzzle it out, it was done: hundreds of gallons of napalm were already cascading and spreading down the pavement.

Out of the corner of his eye he saw a baby snatched from his mother's arms. The baby seemed to fly through the air at running speed, carried away by someone or some force he could not see.

Ah, that would be Cruz, he thought.

Shade leaped from his shoulder, a blur.

The magma rolled forward.

Gas? Gas?

"No," Peaks whispered as the enormity of his error flashed through his brain. *"NO!"*

Hundreds of gallons of gasoline, some on the sidewalk,

some on the street, and far too much in the hair, clothing, and skin of a thousand helpless people, ignited.

Cruz set the baby down on the sidewalk. It was the best she could do.

She started to run back to see whether she could drag anyone else to safety. . . .

The explosion knocked her on her back.

She felt a wave of searing heat. She gasped, and for a moment there was no oxygen to breathe and she was like a landed fish. She rolled to shield the baby, but the explosion was already past. The blue blanket singed. The baby's little knit cap crisped. Cruz used her body to smother the flames. The baby's eyes opened, unfocused blue. His cupid's bow mouth gasped for air.

Cruz pushed herself up, found oxygen, filled her lungs, and raised the infant to her mouth. She blew air into it, watched the baby's lungs fill. The temporary vacuum was followed by an inrush of air carrying the stink of gasoline and charred flesh. Cruz held the child and looked helplessly at a scene from the nightmares of a madman.

Men and women stood, screaming, howling, but unable to move. Their hair burned like they were torches. Their clothing curled and crisped, revealing blistering flesh beneath.

"God, no! God, no! God, no!" Cruz cried.

Human fuel, hair and fat, was lit by burning gasoline.

Cruz turned away, held the baby close, and ran.

CHAPTER 28
A Bonfire of Innocents

"NO!" DEKKA YELLED as she slammed on the brakes and skidded to a halt. She was out of the door in a heartbeat, but by then Armo was out and running.

He ran straight at the burning mass, arms outstretched. He was like a harvesting combine, knocking people back and scooping them up. He ran with four burning people, hurled them onto the unburned sidewalk across the street, and threw himself bodily on them, using his mass to one by one extinguish the flames, even as his fur singed and burned.

Shade Darby was suddenly there, right in front of Dekka. She pointed, her arm vibrating like a tuning fork. "Dekka! Shred! Smother!"

Dekka followed the direction of her arm: the overhang!

She raised her hands and roared like the mother of all lions. The overhang began to shred, bits of steel and plaster and wood and gravel. Dekka sprayed it over the burning people, a fire extinguisher of debris.

Too little. Too late.

Dozens, maybe hundreds had already died. More would be scarred for life.

Her effort had saved some. But only a very small . . . some.

"Armo!" Cruz appeared, a baby in one arm, kneeling over Armo. She batted at flames that had caught in his fur. "Are you okay? Armo!"

He blinked up at her.

"Take care of the baby!" he yelled, leaped to his feet, and went charging back into the burning crowd. He grabbed burning people and literally threw them clear of the gas. He bear-hugged people, smothering the fire on their clothing and flesh. His feet were covered in burning gasoline, but he roared on, oblivious to the pain, fearless, mad with horror and rage.

Shade tried to think. Tried to reason. Enough wind and she might deprive the fire of oxygen as she had in leaping to snatch Dillon's sparking toy. But how? If she ran around and around, would she just draw the fire ever outward?

She was watching human beings burn in what to her was slow motion. She could see individual blisters forming on cheeks. She could see hair go from singed to aflame. She watched mouths desperate for air inhale nothing but fire.

She froze for what felt like a terribly long time. Her brain just seemed to shut down. For a moment even the Dark Watchers were unnoticed.

Then she saw Armo, lumbering in near-comic slo-mo, gathering up burning people, and she moved.

Shade snatched two people, one with each hand, and ran. Ran down the line of tanks, ran so fast that the people she pulled did not drag along the ground, but flew. Her speed extinguished the flames but both people, two women, one older, one barely Shade's age, were covered in raw red flesh.

It was about half a mile to the fountains and man-made lakes in front of the Wynn casinos. Shade skidded to a stop and simply threw both burn victims into the water.

No, no, no.

Peaks turned away. Turned and ran in great, ground-pounding leaps.

No, no, no!

My God, they would think he had done it! They would think he had burned those poor people! They would think he was in league with the Charmer!

No!

The whole world had seen the Ranch. The whole world had seen him rampaging around the Port of Los Angeles. But he could rationalize those, he could try and explain, he could . . . he could someday face his children . . .

I didn't do this! I didn't know!

He had been trying to defend himself, that was all. He had tried to defend himself against the Rockborn monster Shade Darby.

Would his kids see the video?

Would they blame him?

He ran, and as he ran a tank shell raced after him. It struck him in the spine and exploded.

All fifty feet of him flew forward under the impact. He slammed down hard, crushing a car beneath him like a soda can. He tried to stand, but his legs would not work. He twisted his massive reptilian head and stared at the bottom half of Dragon, twisted, skewed, attached now only by skin and viscera.

And liquid fire spilled from his split gut, bubbling out like a volcano.

No! No! He couldn't die like this. He couldn't die with the whole world thinking . . . but his mind . . . his thoughts . . . the Dark Watchers . . . No . . .

He felt the light of his mind flicker and fade.

He formed one last, desperate thought.

De-morph!

Francis Specter stood helpless, paralyzed by the sheer, sickening horror. In morph, Francis's world was bizarre and twisted, lines of light, geometric shapes, but none of that mattered to her now, because her power had made the dying visible in a way no human had ever seen. She saw at once the outsides and the insides of the burning. She watched fire eat its way into their muscle and tendons. She saw the way steam formed pockets beneath skin and within organs. Saw those organs burst.

Malik was beside her. He stood frozen, watching.

"Fire," Malik said. Like that one word was everything. He touched his arm. He looked down at his uncanny flesh. Then he looked at her and she saw his eyes and the pink mass of brain behind it. Saw his mouth move and the tongue within and the squeezing and releasing of his esophagus, and the vibration of his vocal cords.

"Take me to him," Malik said.

"To who?" Francis cried, her rainbow eyes streaming tears.

"*Him,*" Malik said. "He's in there. It's why I asked about your clothing—you can move objects with you. So move me, Francis. Move me!"

Francis looked up at the gold tower. Up and behind and around and through it. There were lots of people still in there, some in the hotel rooms, many on the bottom floor. She saw, too, that the fire was inside the lobby, spreading. The reception desk was already smoking. The art on the walls browned and curled.

"Take my hand," Malik said.

She did.

"Do you see him?"

She searched her field of view. Everything was exposed to her when she focused. "I don't know!"

"Take me inside."

"I don't know if I can!"

Malik took her shoulders and turned her to face him. "Listen to me. I know what fire is. I know what these people . . . the pain . . . the fear . . ." He closed his eyes, shook his head slightly, as if warding off some bit of bad advice. "If you can carry objects like clothing with you, I think you can move me."

Francis took his hand again. She targeted a spot within the baffling 4-D maze of her reality, and said, "Here goes nothing."

For a moment of time, a mere moment, Malik experienced a maze of lines and shapes and bizarre visions. And then, suddenly, he was standing in a restaurant off the lobby.

Smoke hung thick and acrid in the air. A man and his family cowered beneath a table.

"Where is he?" Malik asked the cowering man.

The man could only shake his head, too overwhelmed to think. But his son, who looked to be about ten years old, said, "I heard he was on the top floor!"

"Thanks," Malik said. "Let's go, Francis. And whatever you do, don't drop out of morph!"

Thirty seconds later they exited the elevator into an empty hallway. "Blood trail," Malik said, pointing at a red smear leading down the carpet.

The door to the suite was open.

Inside, two cheerleaders stood over a writhing reptile in formal wear who had already saturated the bed covering with his blood.

"Dillon Poe?" Malik asked.

The cheerleaders stepped back and Dillon's eyes widened. "Who are you?"

"Who, us?" Malik asked, his voice low and silken. "We're

the ones coming to save your life, Charmer."

"What?" It was a sob.

"You're losing a lot of blood," Malik said. "But, see, what you don't know is that each time you morph—you know, change—your body is renewed."

"I . . . what?"

"De-morph, dumb-ass. The bullet wound is to the morph, your own body will be fine. And then . . ." He shrugged. "You can re-morph. All better!"

"Why would you . . . why are you helping me?" Dillon was in pain but still smelled a rat.

"Simple," Malik said. "The Dark Watchers, Dillon. You know who I mean. I'm . . . with them. I can't de-morph; if I do, I die an agonizing death. So"—he shrugged—"if you can't beat 'em, join 'em."

"*They* asked you to save me?"

"Why else would I be here?"

Malik sensed Francis's worry. Would she know to play along?

"They like you," Francis said. "They think you're, you know . . ."

"Funny?" Dillon croaked.

Francis blinked. "Yes. Funny."

"Oh, thank God," Dillon said. "I just have to . . ."

Malik watched as Dillon Poe, the nerdy-looking kid who wanted to be a comedian, slowly emerged from the snake. He watched the bullet wound close, and then disappear.

Dillon blinked. He sat up. He flexed his fingers as if

checking that they were real. He touched the place where the bullet had gone. His ridiculous tuxedo, the outfit he'd thought would give him some class, was still soggy with his blood. But the wound was gone.

"And now I can just morph again? Hah! Hah!" He jumped to his feet. "Oh, they think they've seen the worst I can do. Just wait!"

"You could re-morph," Malik said. "But I have a deep and powerful hatred of fire, and an even deeper hatred of the kind of sick creep who would burn innocent people."

Dillon smirked. "Well, too bad."

"Yeah," Malik said. "Too bad." He closed his eyes and focused on the no-longer-transformed and entirely vulnerable young sadist.

Dillon screamed.

"Anyone here have, like, super night vision?" Justin asked. He was on his feet, steadying himself with a hand on Tolliver's tank body and staring intently toward the east, toward the moon, toward that fleeting shadow he'd glimpsed.

"What is it?" Tolliver asked gruffly.

"I saw something."

"Step back, I need to turn to aim my sensors," Tolliver said. Tolliver had an array of sensors meant to improve his usefulness as a weapon.

It was no easy thing turning Tolliver on the crowded flatbed truck. It was like watching a very old person try to execute a three-point turn on a narrow street.

"Ahhh!" The pain chip twisted Justin's nerves for a second time. "Am I the only one with a chip?"

"Mine is still in," the turtle woman said. "But I'm not getting hit."

Three others said the same.

"I'm not getting anything on my sensors. What is it you thought you saw?"

"Like a plane or something," Justin said. "Probably nothing."

Tolliver had no face and no facial expressions, but he muttered something, and his tone worried Justin.

And then, again, the stabbing pain. But this time it had a rhythm to it. On . . . off . . . on . . . off. And still it was only affecting him.

"Wait!" Tolliver said. "I'm getting something. Definitely something off to our nine o'clock."

"What is it?" someone asked.

And again, the rhythmic stabbing pain, faster this time. On-off-on-off.

A signal! Someone was trying to tell him something.

"It's a goddam drone!" Tolliver said. "There!" He pointed his mechanical arm, and at that second Justin saw a small but distinct flare, a jet of flame.

The stab! Urgent this time, unrelenting.

The pieces came together in the blink of an eye. Justin instantly began to morph. His sword arm stretched out. His skin was replaced by chitinous armor. His other hand became a claw. And the instant he was more Knightmare than Justin, he leaped from the side of the truck.

It would certainly have hurt Justin very badly—jumping off a moving truck doing sixty would break his bones and scrape his flesh and quite possibly smash open his head and kill him.

The half Knightmare hit pavement, though it felt more as if the road surface had jumped up to hit him. The impact emptied his lungs and shot a different pain through his spine, but his armor did not crack, his sword arm did not shatter, and Justin DeVeere did not die.

Ka-BOOM!

The truck was a few hundred yards down the road when the Hellfire missile found it. Justin lay on his back and did not see the moment of impact. But he felt the concussion and the rush of superheated air.

And he saw bodies twirling through the air.

He jumped up, now fully Knightmare, and saw the truck engulfed in flame. It ran on for a few feet before veering off the road and coming to a stop.

Knightmare ran to see, equal parts shaken and curious. He stumbled and fell when his feet tangled in the viscera of the turtle woman.

A bush had caught fire, and a part of Justin registered the sight and connected it to the biblical tale and imagined trying to re-create it. But even he could not distract himself from the horror smeared down the highway.

He found Tolliver. The tank man was on his side. His missile launcher was crumpled, his sensors all blown away. The back of Tolliver's steel body burned.

Knightmare knelt down and peered at the slit and to his shock saw Tolliver's eyes open and aware.

"Who are you?" Tolliver asked. His voice was faint, weak, as if whatever pumped air through his voice box was on its last wheeze.

"Justin," Knightmare said in his booming morphed voice.

"The kid?"

"Yeah, the kid," Justin acknowledged.

"Huh." The next sound may have been a laugh. "I'm finished. Friendly fire! Damn it all."

"I'll see if there's a fire extinguisher in the truck cab."

"No. No," Tolliver said. "This is where it ends. Use that blade."

"What are you . . . what?" Justin drew back. Was the marine asking him to finish him off? He wasn't a murderer! He'd killed people, yes, but not in cold blood, only to defend himself!

"Use. The. Blade," Tolliver begged.

Justin swallowed and looked around guiltily, as if someone might see. The fire flared hotter.

He stood back, giving himself room, and brought his blade arm around. Was it thin enough? Would it fit? He placed the tip of his blade on the lip of the slit in Tolliver's armored bubble.

It would fit.

"It's okay, kid," Tolliver said. "Semper Fi!"

Justin plunged his blade into the marine's face.

CHAPTER 29
One Less Hotel

"ALL DUE RESPECT, I'm going to need that order in writing from someone upstream in my chain of command, General."

The death of Frankenstein Poole had left the army column briefly leaderless. But the army is good at chain of command, so Poole's authority swiftly devolved to Major Gary Andrews. And he had just been given an order by General DiMarco.

DiMarco was not in Andrews's chain of command.

Andrews was currently just behind the lead tank, in a backup JLTV, from which location he had just seen hundreds, maybe as many as a thousand human beings set on fire. Then, within mere minutes, seconds even, he had seen a sequence of events he would never be able to make sense of. He'd ordered a round to be fired into the massive T. rex–looking creature, but beyond that, he'd been helpless.

"Grow some goddamn balls, Major! You've got half a dozen mutants right there in front of you! Kill them!"

The major held his headset a bit away from his ear to save

his eardrum the assault of DiMarco's fury. Andrews waited, and when DiMarco paused to take a breath, he said, "General, I understand that you have direct authority from the Pentagon and the White House, but I am not able to carry out this order without proper written orders."

No way in hell was he going to do what DiMarco wanted. It would be absolute career suicide if it turned out DiMarco was nuts. And from what Andrews had seen of the Ranch from Shade's YouTube video, he was willing to bet good money that DiMarco was off her rocker.

And then he was handed the printed order, signed by the army deputy chief of staff, no less, directing him to obey any and all orders from DiMarco.

Andrews looked at his adjutant. "Jesus H."

"Yes, sir."

"This is a direct order," Andrews said. He fell silent for a moment, precariously balanced between what felt like a very illegal order, and the reality that disobedience would mean a court-martial.

Then, he gave the order.

The screams had been terrible.

The silence was worse.

Some still lived, lived and cried in agony and yet could not move away. Those who'd had their personal hells extinguished by Dekka's shredding coughed and crawled. But what had been a thousand voices was now just a few.

Armo stood panting, his chest heaving. His white fur was streaked black. Cruz stood beside him, de-morphed so that the baby in her arms would have a face to look at. She was past tears. Tears were not sufficient testimony to the unspeakable tragedy before her.

She could not look at the smoldering bodies. She looked up at the palm trees that lined the street. They were leafless black toothpicks.

Dekka stood, seemingly indifferent to the fact that her own morphed fur smoldered and smoked in places.

Shade blurred to a stop. She held a red fire extinguisher, almost laughable in this setting. She sprayed white foam over Dekka's back. Then threw the fire extinguisher away to skitter across the pavement.

"My God," Dekka said. "My—"

But her last word was obliterated as the whole world erupted in a stunning, rolling series of explosions, as the tanks opened fire at point blank range on the Triunfo.

Gold-filmed glass windows blew out, showering shards like a hailstorm.

BAM! BAM! BAM!

Round after round blew away pieces of the hotel. It was deliberate, professional destruction. They were piece by piece, floor by floor, destroying the gold tower.

Dekka yelled, "Malik and Francis!"

A buzz came from Shade, and she was gone on a hurricane wind.

Dekka ran down the army column, hands before her like a faith healer in feline cosplay. She aimed at the long barrels spitting fire. It wasn't hard, it didn't take long, to shred just enough of a barrel to stop it firing.

She ran and shredded, screaming, "Stop it! Stop it! You're killing people!"

Machine gunners swiveled to chase her with .50-caliber rounds, but she stayed close to the tanks, making it hard to target her.

Tank after tank, a few seconds each, but all the while the army column stabbed at the Triunfo, and the hotel erupted again and again.

Shade ran up the stairs. No way she was trusting an elevator, and anyway, it was far quicker to run sixty-four floors than to wait on an elevator.

Floor by floor, turning, leaping when she could, snatching at handrails to hurl herself upward as the cement-block walls of the stairwell cracked and buckled under the army's brutal assault.

She was at the door of Dillon's suite in seconds. She stopped to listen and heard an eerie, mewling howl within.

Shade stepped inside.

Francis crouched under a desk, covering her ears against the cacophony. Malik sat calmly in a chair.

And Dillon Poe, the Charmer, writhed in agony on the floor, yelling, "Kill me! Oh, God, please! Kill me!"

Ka-BOOM!

A near miss hit the floor below, shattering the windows, making the walls and floor jump. Francis cried out in terror, her eyes streaming tears.

Malik, still eerily calm, nodded at the suddenly absent

glass and said, "Well, Dillon, it looks like someone opened the window for you."

"Aaaaarrrggh!" Dillon shrieked. "Make it stop! Make it stop!"

"Malik," Shade said, slowing her voice.

It was mesmerizing watching Dillon's face. He was like a sinner in a medieval painting of hell, his face almost immobile in a grimace of bared teeth, strained tendons, and muscles clenched so hard his arms and shoulders and neck looked like they might crack like dry twigs.

Malik's expression, slowly turned on her, was unlike anything Shade would have thought possible from Malik Tenerife. His eyes were hot and pitiless.

"He burned those people," Malik said. "He burned them alive."

Shade wanted to tell him to stop. She could see the detail as Dillon's fingernails tore at his face, drawing bloody lines on his flesh.

Malik had a pocketknife in his hand. Not his, Shade was pretty sure; it must have belonged to Francis. Malik slowly opened the largest blade.

He went and knelt in front of Dillon.

"We're sixty-four floors up. You can jump. Or you can make sure your voice is never a problem again."

Could Dillon even understand? He was in a living hell of pain.

I have to stop this! Shade thought. *I have to . . .*

It was not pity for the Charmer. It was fear of what this act would do to Malik. But her words did not come. Something both terribly just and terribly wrong was taking place. Something morally indefensible but cosmically right. In the back of her head, the Dark Watchers seemed to lean forward.

Did the Dark Watchers want this? Were they enjoying Dillon's pain?

Malik grabbed Dillon's hand, a desperate claw, and closed his fingers around the knife. "Jump . . . or cut."

"Malik!" Shade said, but failed to slow it down, so that he'd have heard nothing but a millisecond buzz.

I can stop this.

Dillon screamed and cursed. And stuck out his tongue.

The world will never be safe unless he's dead or . . .

Dillon had thought the bullet wound was pain. The bullet wound was nothing.

Nothing!

He was burning alive! The pain coming from every nerve ending, flooding and overwhelming his brain with an urgency unlike anything he'd ever felt. His entire body was under a blowtorch.

He felt the impact of the tank cannon blasts and prayed they'd kill him.

Then, the window! *Yes, yes, jump!*

But what was in his hand? What was the sleek-skinned black boy saying?

Cut and live.

Cut and live!

Flashes of memory.

Let's make sure you never call me or anyone else names again. Bite your tongue in half.

The sound of teeth grinding on gristle.

Never again to speak. Never again to bend anyone to his will.

Never again to tell a joke.

With all that remained of the Charmer's will and strength, he crawled on hands and knees, crawled to the broken window and the whistling night wind.

Below, tanks firing.

Fire burning.

The pain!

He did not leap, he just kept crawling. Crawling until his hands had nothing to crawl on. He tipped forward. His thighs slipped over broken glass, the cuts irrelevant.

And he fell, screaming.

Malik looked at Shade. He said nothing.

Shade de-morphed to be understood and said, "Francis? Get Malik and yourself the hell out of here."

The tanks went on firing, round after round, but as Dekka wreaked her own careful destruction, the firing slowed and finally stopped.

Shade watched from across the Strip, now blessedly out of morph and cut off from the insidious Dark Watchers. Armo, Malik, and Francis stood defeated and exhausted.

"Cruz!" Shade yelled.

"I'm here!" Cruz stepped out from behind Armo's bulk, carrying the baby in her arms.

"Thank God you're all right," Shade said.

Cruz nodded. In a low voice she said, "You don't believe in God, Shade." She shook her head. "And this is not the day to start."

"They enjoyed it," Malik said. No one but Francis had any confusion about who *they* were.

Shade narrowed her eyes. "I know. I felt it, too."

Armo shook his head. "I didn't think things like this really happened."

"It happened," Shade said. "It happened and we couldn't really stop it, could we? I mean, we saved some lives, and we stopped the Charmer, but look at the cost. Look at what we didn't do!"

She spotted a lone figure walking, a sturdy-looking young black woman stumbling from weariness, her head down. She stumbled, fell to her knees, and seemed unable to stand.

Armo, now merely human and clothed in nothing but scraps, ran to her and lifted her in his arms. He carried her back and sat her on the curb, where she hung her head in her hands and cried quietly.

"It's okay," he said. "It's okay." But as he spoke he shook his head, his body denying his words.

Dazed, soot-covered people who had escaped the flaming wreckage of the Triunfo seemed drawn to them, kept a respectful distance, but clustered around them.

Shade heard sirens nearing. After everything, after a day

and a night of unrelenting horror, there were still men and women rushing to help.

As if the sirens were a signal, the six Rockborn walked away, as behind them the hotel burned and crashed.

I saved you, at least, little pink person. I saved you.

Cruz stumbled behind Shade and Dekka, no one speaking. No one but Armo, who said, "I'll carry him for a while."

He took the swaddled bundle from Cruz, but the baby started crying, and after a moment of futile cooing, Armo handed him back to Cruz.

I saved you. Just you.

Cruz imagined herself with a baby of her own. Adopted, of course, but what did that matter? Wasn't the point to have someone to love, who you hoped at least would love you back? Wasn't that everything that really mattered?

Cruz felt the tears start again. Maybe they had never stopped. Maybe they never would. She had seen things that no human being should ever see. Things she would never forget, though if she could push a button and just delete . . .

The day's shock and violence was a fresh wound laid over many earlier ones. And this was life now, wasn't it? Violence and pain and fear. That was it now. The old world was dead, wasn't it? Nothing would ever be good or right again.

But still Cruz formed pictures in her mind. There was a beach. It was maybe mid-morning, so the sun was shining bright but wasn't yet really hot. The water was calm, the waves just lapping rhythmically, not crashing.

And Armo—or some reasonable facsimile—was walking hand in hand with their baby.

Jesus, Cruz, mawkish much?

She knew she was retreating into fantasy. Well, why shouldn't she? When she thought about someday writing stories and even books, hadn't part of that always been escapism? Hadn't she always wanted to create worlds where people could just love each other? Hadn't she always known that her only happiness would be in some fantasy world?

The baby burped. It had fallen asleep.

"We better go find someone to take care of you," Cruz whispered.

"Nice baby," Armo said. He was walking beside her. "And I didn't even know you were pregnant."

It was a feeble joke, but Cruz gave him a tear-streaked smile. She sighed. "Well, pregnant is one thing I will never be, I'm afraid."

"Oh, right," Armo said, nodding sagely. "But you could always adopt one. I hear there are plenty. You can just . . ." At this point he lost the thread and ended up by saying, ". . . I mean, babies can't be that hard to find, right?"

Dekka said, "We need to find someone to take care of it. Him. It's a boy, right? We are not the safest babysitters in the world."

Shade frowned. "Hey. Not all of the Charmer's slaves died. There must be hundreds at least running around. But look."

Cruz did, and realized that there were people on the sidewalks, civilians, but no one was attacking. Some of the people had blood on their chins and necks from attempting to bite and eat others. Many had wounds of their own.

They walked down the Strip, heading for Caesars, hoping to find someone there to take the baby, hoping almost as fervently to find showers and food and beds. They walked, each de-morphed with the exception of Malik; Cruz and Armo in front, Dekka and Shade next, Malik and Francis bringing up the rear.

"Thank you!"

It did not at first occur to Cruz that the shout was meant for her.

"Thank you! Thank you!"

More shouts. And someone started applauding. Ragged, tattered, bloodied bands of survivors lined the sidewalk, with more coming to join them.

"Shade Darby!"

"Berserker Bear! You kick ass!"

"Go, Lesbokitty!"

"No, no, no," Dekka said, but under her breath. "That will not stand. I am not wearing that name the rest of my damn life."

By the time they reached Caesars, they were leading a solemn parade, a crowd of hundreds. Wilkes, the security chief, came out to meet them.

iPhones were raised. Video was taken.

"Say something!" someone yelled. And Cruz realized from the ensuing silence that they all wanted this. Needed it, maybe. These damaged people needed someone to say something. Something to make sense of it.

"You should say something," Cruz said to Shade. "Or you, Dekka."

"I don't do speeches," Dekka said.

Shade shook her head and smiled a sad, wistful smile. "I don't think it's me they want to hear from, Cruz."

CHAPTER 30
The Speech

"HI. UM . . . MY name is Cruz. I want to tell you first of all that Dillon Poe is dead."

The rapt audience cried, "Bastard!" and "Murderer!" and a few other insults directed at the villain.

"Malik and Francis here"—Cruz waved to indicate them—"they went into that place while it was being blown up. While it was burning. And they . . . they took care of him. He's gone."

The applause was loud, bordering on frenzied.

"Look, we tried to . . ." Cruz shook her head. "None of us ever thought we'd be here. You know? That we'd be what we are. Now. Freaks or mutants. Rockborn. Whatever you want to call us."

"Heroes!" someone shouted.

"No, no," Cruz protested, urgently. "We didn't succeed, we didn't stop him, we didn't . . . all those people. We couldn't . . ."

The tears came again and she didn't brush them away. She needed tears. It felt like the whole world needed tears.

"You tried," a voice said. It was a calm voice, quiet, but carrying all the more authority for that reason.

Various voices shouted, "You saved the baby," and "You killed that monster!"

Cruz shook her head. "But we should have . . . Maybe if we had, I don't know . . . We just should have . . ."

A woman's voice from the back of the crowd said, "Save one life, save the world entire."

"We were helpless. You saved us!"

Cruz frowned in confusion. She looked to Shade for help, but her friend seemed amused and shook her head slightly.

Dekka leaned forward and whispered. "They want a hero, Cruz. They *need* one. Don't fight it."

Cruz swallowed and nodded to herself. "Okay. Okay. Okay, look, we tried. You're right, we tried. We wished we could do more. We wished for, boy . . . for a lot of things. But I guess it's too late for that now. We have to look forward. You know? All of you the same. You're going to have to find some way to deal with this, to process it. To forgive. To forgive yourselves. What many of you did you were forced to do. You're never going to be able to forget. Neither will we. I won't." For a moment she couldn't go on. "But even if we can't forget, we have to be clear on who the villain was here, who is to blame. And it wasn't you people."

Wilkes, the casino security chief, stepped up with a baby bottle. She handed it to Cruz.

"I don't suppose you're a mommy?" Cruz asked her.

"Better yet," Wilkes said, "I'm a grandma."

"Will you . . . ?" Cruz asked. "I'm so tired. I'm afraid I might drop him."

Wilkes accepted the baby.

Cruz nodded. She closed her eyes and had to fight the urge to lie down right there, right then, in the door of Caesars Palace.

"What now?" a voice demanded.

Cruz shook her head, baffled. "What?"

"What now?" the voice repeated. "What are you six going to do?"

Cruz looked at the others beside her. At silent Malik. At Dekka standing like one of the pillars of the earth. At Francis, just a kid with a power almost impossible to describe. At Armo, practically in a loincloth.

As soon as they turn social media back on, that boy is going to have a very large fan club. And I'll be its president.

Finally she looked at Shade Darby.

Shade, who had swept Cruz up in the wake of her obsession.

Shade, who had led Malik to disaster.

Shade, who had led Cruz to become . . . *a hero.*

"What are we going to do?" Cruz repeated. She shrugged. "I guess we're going to try and save the world."

CHAPTER 31
Aftermath

IN THE SUITE atop Caesars, they drank beer and vodka and whiskey from the minibar and ate room-service food. Management had sent up a spread fit for royalty. But they ate and drank in silence. Whatever words any of them had were not worth the effort to speak.

Wilkes had taken charge of the baby, the still-nameless baby whose parents had almost certainly died in the fire.

The army's tank column was withdrawn. The National Guard, the Nevada State Police, the traumatized Las Vegas Police, and the hastily deputized California Highway Patrol restored order in the city. Two looters were shot dead, and that ended the looting.

Fire departments and EMTs from all over Nevada, southern California, Utah, and Arizona flooded Las Vegas with ambulances and medevac helicopters. Every burn unit in every hospital west of the Rocky Mountains was filled to overflowing.

Reassuring speeches flowed from Washington, D.C. No one believed them.

And Dekka, Shade, Cruz, Francis, and Armo slept through it all.

Only Malik lay awake, half hearing the low drone of the television news. His mind was full of the Dark Watchers and his own churning thoughts. From time to time he would turn to look at Francis.

Francis Specter, the girl who could move through a fourth dimension.

Francis Specter, the girl who morphed untouched by the Dark Watchers.

Only Francis.

Because Francis was a mistake. Francis was random chance, an anomaly, a freak among freaks.

You're afraid of her.

Silence.

She wasn't in the plan, was she?

Silence.

Do you get movies there? Ever see Star Trek? *There's a famous line.*

Silence.

Although it was actually from Herman Melville.

Silence.

Would you like to hear it?

Silence.

"To the last, I grapple with thee . . ."

Silence.

Malik, ever-controlled, ever-logical Malik felt something growing inside him. Something built out of the memories of burning men and women; out of clearer, sharper images of Dragon's fire rolling toward him; the intolerable memories of pain.

Hatred. Rage.

His teeth clenched until they might crack. His hands were fists. Tears welled in his eyes.

"From Hell's heart, I stab at thee!"

"Do you like it?" Malik spoke aloud. "There's more. You want the rest? Do you? Do you, you filthy bastards?"

Shade, asleep on the couch, shifted, opened her eyes, and sat up.

"'For hate's sake.'" Malik's voice was a chain saw on metal. "'For hate's sake, I spit my last breath at thee!' Do you like that quote? Do you?"

Shade stood over him. She laid a hand on his quivering shoulder.

Malik sat up. He glared at her defiantly. "Don't say anything, Shade. I don't want to hear it."

Shade moved her hand up his neck, cradling his cheek.

"My God, Shade. My God, what do we do?"

Cruz woke hours later, confused as to where she was. On a bed? How . . . and the memories came like a tidal wave of horror.

Francis was in the little kitchen, brewing coffee.

"Hey," Cruz said.

"Hey. Want some?"

"Like a drowning woman wants a life raft," Cruz said. She took a cup and scalded her tongue. "What's that noise?"

Francis grinned. "Armo snores. Dekka, too."

"It's like they're a really bad musical act."

Francis laughed, and her laugh seemed to flow into Cruz. Cruz grinned despite herself, despite a million images threatening to overwhelm her. "You've fallen in with some crazy people, kid."

"Well, I guess any family I'm part of will have to be crazy."

Cruz frowned at the word "family." Was that what they were? "Hey, where are Shade and Malik?"

Francis arched a brow that was too knowing for her age. She nodded toward one of the bedrooms, where a door that had been open was now closed.

Cruz sighed. "Well, it's about time."

She gave herself the simple but wrong pleasure of gazing at Armo, who lay on the pull-out sofa, having wrapped himself in a sheet that, fortunately from Cruz's perspective, revealed a shoulder and almost too much of a thigh.

"Some family," Cruz muttered.

"What was it?" Sam Temple asked. He'd just hopped off the treadmill in the breakfast nook he and Astrid had converted to a home gym. He'd been using the treadmill and the weights religiously since the world had gone crazy.

Astrid came from the front door holding the FedEx envelope behind her back. "Nothing. Just some kids collecting money for their soccer team. I gave them five bucks."

"You're a patron of school sports, babe. Don't worry, I won't tell anyone."

Astrid said, "You know it's not like I hate sports, I've just never cared what people did with balls."

"I'm going to pass on the chance to make a crude joke," Sam said, and laughed anyway.

Astrid moved on through to the bathroom adjoining their bedroom. She locked the door and sat on the closed toilet, contemplating the FedEx envelope on her lap. She was pretty sure she knew what was in it. She knew who had sent it despite the fake name on the packaging slip.

Should she be grateful to Dekka? She had vowed to keep Sam out of it if she could. But the world was disintegrating, so maybe Dekka had thought it was her last chance to send mail and have it reach its destination.

Or maybe Dekka had reassessed the situation and reached this grim conclusion. Astrid knew that Dekka had never liked her, and the feeling was mutual. But like was not the same as respect, and she had deep respect for Dekka's judgment, a respect born of too many dreadful and dangerous experiences.

If it has to be: me.

It had been all Astrid had time to write on the note she'd slipped to Dekka as she and Armo had left. She wished she could have provided more guidance, more if-then scenarios. But in the end she'd had to leave it to Dekka.

"Well," Astrid muttered, "if I had to trust anyone . . ."

Drake would come. With the world in meltdown, he would come. He no longer needed to be prudent. He no longer needed to fear discovery.

Sam had bought a twelve-gauge shotgun the day before, a dangerous, matte-black object with no purpose but to kill. But they both knew that Drake could be blown apart, slowed, but not stopped. Not by any weapon they knew of.

There was a plague of monsters loose in the world, and Astrid feared them, but with her usual logic had seen that she and Sam were just two of potentially millions of victims. But she had no such logical defense against Drake, because Drake was not just a monster; he was her monster. Sooner or later, Drake would come for her. And Sam would fight him, but without the power he once possessed, he would fail. And Astrid would be Drake's to do with as he wished.

She licked her lips, and her fingers shook as she tore away the sealing strip and pulled out the contents: a plastic sandwich bag containing what looked like perhaps a tablespoon of gray powder.

"Hey, can I come in and shower?" Sam was at the door.

"Just a minute." Astrid slid the baggie back into the envelope and stuffed it beneath the sink, behind the Comet and the Scrub Free.

She opened the bathroom door.

"Sorry, I'm out of shape and sweaty," Sam said, pulling his T-shirt over his head.

"Well, then, a shower is just the thing," Astrid said. She held up a fresh bar of soap and smiled. "I could help."

Dekka was the last to wake, and when teased about it grumbled that she was the oldest one there, after all.

"Yeah, you're way old, Dekka, practically legal drinking age," Shade teased. She was in an easy chair, sharing it with Malik, the two of them squeezed together in too little space.

"Oh, so *this* now?" Dekka said sourly, seeing them. She shook her head, but her disapproval was fake and no one believed it. Francis handed her coffee. "I remember when I didn't drink coffee," she said, taking it gratefully.

She glanced at CNN on the TV and read the chyron scroll at the bottom.

Four hundred and nine confirmed dead in Las Vegas.

Death toll expected to mount into the thousands.

Hospitals overwhelmed.

Red Cross urgent requests for blood donations.

But the picture above the crawl was not of burned bodies and hollowed-out buildings. It was of Cruz walking down the Strip with a baby in her arms, followed by a scarred, soot-covered, exhausted band.

"Who's got the remote? Turn it up."

". . . the one bright moment coming when a Rockborn mutant identifying herself as Cruz brought a baby out of the inferno . . ."

"Like you said, Dekka, they *need* a hero," Shade said.

"We need one, too," Malik said. "We have a face now. Something people can hold on to and think maybe they shouldn't just exterminate us."

"Cruz is the official face of . . . of whatever we are," Armo said. He grinned his goofy-sweet grin and added, "At least it's a nice, friendly face. Not like . . ." He hooked a thumb toward Dekka, who calmly lifted a cushion and threw it at him.

"They're going to come up with a name for us, you know, and it'll probably be as bad as Lesbokitty."

"A name for us?" Francis echoed. "Like the Rockborn Gang?"

One by one, faces turned to Francis. She shrugged and blushed.

"Sorry," Francis said. "I was living with . . . my mom . . . like a . . . well, it was a biker gang. It was the first thing that popped in my head."

"The Rockborn Gang," Shade said, her arm around Malik's neck.

"There are worse names," Malik conceded.

Dekka picked up the phone. "Yeah, front desk? Can you connect me to CNN?" She drank more coffee while she waited. "Hello? This is Dekka Talent." Pause. "Dekka Talent. You know . . . Jesus H. Lesbokitty, dammit, get me the newsroom." With her hand covering the mouthpiece she said, "If I ever find the Twitter moron who started that, I will . . . Hello? Yeah, this is Dekka Talent. Two things. One: if you call me Lesbokitty I will fly to Atlanta and shred your office. Two: we are the Rockborn Gang. Yes. Gang. And . . ."

Dekka stopped, held the phone away from her ear. "I got cut off. Or something. It's just static."

"Look," Armo said, pointing at the TV. CNN was just snow. Armo took the remote and switched to MSNBC. MSNBC came out of New York.

CNN was in Atlanta. It was two hundred miles from the coast where, MSNBC was reporting, something—something very bad—had happened.

ASO-6

PETTY OFFICER DEB Forte, battered, bruised, bleeding, frantic with dread and certain that she was the only person who could end the *Nebraska*'s suffering and save the world from whatever monster had seized the boat, made her final connection.

She had been wedged in an impossibly tight space atop the nose cone of a Trident II rocket. She had removed the cladding and uncovered the eight steel cones like baby birds in a nest. And even as the *Nebraska* was dragged and pummeled, she had used her soldering iron, her tool set, and her knowledge of primitive computer systems.

Then she had climbed down and stretched out on a bulkhead currently serving as a floor.

In her hand she held a switch.

She prayed. Prayed for her husband and her family. She prayed for her little girl, visiting her mother in Kansas.

She prayed for the forgiveness of her sins. Including the sin she had no choice but to commit.

She threw the switch.

In a millionth of a second she, the *Nebraska*, and every living thing within ten miles of Savannah, Georgia, was reduced to atoms.

ASO-7

ANOMALOUS SPACE OBJECT #7 passed the orbit of the moon, tumbling toward Earth.

ACKNOWLEDGMENTS

I GET TO be the name on the cover of this book, but I didn't edit it, or market it, or choose the layout, or design the cover. There are a whole bunch of people doing a whole lot of work to turn my words into your book. So, if you enjoyed this book, please know that your enjoyment is the product of an excellent team: VP/publisher and editor, Katherine Tegen, assistant editor Mabel Hsu, senior production editor Kathryn Silsand, executive managing editor Mark Rifkin, senior designer David Curtis, senior art director Amy Ryan, cover artist Matthew Griffin, production coordinator Meghan Pettit, production manager Allison Brown, senior director of marketing Bess Braswell, marketing manager Audrey Diestelkamp, associate director of publicity Rosanne Romanello, copy editor Maya Myers, proofreader Jessica White, and cold reader Mary Ann Seagren.